2
8

—
—
—
—
—
—

This
lates
peri

- Pl
- Vi

THE BAGHDAD
RAILWAY CLUB

THE BAGHDAD RAILWAY CLUB

ANDREW MARTIN

ISIS
LARGE PRINT
Oxford

First published in Great Britain 2012
by
Faber and Faber Limited

Published in Large Print 2012 by ISIS Publishing Ltd.,
7 Centremead, Osney Mead, Oxford OX2 0ES
by arrangement with
Faber and Faber Limited

British Library Cataloguing in Publication Data
Martin, Andrew, 1962–
    The Baghdad Railway Club.
    1. Stringer, Jim (Fictitious character) - - Fiction.
    2. Baghdad (Iraq) - - History - - 20th century - -
    Fiction.
    3. Detective and mystery stories.
    4. Large type books.
    I. Title
    823.9'2–dc23

ISBN 978–0–7531–9084–5 (hb)
ISBN 978–0–7531–9085–2 (pb)

Printed and bound in Great Britain by
T. J. International Ltd., Padstow, Cornwall

Acknowledgements

I am grateful to Lieutenant Colonel Parkinson of Sandhurst Etiquette and Media; to Richard Smith at the Foreign and Commonwealth Office; to Michael Harvey of the National Media Museum, Bradford; to Alan Renton, curator of the Porthcurno Telegraph Museum; to Mr Roy Smith of the Oasis Camel Centre, Halesworth, Suffolk; to Mr David Payling and Mr Roy Fenton. All departures from historical accuracy are entirely my own responsibility.

Part One

London and York

CHAPTER
ONE

In a quiet and dark corner of London, with the rain falling, I walked up to the doorway of 92 Victoria Street, and read "Railway Club, Upper Bell." The lower bell was for William Watson, Tailor. Alongside the Railway Club bell was a wooden frame with a glass front. An announcement was pinned inside:

THURSDAY JANUARY 25TH, 1917 AT 6.30p.m. "HUMOUR ON THE RAILS". A TALK WITH LANTERN SLIDES BY MR JOHN MAYCROFT, AUTHOR OF "HUMOURS OF A COUNTRY STATION", "OUR BOOKING OFFICE", "DOWN OR UP" & C. & C. MR MAYCROFT IS OUR PRINCIPAL RAILWAY COMEDIAN. TEA AND COFFEE WILL BE SERVED.

Alongside the notice was fixed a cartoon showing two women in a station restaurant. The first was pointing at a plate and saying, "These cakes are all quite stale, Miss Hunt. They've been on the counter a fortnight." The reply came, "Would you mind taking them to the Second Class refreshment room?"

What exactly John Maycroft had to do with this jollity was not indicated.

Victoria Street was lit by lamps turned down low. A man on a bicycle approached along it. There was no headlight on the bike, but when the bicyclist had gone past, I saw that he displayed a red rear lamp in accordance with the blackout regulations. It was evidently more important to see a bicycle going away than it was to see it approaching. The rain increased as the bicycle faded, and I was reminded of the new silk umbrella in my hand. It was a Peerless with an ash handle, and I'd bought it with money sent me by my father on his learning that I had been made up from corporal to captain as a result of my railway work in the Somme battle. "A quite remarkable leap", Dad had called it.

The money — a cheque for ten pounds — had come with a London Handy-Map and Guide and a note insisting the wife and I were to travel south for a bit of a spree. He knew I'd been "through it" on the Western Front, broken my thigh bone and all the rest of it, and he believed I deserved a treat. The wife and I were to stay for two nights in the Midland Grand Hotel, no other would do, and we were instructed to take a second-floor room, the first-floor rooms being more like suites, and the third-floor "inclined to be pokey". (Dad himself had been to London on exactly two occasions, and both times he'd stayed at what was familiarly called "The Mid-Gran".)

In retirement, Dad had come into money, or at least a means of making a good deal. After selling his butcher's shop, he'd set himself up as the business agent of the model boat makers of the Yorkshire coast

— The Ancient Mariners, as he called them, and they were in the main retired fishermen even older, and much less presentable, than himself. (Dad was seventy.) He'd done so well at this that it appeared he'd made a mistake in having worked as a butcher for the best part of fifty years.

I put the umbrella up and, well . . . It worked. But standing underneath it, I felt a fraud.

It was only just gone six; I had half an hour to kill before "*Humour on the Rails*", so I crossed the road and drank a glass of London Brown beer and smoked a cigarette in a pub called The Albert. When I returned to number 92, there were two men on the doorstep: an elderly party and a young chap perhaps in the early twenties. The elderly party was singing the praises of John Maycroft — of "*Humour on the Rails*" fame — even as he *took down* the notice advertising the man's talk.

"He's awfully good, you know. He gave the talk at Cambridge. I'm led to believe it was an absolute riot."

"*Where* at Cambridge?" asked the other, who wore a thick muffler.

"At Cambridge — at the University, you know," said the first chap.

"At the Cambridge University *Railway Club*?" asked the younger one, evidently a stickler for fact.

The older chap looked flummoxed, but I got him off the hook by asking, "Is the talk cancelled?"

"Postponed," he said without looking at me (which the young one made up for by staring). "But we've been able to get a fill-in at short notice."

And as he spoke, he pinned up a new notice in the box:

RLY. CLUB
  JAN. 25TH, '17
  THERE HAS BEEN A CHANGE TO THE ADVERTISED PROGRAMME. TONIGHT AT 6.30, MR NOEL DOWNES OF LONDON UNIVERSITY LECTURES ON "THE BERLIN-BAGDAD RAILWAY".

There had originally been an "h" after the "g" in "Bagdad" but this had been cancelled out by the overtyping of an "x".

The younger chap asked me, "Are you a member of the Railway Club? Because you won't get in if you're not."

"Oh, I think an exception will always be made for an officer," the older man cut in — and I wondered how he could tell, since I was not in uniform, and my Northern accent was stronger than is commonly found amongst commissioned men. I was pleased, anyhow.

The younger one softened to the extent of saying, "It's members-only but they generally don't ask for cards to be shown."

"I am a member," I said, "and I do have a card."

"I haven't seen you before," said the younger one.

I'll bloody clock you in a minute, I thought, while saying, "I'm a corresponding member."

"Where do you live?"

"York."

I was thinking about The Albert public house. They served topping beer at only tuppence a pint, *and* they ran to hot dinners. Did I really want to hear about the Berlin-Baghdad railway? It was a scheme, as I recalled, that had come to grief in the war, like many another: a German attempt to connect with . . . what was it called? Asia Minor. At first we hadn't troubled about it, but as Germany became the enemy we'd tried to block it. The thing had never been finished, as far as I knew — had never reached Baghdad, anyhow. There was fighting over there now of course — us against Brother Turk and the Huns, with the Arabs somewhere in between, and more men dying of heat than bullets. An engine driver I knew called Kemp had gone out to Egypt with the East Yorkshires. He'd reasoned that you couldn't dig trenches in sand, so he reckoned he'd be better off than the blokes in France, but I heard that when he came back for his first leave, he'd lost two stone, and spent the whole time looking for a mosquito net in the York stores — without success. He'd seen the Sphinx, and reported it no higher than a tall tree. As to the digging of trenches . . . It *was* possible in sand.

The elderly party was now unlocking the door, and a couple of blokes were approaching along the dark street. They looked like Railway Club types. I stepped off the doorstep of 92 as they came up. The elderly party explained to them about the change in the programme, and they took it easily in their stride. In fact, they didn't look at all surprised. Then all the four blokes went in. I saw a couple of others coming up, and I eyed The Albert pub behind them. I was just starting towards it when it seemed instantly to disappear from the street. All that had happened ... the lights had gone out. It had closed, as any pub was liable to do at any time in the war. There seemed nothing for it: I turned back towards number 92, and walked in.

The talk was given in the Club Room of the Railway Club, the holy of holies. Downes, the speaker, had pitched up while I'd been along the corridor in the Gentlemen's, draining off my pint of London Brown.

He turned out to be a slightly built, sandy-haired fellow, who wore a thick guernsey beneath his suit-coat. The elderly party who'd been on the doorstep was called Mr Short, and he was the Deputy President of the Railway Club. The *President* sent his apologies, as did John Maycroft, the humorist, who was "unavoidably detained on the south coast". Short was still cut-up over this loss and Downes, sitting beside him ready to start his talk, put a brave face on it as Short said how he personally had been "particularly looking forward" to hearing of the lighter side of the railways. There was then some Railway Club business.

We were all reminded that the monthly meetings were continuing during the Crisis, even if it had been necessary to suspend the annual dinners. One of the members, Mr N. McCracken, had recently distinguished himself by winning the M.C., but then again, two members had been killed in action during the past month. It appeared, from listening to Short, that the Railway Club was at one and the same time both the leading railway society in the world, and desperately in need of new members. Therefore, a recruitment drive would soon begin, and we were all reminded that serving men paid only half the subscription. Short was sorry about the absence of tea; a collection for War Relief would be taken after the talk. He then gave the floor to Downes.

I spent the opening minutes of his talk wondering why the fellow wasn't serving with the colours, since he was about of an age with me — early thirties — and why the fire wasn't lit, since the room was chill, and with a feeling of damp. I then looked all about the room, the pale green walls of which were covered in railway photographs and drawings, not over-clean. Some of the photographs showed the Railway Club members on the steps of signal boxes, or the tops of footbridges, and I believed that I recognised some of the faces in the room from these photographs. There were fourteen in the audience, including Short and his inquisitive young pal from the front door. Most had cigarettes on the go, but I'd smoked my last Virginian in The Albert. Amongst the clutter of pictures on the wall was a cigarette machine — Churchman's, but they'd do, and I wondered whether it would be all right to stand up and put in my sixpence for a carton.

The man Downes still hadn't hit his stride. He was now saying how, although he knew they'd come for an evening of laughter, it was important to understand why so many of our men were dying out East, and how the Berlin-Baghdad railway was part of the reason we were over there.

I realised that the fellow sitting next-but-one was leaning towards me and holding out his own packet of cigarettes — some foreign brand I couldn't quite make out. There were only two left, so I whispered thanks, and indicated that he should hold on to them. But he insisted, albeit without speaking, and followed up with a light. The cigarette was short and the tobacco strong, but of good quality — not burning to the throat. It was clever of him to have spotted that I was after a smoke.

I now turned again towards Downes, whose early hesitancy had fallen away. He was leaning forward from his chair, and speaking with urgency. "The land of Mesopotamia," he said, ". . . is it really worth fighting for? It seems on the face of it nothing more than a waste of sandy desert." He looked at us one by one as though honestly seeking an answer to his question, and it seemed to me that he had some sort of illness. Otherwise he would have been standing to give the talk. Yes, he was too pale. One leg sagged against the other, and the railway club lectern stood disregarded behind him.

"But one hundred miles north of the Persian Gulf lies a veritable lake of petroleum," said Downes. "The Anglo-Persian Oil Company was formed to exploit it, and that company supplies three-quarters of the oil used by our navy. As you all know, however, the German navy is equally dependent on oil . . ."

The oil was in Persia — next door to Mesopotamia and supposedly neutral. But it was only *just* in Persia, and might easily have fallen into the hands of the Turks, the allies of the Germans and the controllers of

10

Mesopotamia. They might interrupt the pipe and take the oil, so we had sent a gunboat at the start of the war, and this had been followed in pretty short order by an expeditionary force of the British Indian Army.

What was the reason for the Turkish alliance with Germany? Downes was asking the question, and had begun supplying the answer when the quiet man who'd passed me the cigarette said, almost in an under-breath, "No choice in the matter."

Downes half nodded at this half answer, and hesitated for a fraction of time to see whether the speaker wished to elaborate. Evidently he did not, and so Downes spoke on himself. The Germans and the Turks shared a common fear of Russia; and Germany might have attacked Turkey if it had not formed the alliance. Turkey had to choose one side or the other, and she seemed to have picked the winner, back in 'fourteen. Also, Turkey and Germany were building a railway together.

It was the Germans who put up the money for a line leading out of Constantinople in the direction of Baghdad in 1888. That had got the ball rolling, and between them the Germans and the Turks had got up various schemes of funding to *keep* it rolling.

"In 1903," said our speaker, "a number of German banks created the Berlin — Baghdad Railway Company. This alarmed the Russians, the French, and especially ourselves." Downes surveyed us gravely: "Can you all see why?" He leant, or rather lurched, further forward. "*Can* you?"

Someone, embarrassed, muttered, "On account of the oil."

"That's part of it," said Downes, "and perhaps the main part. But imagine Germany with a direct route to its East African colonies. Imagine her being able to bypass the Suez Canal. Imagine the Germans as rulers of Asia Minor, hand in glove with the Ottoman Empire in a territory unassailable by sea power, and with the whole of the Orient opened up before her!"

We all looked glum at that. Here was the very opposite of *Humour on the Rails*.

"The line", Downes continued, "creeps forward towards Baghdad, even while the fighting carries on. It has to date reached almost as far as Nusaybin, a hundred miles east of Aleppo."

"Never heard of either place," a bluff voice said. "Haven't the foggiest notion where they are."

"I shall be passing out a map," said Downes, rather shortly. "In addition, a branch creeps north from Baghdad to meet the section coming down from Nusaybin. The gap between the two lengths of line is some two hundred and fifty miles."

He sighed, either at the situation in Mesopotamia or because he was obliged to now reach down for the walking stick that lay under his chair. He rose with difficulty to his feet and made one pace forward — a sort of arrested stagger. He took one of the papers from the sheaf in his hand, and roughly pressed it on the nearest man in the front row. He in turn passed it to his neighbour, and it came to me a minute later.

Aleppo — which I'd never heard of either — turned out to be in "Upper Syria". One part of the Berlin-Baghdad railway came down — rather shakily — from Turkey and went there. It then drifted right towards this place Nusaybin, which was in "Upper Mesopotamia". The other part crawled up from Baghdad towards a spot called Samarrah, petering out somewhere between there and a spot called Tikrit. Both Samarrah and Tikrit sat on another, more wriggly hand-drawn line signifying the River Tigris. Baghdad itself was on that river, as were the only places marked on the map as being *south* of Baghdad, namely Kut-al-Amara and Basrah.

Downes, having regained his seat, watched as we passed the map amongst ourselves. "The labour on the Nusaybin stretch," he said, "is supplied by British prisoners of war, taken after the fall of Kut, then force-marched north." Again he eyed us individually, as though asking each man: "You can see that I'm crocked. But what are *you* going to do about it?"

The fellow who'd said he hadn't heard of Aleppo — and who had the map in his hand just then — spoke up again.

"But hold on, chap," he said, "you're being too depressing. Don't you read the papers? Townshend's gone. Maude's the chap now, and the War Office is giving him everything he wants. Part of his army's outside Kut as we speak. He's already nibbling at the Turks, and the big push up from Basrah is bound to come soon, then we'll be into Baghdad and running the whole show in Mespot." He flicked the back of his hand against the pessimistic map, making a sharp crack that threatened to tear it.

The name of Kut was just then in all the newspapers, as it had been nearly a year before. On that previous occasion, our forces under General Townshend had been besieged there, and had finally surrendered, not that any such word had appeared in print. Instead there had been talk of "the end of a heroic defence" or "the conclusion of a siege". Now we seemed likely to have our revenge, and Kut, gateway to Baghdad, would soon fall.

"If we take Baghdad . . . where does all this leave the Berlin-Baghdad railway?" It was the inquisitive kid in the muffler who spoke (and he still wore the muffler, too).

"Up the pole!" said the bluff man. "It'll be the *British*-Baghdad Railway!"

He was pleased with that, and he looked round at us all.

"Tell that to the British prisoners blasting tunnels in the Anatolian mountains," said Downes, and the bluff fellow scowled.

. . . And he did not clap when Short rose to his feet to give the vote of thanks to the speaker, and to say that next week's talk would be on "Byways of Bradshaw — some curiosities of the railway timetable". The War Relief collection was taken, and the audience filed out. But not the quiet man who'd given me the cigarette. He was talking to Downes, who at first was standing, painfully, with his stick, but the other politely urged him to sit down. It seemed that, in his quiet way, he had a good deal to say.

I trooped down the stairs behind Short and his friend in the muffler, who said, "Shouldn't all that have come under Official Secrets? It was a bit near-the-knuckle, anyhow. And did you hear that fellow sticking up for Johnny Turk? I suppose they 'didn't have any choice' about giving our boys what for in Gallipoli?"

"Apparently", said Short, "Mr Hayward does a very good skit about a rather dim fellow who comes up to London from the country, and buys a ticket for the Central Line on the Underground. He says to the clerk, 'But there's no destination stated.' 'That's correct,' says the clerk, 'all our tickets are alike.' 'But how,' says the rather dim fellow, 'will I —'"

"'. . . Will I know where I'm going?'" put in the younger man. "It's an old joke."

And he was still scowling.

In our third-floor room at the Midland Grand Hotel, the wife was looking down at the carpet with arms folded in disapproval.

"You'd have thought it would be a *fitted* carpet," she said, kicking away at the end of it.

I ought to have known that, given the chance to have a holiday in one of London's premier hotels at someone else's expense, she'd object. She was a snob like Dad — the trouble was, she was snobbish about his snobbery.

"I think the rooms above have only got linoleum," I said.

15

"Well, that's no comfort to me," said the wife. She walked over to the window, and pulled back the curtain. "And what's *that?*" she said, looking down.

"The Midland Road goods yard," I said. I'd been watching it myself from the window a moment before. Assorted lights burned down there: orange-glowing braziers, the red and green lamps of low signals. The pilot engine had been nudging a rake of twenty empty coal wagons, as though positioning them to the very inch, and the great gouts of steam that had come rolling up through the blackness had seemed to signify the tremendous *brainwork* involved rather than the mechanical effort.

"Well we've got an excellent view of it," said the wife. "I suppose they'll be shunting all night?"

It was difficult to think of an answer to that, apart from "Yes".

It was a good room, I thought: the wallpaper was the colour of a sweet wrapper: red and green stripes, nicely offset by the black wrought-iron fireplace, where a strong fire burned.

"What was the talk like?" I enquired, for the wife had gone to a talk as well, on what we had decided would be the "cheap night" of the three we were to spend in London.

"It was called 'Problems of the War'. And it was extremely rambling — went on for two hours."

She looked harder through the window. "I believe they're just moving those wagons about for the sake of it. The problem of the war", she said, sitting down on the bed with a sigh, "is the *war*."

The talk she'd attended had been given by some London sub-division of the Co-Operative Society. She worked for the Co-Operative Women's Guild in York, and the movement generally was pushing for a scheme of food rationing. Since the Co-Operative stores did not make a profit (but redistributed income to their members), they could afford to come out against profiteering and unequal distribution of food. But the wife found the whole matter "a great bore", and had admitted as much to me.

The complications of war politics had drained away some of her radical energy. She was still part of the push for women's suffrage, but her particular group had dropped most of their campaigning for the duration. She might go either way — towards the all-out anti-war camp of the Independent Labour Party, or into the bloody Conservative Party for all I knew. Certainly she was coaching up our boy, Harry, for the best of the York grammar schools; she'd been overjoyed when I'd received my commission, and when we'd booked into the hotel, and the clerk had said, "Mr Stringer, is it?" she'd cut in, saying, "*Captain* . . . Captain Stringer."

She was now stretched out on the bed with her book. She was reading *Little Women*, and not for the first time. It was her protest book. If I saw it in her hand — it or *The Collected Plays of George Bernard Shaw* — then I knew I was in for the silent treatment. She was boycotting love-making — this ever since I'd been to the medical board and received the option of rejoining my unit in France or going for a four-month spell of officer training at a pleasant-sounding place in the countryside (for it seemed I could either *learn* how to be an officer, or just go off and *be* one). I had opted for the front.

"You don't want people to think I'm a shirker, do you?" I'd said, to which the reply had come, "You've done your bit, Jim. You've got half a hundredweight of metal in your leg."

From the Midland Road goods yard came a repeated rapid clanging, and the pilot engine gave three shrieks of its whistle, as though in panic.

"Let's go for a drink," I said.

"Where?" said the wife, not looking up from *Little Women*.

"Well, I don't know if you noticed, but there's about a dozen bars downstairs."

"There *are*. There *are* about a dozen . . . And don't call them bars."

But she'd put down her book.

She got up and I watched her change her dress. When she'd finished, she said, "I'm not drinking alcohol, you know."

We went out of the room, along the corridor a little way and came to the great wide curving staircase. There were lifts at the Midland Grand, but the staircase was the big draw. It seemed to come down from the heavens, for the ceiling of the stairwell above was painted pale blue and decorated with gold stars. The balustrades were all fancy ironwork. Electric chandeliers swung over our heads as we descended past plaster carvings and assorted artworks. The hotel was like a

18

cathedral in the days when they were still painted — a cathedral with electric light and giant steam radiators. Half the guests seemed to be treading the staircase and looking about in wonder, for nobody *talked* on the staircase. You got the idea that having descended, people turned about and ascended again, just for the thrill of it. About half the men on the staircase were in uniform, and most were with women. A fellow captain came towards me, and we smiled. The captain's wife looked at my wife's dress and vice versa. As we crossed with the other couple, the wife put her arm in mine — which meant that her dress had beaten her opponent's.

Piano music floated up from . . . was it the coffee lounge, or the men's smoking room, or the women's?

"There's a man in the billiard room," I said, "who's paid to chalk up the scores. He's called Bartlett. He was in France himself and he stopped something at Loos. *He* has a lot of metal in him as well, and he says he gets a terrible pain whenever it's foggy."

"How do you know?"

"How do I know what?"

"Oh, I don't know . . . That he's called Mr Bartlett."

"Because he introduces himself to the players before the game. If he just started chalking up your scores *without* introducing himself that would be rude."

"Is that all he does?"

"He also puts up the war news in the Mahogany Room."

"Then let's not go there."

We were just then coming around the final bend in the staircase so that the whole ground floor came into view, which was a series of islands, each one with its potted palm, a cluster of chairs . . . or perhaps just a small palm on a stand next to a single man in an armchair. Almost anything you could do in any of the lounges — smoke, drink, eat, read the paper — you could also do out here, on public show. As we stepped off the staircase, a man in uniform, unaccompanied by a woman, stepped on to it — a dark, pleasant-looking, modest sort of chap with a cigarette held in long fingers and a rolled-up magazine under his arm. He gave the quickest of glances to the wife, but not to me, and only when he'd gone past did I identify him — and this by the particular tang of the cigarette smoke trailing behind him. It was the fellow from the Railway Club talk: the man who'd seemed to have a soft spot for Johnny Turk.

I turned around, but he gave no glance back.

On the ground floor, we drifted over towards the dining room and I read the menu mounted on the stand outside. The wife looked it over, and it was all a matter of "potages", "poissons", "relevés", all in French. But then a man in a tail-coat blocked our view of it: "Will you be joining us, sir? Madam?"

"No thanks," I said, "we've already eaten."

I didn't let on that we'd had steak and onions on the Euston Road, but the man smiled in such a way as to suggest that he knew anyway.

"You should have said, 'No thanks, we've already banqueted,'" said the wife, as we drifted off.

We went into one of the coffee lounges, where I told the wife she *would* be drinking alcohol, and ordered, at

20

a cost of nine shillings, what turned out to be only a half bottle of champagne.

"I thought the price was a bit too reasonable," said the wife, when it arrived on its tray, looking rather small — not that she took more than half a glass herself, but it was enough to get her started on a bit of York gossip.

"You know that Mrs Knight-Squires is working as a tram driver?"

"No, I did not."

I *did* know that Mrs Knight-Squires was a patron of the Co-Operative Society, even if she was too grand ever to shop at a Co-Operative store, and altogether the most unlikely socialist imaginable. I also knew that the York Council Transport Committee had been hoping to train up women to replace the men who'd gone off to France.

"She passed a test, and they put her on directly. The number nine, you know, so she's up and down the Hull Road all day."

"Lot of pubs on that route," I said, "pretty low ones as well."

The wife nodded, took a quick sip of champagne.

"Doesn't bother her in the slightest."

"But how does she cope with all the drunks?"

"Well of course, she has a big strong conductor to deal with *them*," said the wife, ". . . her good friend Mrs Gwendolyn Richards."

She burst out laughing, and looked all around the coffee lounge; then she burst out laughing again, at the end of which she was rather red. After our drink, we took another turn through the entrance hall, and the islands of seats were more populated now.

"Shall we go back up?" said the wife, which was a promising remark.

We closed once again on the foot of the staircase, and I noticed a strange little set-up that didn't seem to have been there before. It was a wooden replica of an Arab's tent, or something of the kind. It was brightly coloured, with a fairground look to it, and a dome on the top that finished in a point. The signs announced "Cigarettes from the East", and "Coffee from the East". A man stood inside the wooden tent. He wore a stripy tunic shirt that came down to his knees, with perfectly normal trousers and boots beneath. He was quite dark-skinned. Well, he was "from the East" (I supposed).

"Coffee?" he said, "cigarettes . . . from the Biblical lands?"

I was about to decline, but he pressed the matter.

"For after dinner, perhaps? I trust you are enjoying your stay, sir?"

There was nothing of the East about his actual voice, as far as I could make out, but in the form of words there may have been.

I shook my head. "Thanks awfully, but . . ." He half bowed at me, and we walked on.

"I don't think there are *many* cigarettes smoked in the Bible," said the wife, as we began to climb the stairs. "But then again, that man *is* a Mohammedan."

"Not a real one," I said.

"I think he is," she said; "I was wandering about on the top floor this morning, and I saw him."

The top floor was where most of the staff had their rooms.

"What were you doing up there?"

"Wandering about — I told you. He was kneeling on the floor and facing that direction," she said, pointing.

"King's Cross station," I said.

"Mecca, you idiot."

"I know," I said, "I know."

The drink did its work, and we had our tumble on the bed. It was a very good bed, being well sprung, and the fire had been banked up while we'd been downstairs. The goods yard had not gone away though (I had glanced down and seen that they were now moving great quantities of beer barrels) and the pilot engine, which seemed to be very badly fired, would repeatedly blow off its excess steam. I'd thought, or hoped, that I had so transported the wife that she hadn't noticed the racket, but at the moment we concluded the business, she said, "What *is* going on down there, Jim?"

She got off to sleep pretty quickly even so, whereas I could not. The comfort of the room only brought to mind its opposite: the Western Front . . . or maybe the noise of the goods yard had stirred something up. Anyhow I kept imagining what a five-nine crump might do to the spires and pinnacles of the hotel.

I lay awake for the best part of an hour before deciding to return downstairs.

The clock gave a single chime as I put on my suit. There were still a fair few on the staircase, but now they were all coming *up* — men and women in beautiful clothes, smiling and walking with a sleepy trudge. I went against the tide, with my right hand on the banister. (With memories of the front, my right hand had begun to shake, and I held the banister to steady it.)

At the foot of the staircase, I turned and saw the Eastern gentleman — the real Mohammedan — standing outside his tent-like quarters. He held a looped cord on which hung a couple of dozen small metal coffee cups, and he was speaking to the man who had been at the Railway Club, the man with the weird brand of smokes, which I now saw must have been purchased from the Mohammedan, with whom he seemed on the best of terms. He — the Mohammedan — was smiling, and he seemed to say, "You are right, my shepherd, you are perfectly right," and the other — who still held his magazine — was nodding and colouring up, as though *embarrassed* at being in the right.

I observed this from across the lobby, in which only one or two of the islands were now populated. The man from the Railway Club happened to glance my way, and I knew that he now *did* recognise me, and at this for some reason he coloured deeper. It may have been just shyness, but he seemed somehow *helpless* at that moment. I felt it would be impossible to walk away from him, even though I also knew he would not necessarily welcome an approach. But I *did* approach, at which the coffee-and-cigarette man said something in a low voice to my quarry, and moved away.

"Shepherd," he said, extending his hand. "We were at the Railway Club earlier."

He was a handsome fellow in the later thirties or early forties, slightly built, with crinkly dark hair. I gave him my own first name, but "James" instead of Jim. He gave every indication of being a high-ranking officer. I had him down as a major at least, but it didn't do to ask.

"Thanks for the cigarette," I said. "A very decent smoke . . . It came from there, I suppose?" I said, indicating the Eastern tent.

Shepherd nodded, but said nothing. Was it a social mistake for a fellow to show knowledge of where another fellow bought his cigarettes? Shepherd was perhaps on the point of utterance when the man who'd occupied the kiosk swept across the lobby towards the front door, having collected his coat from somewhere. (It was a blue greatcoat — nothing in the least Mohammedan about either it or his grey felt hat.)

Seeing me looking at the man, Shepherd said, smiling, "His name isn't . . . Abdullah, you know?"

I thought: *I never said it was.*

"Care for a drink?" he said, and I saw that this was the way of it with the man Shepherd: he was shy but well mannered. He would try to make up for any display of shyness, or the awkwardness consequent upon it, with a generous offer.

A quick inspection of the lounges off the lobby told us that the Mahogany Room was the only one still boasting a fire. A dozen men sat in there, smoking hard. The first chairs we came to were set either side of a low table, and I could see Shepherd thinking, *If we sit there, I will be interrogated,* but we took those seats anyway. Shepherd set down his magazine, which unfurled itself to reveal . . . well, of course it was a copy of *The Railway Magazine* — the February 1917 number, I had it myself at home. He took his cigarettes from his top pocket and again offered me one. He set down the packet on the table. There was some writing in a foreign script, and a picture of a dark-skinned man in a fez hat walking through a pale-coloured desert at night with a rather paler woman in a red dress at his side. The man's fez was the same shade of red as the woman's dress. In the sky above hung a crescent moon and four stars. A waiter came; we ordered brandies (I didn't care for spirits myself, but I knew they were the right thing to have, late on in a good hotel), and then sat back for an interval, blowing smoke and smiling. I was trying to look like an officer. Shepherd had no trouble in that regard, yet his shyness — or something else — prevented him from opening the conversation.

We both found that we were contemplating the magazine. The covers of *The Railway Magazine* were always either blue or green, and this one was green. Across the top of it — as usual — was an advertisement for "The United Flexible Metallic Tubing Company Limited. Works: Ponders End, Middlesex."

Shepherd put his hand towards it, saying, "Good old *Railway Mag.*"

"I have it on subscription," I said.

"Me too," Shepherd said, blushing again.

. . . But having said this, he once again blushed, which suggested there *was* something shameful in it after all. Yet there couldn't be if Shepherd did it. I was promoting him in my mind as the seconds went by. Only a lieutenant colonel — say — could afford to be so awkward.

Another silence fell between us.

"I was *in* it once," I said, indicating the magazine.

"*Were* you?" he said, and it was genuine interest too.

I believe I then spoke for about ten minutes continuously. I began by telling Shepherd of how I was a railway detective by profession, having been deflected from a career on the footplate by an accident involving an unwarmed engine brake and the wall of an engine shed in Sowerby Bridge, near Halifax. (On the basis of this data, I realised, he must be wondering how I came to be a commissioned officer, for I assumed he did credit me with being an officer of some sort.)

I told him how the police office I had worked in was situated at York station . . .

"On platform four," he cut in, "I know it."

I then started in about how a journalist had come from *The Railway Magazine* and written us all up, giving prominence to my governor, Chief Inspector Weatherill, and giving me second billing in a way designed to cause maximum embarrassment: "The sharpers and dodgers of York station have learnt not to run too close a risk in the immediate vicinity of Chief Inspector Weatherill, and his close associate Detective Sergeant Stringer . . ."

At this, Shepherd smiled, but I believe he was smiling at the words of the journalist rather than at my own recollection of them. In other words, he was not laughing at *me*.

"Go on to the war," said Shepherd.

I told him the North Eastern Railway had formed its own battalion . . .

"The Seventeenth Northumberland," he again cut in. I nodded, and waited for him to say, ". . . known as 'The Railway Pals'," and he got points with me when he *didn't*. I told him that in the second half of the Somme campaign my unit had operated trains to the front from the railhead at Aveluy.

"Little trains?" he said, again with excitement.

"The two-foot railways," I said. "They're everywhere now."

"Were you running the Simplex twenty-horsepower units?"

I shook my head.

"Never touched the Simplex tractors. Never saw one, or any petrol engine for the matter of that. We were riding the Baldwins."

Blowing out smoke, he said the one word, "Steam," and sat back. He eyed me for a while, sat forward. "Are they good runners, the Baldwins?"

"They're good *steamers*," I said, "but the boilers are set too high."

"So they're unstable."

I drained my glass of brandy.

"They fall over," I said.

I told him how I'd got crocked, but not about the bad business I'd struck in my own unit — the matter of the bad lads within it. He listened, it seemed to me, carefully, and not just out of politeness.

His knowledge of railways might have put him in the Royal Engineers. But they were in the thick of the railway construction, and he'd asked his questions as an outsider. He held back, anyhow, which was his right as the senior man. But he again tried to make up for any lapse in manners by returning to the question of the cigarettes, which he had seen had interested me. Indicating the packet on the table before us, he said, "By the way, if you're a regular here, you'd know that it used to be 'Turkish cigarettes' and 'Turkish coffee'."

I nodded.

We were at war with Turkey. You might as well try and sell "German sausages" as "Turkish cigarettes", and this accounted for "Smokes from the Holy Land" or whatever the phrase had been.

"I'm surprised the fellow can still lay his hands on them," I said.

"Oh, he can't of course," said Shepherd. "His stock's running very low . . . And they're becoming rather dried out. With the fires and the steam heating," he said, leaning forward, "it's very hot in here, whereas a cigarette wants moisture in the atmosphere."

I nodded, thinking: *Well of course it's very hot in Turkey as well.* But perhaps it was the humid kind of heat.

A long interval of silence. Then Shepherd suddenly asked another railway question: "How portable are the two-foot tracks?"

"It takes four men to lift a length," I said.

"Not portable enough."

I said, "You could get away with lighter specifications if the engines were more stable." And then I tried a bit of philosophy: "Railways are called 'The Permanent Way', but in France just now, we don't want them permanent. We ought to be able to pick them up and move them in just the same way a boy takes up his model railway when it's time for bed."

He nodded slowly, saying, "Well it's time for *my* bed," but I fancied he'd liked that answer I'd given him.

He stood up; we shook hands again, and he walked off.

By now, the Mahogany Room was quiet — only half a dozen men left in it. A footman was clearing out the fire, which was a way of getting stragglers to get off to bed. But I wondered about another drink. I turned and saw, standing at the bar, Bartlett, the fellow who chalked up the scores at billiards. He was talking to the barkeeper, with a glass of something on the go.

As I approached the bar, he said, "Evening sir. Very fine gentleman, the lieutenant colonel."

"What is he?" I said. "Guards?"

"*Grenadier* Guards," said Bartlett. "Been involved in some marvellous forward moves, has Lieutenant Colonel Shepherd."

Well, he would know, being the man who pinned up the war news. I looked across at the green noticeboard, and saw in the headlines over and over again the wrong-looking word "Kut".

"He was decorated," Bartlett was saying. "D.S.O."

"Any chance of a drink?" I asked the barkeeper.

"The Mahogany Room closes at two, sir," he replied. "It's ten after now."

"War regulations, sir," said Bartlett; but the barkeeper set another brandy before me. "Anyhow," Bartlett added, "that's what we say to those chaps not *in* the war."

"I'm obliged to you," I said to the barkeeper, and put a half crown on the bar, which he pushed back my way.

"What's the name of the chap who sells the cigarettes?" I said, pushing the half crown back.

"Mr Ali," said Bartlett. "*Coffee* and cigarettes, it is."

"What is he?" I said. "I mean . . ."

"I would say he was foreign," said Bartlett, "but friendly."

"But where's he from?"

"Well now I don't think you'd be far wrong if you said he was an Arab."

"Or something of the sort," put in the barkeeper.

The fire had quite gone out, and the steam heating had evidently been turned off in the public rooms.

"It's rather cold in here," I said.

CHAPTER
TWO

In the police office on platform four of York station, I was sitting "in state", so to speak, observing the work of my old office with my bad leg up on the desk. This was to remind everyone that I was an officer on convalescent leave, as yet with no news of when I would return to my unit, and not to be troubled by the question of what was or was not in the Occurrence Book, or by the fact that the witness statements relating to an unlawful wounding at the Dringhouses Marshalling Yard had just gone missing for the second time.

I had done my officer training course after all. My commanding officer, Major Quinn, had written from France politely insisting upon it. Six weeks in a country house outside Catterick. The grounds of the place were apparently famous, but I had mainly seen them blurred through window glass, for it had rained almost every day. I had spent most of my time sitting down and being lectured, and sitting didn't suit my bad leg. It got so that whenever one of the officer-instructors said, "Sit down, gentlemen," I'd think he was trying to do me in, and when I was driven out of the place, in the charabanc that shuttled between house and railway station, my limp was more pronounced than when I'd arrived.

Old Man Wright, the clerk of the police office, thought I was putting it on. He might easily have been seventy-five, and he'd been bucked up no end by the coming of a war from which he was exempt. The crisis made it seem a good thing to be a scrawny old man in a dullish line of work. With Chief Inspector Weatherill — my governor as was — it was the opposite case. The Chief loved a scrap. *His* war had been out in Egypt in the eighties, and his great regret ever since was that a fellow didn't come up against too many dervishes on the railway lands of York.

Wright was moving about the office slamming drawers. He didn't take kindly to seeing me with my leg up, but he could hardly say anything about it, for the Chief, sitting at the desk over opposite, had *both* his legs up. He was reading the *Yorkshire Evening Press* about the British occupation of Baghdad. The date on the paper was Monday April 23rd.

"They've got their tails up in Mespot," he said, and I recalled to mind the talk I'd attended at the Railway Club.

"A hundred and twenty degrees it is over there," said Wright, who was perhaps hunting up the missing witness statements. "*Bit* on the warm side."

"Fancy a walk?" said the Chief, lowering the paper.

"It's raining," said Wright, from over near the fireplace, where he was blocking the heat.

But the Chief hadn't been asking Wright, and he continued to look his question at me.

33

We walked through the station with the rain thundering on the great roof. I liked to look up and watch it roll over the dirty glass. As the Chief collared a messenger boy, and sent him off to the Lost Luggage Office with a sixpence and instructions to bring back two umbrellas, I watched an Ivatt Atlantic come in, mixing its own roar with the roar of the rain. It was London-bound, and there weren't many takers for its carriages.

At the ticket barriers, the Chief said, "Where do you want to walk to?" and he named a couple of pubs. Then he said, "But I was forgetting . . . you're a hotel man now, en't you? What do you reckon? Lowther's? The Royal?"

As we stepped out from under the station portico, and raised our brollies, I said, "Let's go to The Moon, shall we?"

The Full Moon was in Walmgate. It was most certainly not a hotel. You couldn't even get a bite to eat there. You could drink *beer*.

Now that I was an army captain, the Chief would constantly set traps for me — giving me opportunities to put on swank, and I did my best to dodge them. He might be a chief inspector in the railway police, but he'd risen no higher than sergeant major in his own days with the colours. This was partly through choice. The Chief didn't want to be doing with writing up reports and dining in the officers' mess. He would scrape his knife against his plate; he didn't know which way you passed the salt.

34

It was a ten-minute tramp to Walmgate. On Lendal Bridge, with the rain redoubling and the river seething below us, the Chief brought his umbrella close to mine, passed me a cigar, and lit both it and his own. We walked on through the darkly shining York streets, under endless sodden Union Jacks.

"Well," I said, as we turned into Parliament Street. "What is it?"

Because he obviously wanted to talk to me about something.

"Tell you in the pub," said the Chief. He liked to draw these things out — a bit of a sadist, was the Chief.

The Full Moon was not full. In fact, it was completely empty and silent. The Chief walked up to the bar, and bawled out "Carter!" which was the name of the landlord — after which the silence gradually returned. Everything was brown, and slightly ticking — the clock, the tables, the benches. After a while, I began to hear the drumming of the rain above the ticking. The Chief swore, called out "Carter!" again, and nothing happened again, but I noticed that the trapdoor in the floor behind the bar was open.

"He's in the cellar," I said.

Presently, we heard the trudge of Carter on the cellar steps, and he began to come up through the trapdoor.

"Chief Inspector Weatherill!" he said, when about three-quarters of him had appeared; but the Chief just said, "Four pints of Smiths."

"Four?" I said. "Hold on a minute!"

"Bloody emergency licensing," said the Chief. "You never know when a pub's going to close. When are *you* going to close?" he asked Carter.

"Not till eight," said Carter, handing over the pints, "but there's no long pulls for soldiers."

We took our drinks, one in each hand, over to the table near the fire. Halfway over the Chief turned back to Carter.

"I hope you don't serve milk do you?"

"Why?" said Carter, "do you want a glass?"

"Of course I don't want a fucking glass of milk," said the Chief.

The Chief had never drunk a glass of milk in his *life*.

"Some pubs are serving milk," the Chief told me, taking out his bundle of cigars.

I took my first sip of the Smiths.

"Well, it's the law," I said. "And you *are* a policeman."

"I tell you, this town's being run by the teetotal cranks and the bloody cocoa men."

The Chief was down on the York City Council, and he now started in about how they'd changed all the lighting out of fear of a Zeppelin attack, but then he stopped talking about that, and said:

"I'm taking you up to London tomorrow."

I eyed him for a while.

"In that case I should tell you that I've developed rather a liking for the Midland Grand Hotel."

"No need for an overnight," said the Chief.

"Is it the War Office again, by any chance?"

No reply. Well, the Chief was busy lighting his cigar.

36

"Henderson-Richards again?" I said.

The Chief knew a man in the Intelligence Section of the War Office called Henderson-Richards. He'd taken me to see him back in 1911, after a case in which I'd stumbled on some government-and-railway business that was to be kept muffled up. Henderson-Richards I recalled as having uncommonly long hair and slipper-like shoes. After talking down to me for a while, he'd made me sign the Official Secrets Act.

"Different bloke," said the Chief, while working the cigar with his mouth.

"Name of . . .?"

The Chief set down the cigar.

"Manners," he said.

"Is he a soldier?"

"Is he fuck."

The Chief would refer to certain young military men who didn't come up to the mark as "boy scouts", but it was a real boy scout who led us up the great staircase of the War Office towards the office of Manners. The kid was about fifteen, and he and his entire troop were doing the work of the War Office messengers who'd gone off to France. We were put in his charge in the great lobby, which was full of men shaking out their umbrellas in a grey light. As we climbed the wide marble staircase, the scout said that his greatest hope was that the war would carry on long enough for him to be in it. But I hardly heard him. I was thinking of what had happened on the train on the way up.

The Chief and I had had a compartment to ourselves: a First Class smoker of course. The Chief always went First — well, he was *The Chief*, and he had the highest sort of staff pass, the one that came in a leathern wallet with an outline of the North Eastern territory embossed in gold. (It looked like the head of a cow.) A little beyond Doncaster, with the wind flinging occasional raindrops at the window, he'd leant forward and handed me a letter that nestled in a ripped-open envelope. It was addressed to me at the police office, and it came from France.

"I opened it by mistake, lad," said the Chief, and I didn't know that I believed him. Certainly he was very free and easy about the mail, often chucking away his own letters unopened, but I also knew he'd been like a cat on hot bricks over the question of whether or when I'd be returning to my unit.

Evidently, the letter had arrived at the police office on the previous Thursday, April 19th, when I'd been at home. It was from Major Quinn, my C.O., and had been despatched from Givenchy. Quinn couldn't give his exact whereabouts, but I knew he was in charge of a detachment helping the Canadians with light railways behind Vimy Ridge. He gave me his best wishes, hoped I'd got something out of the training course, if only a good rest, and expressed the hope I'd be rejoining the unit soon. On the other hand, he had received, on April 10th, a letter dated March 14th, and sent from Baghdad, Mesopotamia, by a Lieutenant Colonel Shepherd, who had evidently sailed for the East within a week of my meeting him. It seemed I'd made quite a

38

score with him at the Midland Grand, and he wanted me to join him in helping run the railways of Baghdad, such as they were. Shepherd himself had been invited out there by a high-ranking officer he'd run across in the early days of the war, and had got the job through "what was really the most tremendous luck". (The old school tie more like, I thought.)

Quinn had pointed out that Shepherd had sent his letter only three days after the fall of Baghdad, meaning to indicate, I supposed, that I ought to be flattered at being in the thoughts of a lieutenant colonel during what must have been what Quinn called "a pretty hectic time". Quinn was perfectly happy to let me go if I was so minded.

At first I'd been silent, annoyed at the Chief for opening the letter, and revolving a hundred questions. Then I'd begun quizzing the Chief. Since he had opened my letter, I'd felt he owed me some answers. But he hadn't seen it like that, and as London approached, and the rain beyond the carriage windows came on in earnest, I'd settled into a mood that was a queer combination of sulk and stirring excitement.

"This is Mr Manners's office," the Scout said, knocking, and his patriotic front cracked a bit when he added, "I don't mind saying . . . he's had some queer blokes in here today."

The shout came from within: "Enter!"

Whereas Henderson-Richards, back in 1911, had had hair practically on his collar, this bloke had none at all, and, his head being so long, he could have done with some. On the strength of his name, I'd expected him to have some manners, which he didn't really. He just indicated a chair for me and another for the Chief, before saying to me: "Now you're off to Baghdad. How did that come about?"

No preamble about whether I wanted to go to Baghdad or not (although I'd decided immediately on seeing the letter that I did want to). No apology on behalf of the Chief for opening the letter; no mention of how the Chief must have telephoned or telegraphed to him or some other department to reveal the detail of it. No explanation of what the letter had signified to the Chief, or how and why it had any bearing on my presence in this office.

Even so, I gave Manners my account of the meeting at the Midland Grand, ending by saying, "I believe Lieutenant Colonel Shepherd must have decided to take me on there and then, knowing the job he had in hand."

"Yes," Manners said when I'd finished. "Well, let nobody say the British Army officer is incapable of improvisation. Tell me, Captain Stringer, what do you think it was that the lieutenant colonel saw in you?"

"I suppose he felt I'd talked sense about the railway logistics of the Western Front."

"Mmm," said Manners.

On his desk was a red pasteboard folder and a buff envelope. I looked at this stationery for a while, and he watched me doing so. Presently, he said, "There is no blinking the fact that we believe Lieutenant Colonel Shepherd to be in league with the enemy."

"Which enemy?" I said.

Now Manners evidently did not think this a clever question — and I could tell the Chief was embarrassed at it, by the way he suddenly crossed his legs, which left him sitting in a position to which he was not at all suited.

"Captain Stringer," said Manners, "it might be as well for you to know in advance of your departure for Mesopotamia that the gentry we are fighting over there are the Turks. Have you got that straight? The *Turks*."

"But the Germans as well?" I said.

"The occupiers of Baghdad were Turkish, I don't think there's any room for doubt on that score. It was the Turks that we banished from the city; it is the Turks who may attempt to reclaim it, and it is the Turks who are occupying the territories to the north and west of Baghdad. Certainly, there are German officers on the Turkish Army Staff — but not many, and their role is advisory rather than executive."

"And the Arabs?"

"The *Arabs?*" he said.

You'd have thought they were completely out of account.

"It's their country, after all."

"I see you are an expert on the region. There is Arab soldiery in the Turkish Army, and there is a cadre of Arab officers. The loyalty of these men to their Turkish masters may be doubted. The position of the Arab citizenry of Baghdad, incidentally, is that they welcome us as liberators . . ."

I nodded.

"For *now*," he added. "As of this week."

He pushed the red pasteboard folder my way. It held my itinerary and passports for travelling east.

Shepherd *had* seemed to stick up for the Turks at the Railway Club meeting; he had certainly been partial to Turkish cigarettes, and he'd seemed quite thick with the Eastern cigarette-and-coffee man of the Midland Grand, but I could not believe he was a traitor. He'd seemed such a thoroughly decent sort. My thoughts raced in a circus as I leafed through the documents, one of many imponderables being: where did the Chief fit in? How had *he* heard of the suspicions against Shepherd?

Manners was speaking again.

"The essential data is as follows. Expeditionary Force 'D' of the British Indian Army — which is to say, General Maude — took control of the city of Baghdad some six weeks ago — on the night of March 11th to be exact. Maude's army advanced on the city by the left and right banks of the River Tigris. In the van of the forces of the left or the west bank was a unit of infantry under the command of Lieutenant Colonel Shep —"

"But hold on a minute," I said, "what was he doing in the fighting? Wouldn't he have been just travelling in the rear to take up his job on the staff?"

"Do feel free to interrupt me with questions, Captain Stringer. Lieutenant Colonel Shepherd got himself attached to the unit as a supernumerary. Perhaps he found the idea of steaming up to Baghdad in the rear to be rather a bore. Or perhaps he had some other scheme in mind."

"How did he get himself attached?"

42

"He knew the commanding officer of the unit, a man called Blake."

"How did he know him?"

"How does anyone know anyone? He met him at a party in London — for all I know at the Midland Grand Hotel. They met again in Basrah, prior to the advance. Anyhow, in the push for the railway station, the unit came under fire and Blake was killed. Shepherd then took command of the unit. He was the only white man left . . . I see you are frowning."

I was.

"There are entirely British units within the British Indian Army," Manners ran on, "and entirely Indian ones. But in most cases the men are Indian, the officers British. The unit we are concerned with was Indian except for Blake and Shepherd."

I nodded.

"Now the picture is confused. It was dawn — the light uncertain, a sandstorm rising. Communications were, so to speak, 'in the air', and the forward patrol on the left bank was rather a jumble. But it seems that its chief elements came from the unit Shepherd was with, and a machine-gun company, the 185th. As these units pressed on, the enemy fell back on the Baghdad railway station, which lies on the outskirts of the town. For days, the Turks had been sending men, armaments and stores from there to Samarrah and points north. The last train to leave the station departed at about four o'clock in the morning on March 12th, and it carried both materiel and men — the last of the Turks put to flight. What concerns us here in this department is that immediately before the departure of that train, a parley occurred within the station between Lieutenant Colonel Shepherd and a Turkish bimbashi."

"What's a bimbashi?"

"A major, let us say."

"What language would this have been conducted in?"

"Almost certainly French. The Turks speak their own version of Arabic, but any well-born Turk speaks French, and we know Shepherd is fluent in it."

Another score chalked up to his name. He had seemed a remarkably modest man, considering.

"Was Lieutenant Colonel Shepherd taking the Turkish surrender?" I said.

"Receiving the chap's pistol and sword you mean?"

Evidently, I was wrong.

"Don't you think it would have been for General Maude to take the surrender?" said Manners. "And for somebody higher than a major to give it? The Turks did not in any case surrender the city of Baghdad, but merely fled from it. Our concern, however, is that Lieutenant Colonel Shepherd *did* take something from the Turkish officer, and that the Turkish officer was given something in return."

"What?"

"A certain amount of . . . *treasure*."

Manners eyed me levelly.

"What form did this treasure take?" I enquired.

"We believe gold coins, possibly other articles as well."

"A large quantity?"

44

"We think so. What was the quantity in *Ali Baba and the Forty Thieves?*"

"I don't know."

"You've never read the story?" He seemed to be quite staggered.

I had in fact gone with the wife and children to see a *film* of the story at the Electric Theatre in York, and it had been very prettily hand-tinted but completely baffling as to plot.

". . . *An amount large enough to be weighed,*" said Manners in a heavy sort of way that told me he must be quoting.

"And what did the Turk get in return?" I asked.

"Perhaps his own freedom for one thing; permission for that last train to depart — and it is believed that certain undertakings may have been made on both sides."

"Undertakings of what nature?"

"Of an unknown nature."

"How do you know Shepherd took this treasure and made these undertakings?"

Manners said, "Any information touching on this affair might be dangerous, both to you and others. I'm sorry if I appear to be obtuse, but there's no point in telling you the little I know at this stage. You'll find out more from a Captain Boyd who is out there, and who is known to this office."

(An intelligence man on the side, most likely — I knew there to be a good sprinkling of those in the officer class.)

I asked, "Was Boyd on the spot at the time? Did he see what went on?"

Manners made a slight head movement, which I took to mean "Yes". I further reasoned that the man Boyd must have been with the machine-gun company — the 185th — since there were only Indians left in the infantry unit. (Unless of course he actually *was* Indian. *Could* you have an Indian called Boyd?)

"This fellow Boyd," I said. "How did he get into touch with you? By telegraph, I suppose. Or did he telephone? Can you telephone from Baghdad?"

"At a pinch, but it's a great performance, involving about half the telephonists in India. No, Boyd wrote to us."

"He wrote you . . . a *letter?*"

Manners looked at me for a long time before responding: "You know what they say, Captain Stringer: 'as safe as the mail'. And Boyd's letter was particularly safe, since he sent it via the diplomatic bag."

"But it wouldn't be any *quicker* that way. It takes nearly four weeks to get a letter from Baghdad," I said, thinking of the letter sent to Quinn in France by Shepherd.

"General Maude himself communicates mainly by post with London," said Manners.

"But that means he must take weeks to get his orders?"

"Slow and steady wins the race, Captain Stringer."

And at this, I finally realised the truth about Manners: he was *humorous.*

46

"I still don't see why Boyd didn't send a wire," I said.

Manners sighed, and looked to the Chief: "A regular terrier this man, Weatherill. In the first place," he continued, turning back to me, "he did wire. The day after the fall of Baghdad, he reported to us that he had an urgent and important matter to mention, and that he required a confidential channel of communication. Without any reiteration of his message, we replied by wire to the effect that he should seek direction from a certain other officer out there."

"A more senior one?"

Manners blanked the question with a slight look of pain, continuing: "After speaking with this other officer, Boyd set down his concerns on paper in greater detail — although still not so very great."

"And he sent them to you in a letter."

"Which we received on April 15th. Mr Henderson-Richards of this department had sight of the letter. Four days later, he happened to be at York station — his mother has a place in the country nearby — when he bumped into Chief Inspector Weatherill here, who is of course a trusted man, known to this office. The two fell to gossiping."

"*Exchanging intelligence*," growled the Chief, and Manners, for the first time, actually grinned.

"The name of Shepherd in Baghdad was mentioned to the Chief Inspector," said Manners, "who only a few moments before had by an unfortunate accident — which in fact was very *fortunate* — read the letter indicating the job offer to you from Shepherd."

Manners now slid the buff envelope towards me.

"Open it," he said.

"Is it the letter from this Captain Boyd?"

"No, although it arises from his letter. It was written for you by one of my superiors, and it relays to you an arrangement made with Boyd."

Inside was a typed note, headed — ridiculously to my mind — "Top Secret". It went on in peremptory fashion: "Captain Stringer to rendezvous with Captain Boyd outside the *Salon de Thé* (restaurant) at Baghdad railway station at 11p.m. on Thursday May 24th. Stringer to observe, 'It is closed.' Boyd to reply, 'The coffee houses by the bridge of boats will do you very well if you don't mind the walk.'"

So I had a little under a month to get to Baghdad.

I handed back the note. Since this arrangement must have been made in the few days since I came into the picture, it must have been made between the Intelligence office and Boyd via telegram. I asked if this was the case and Manners (with the greatest reluctance) nodded. I said, "How secure were those wires?", for there must have been two: one proposing the arrangement, and one confirming.

Manners said, "You need have no anxiety on that score. Boyd did not know the military codes, so his telegrams were sent, as we say, 'clear' — that is in plain English — but you were not named in the wires, and nor was the rendezvous point named. In his *letter* to us, Boyd had already nominated that particular spot as 'safe place' — the station being some way out of town — in which to confide his anxieties should we wish to assign a man to the case. A return to the station would also allow him to show exactly what he'd seen on the night in question."

"So the telegrams were to the effect X will meet you at Y place?"

"You've caught on splendidly," said Manners, who now stood up, walked over to his fire, and dropped the note detailing the arrangement on the low flames. Since it was on the very flimsiest paper, it disappeared immediately.

"By the way, I trust you committed that to memory," he said, with the hint of a returning smile. "Boyd's a good chap — he'll put you in the picture. You'll take your place in Shepherd's office. You'll gather evidence and you'll report back."

"And the aim is to bring Shepherd to book."

"Or put him in the clear," said Manners. "We'll settle for either. But there is another aim equally important, and that is the uncovering of the treasure, and the securing of same for His Majesty's Government."

I'd forgotten about the treasure.

"You will spend a month in Baghdad."

"Not very long," I said, and I knew I sounded relieved, which in fact I was.

"At the end of that period, you will be recalled as a matter of urgency to your unit in France."

All of this raised so many questions that, in the end, I didn't ask any.

"Can I press on you the need for absolute discretion?" Manners said. "Lieutenant Colonel Shepherd is a popular man and highly rated by the command. There would be a scandal in Baghdad if it was found he was being investigated, and that would sap morale badly. Discretion must be *absolute*. Have you packed yet?"

"I've only just found out I'm going."

"You won't be needing a top-coat. I recommend mosquito cream, quinine, malaria tablets and a well-oiled service revolver." He offered his hand. "Enjoy yourself out there. Give my regards to Captain Boyd, and we have a message for him from his lady wife . . ."

"Which is?" I said, scowling rather.

"Oh, just that she loves him, and will he please *write* to her?"

Manners had now walked over to the door, and was holding it open for me and the Chief.

"Hold on a minute," I said, "how do I get in touch with you before the month's up?"

"Ah yes," said Manners, and he leant into the corridor and called, "Boy!"

Part Two

Mespot

CHAPTER
THREE

On our third day of sailing up the River Tigris, I resolved to step from under the tarpaulin overhanging the aft deck of the small British Naval gunboat, *Mantis*, and to remain in the open for some time. I had been told to acclimatise to the sun. Stretched out on a long deckchair some way beyond the tarp was a fellow called Dixon. He was reading a magazine called *The Wide World*, and he had been reading exactly the same magazine in exactly the same spot the day before. He was already acclimatised.

Under the tarp, I tried to predict the heat, but when I stepped into it my prediction was as usual exceeded by an amazing amount. Into the dazzling white sky overhead flew ragged gouts of smoke from the oil-fired engines of the *Mantis*.

Oil-fired . . .

From the quay at Basrah, at the head of the Shat-al-Arab waterway, the refineries of the Anglo-Persian Oil Company had been pointed out to me, but they were only so many low, white drums wavering in the heat haze on the other side of the water, like something burning in white flames. They seemed hardly there at all, and yet ten thousand men of the

British and the British Indian Army were in Basrah on their account. Another forty thousand were in Baghdad. There were in addition garrisons posted along the five hundred miles of river connecting those two spots. In short, the hundred and fifty soldiers and thirty crew aboard the *Mantis* were not in any imminent danger of attack — not from Brother Turk anyhow. He'd been driven north of Baghdad by the forces of General Maude. And if any *Arab* tribes encountered on our way might be thinking of having a crack at us . . . Well, they would have the six-inch gun on the foredeck to reckon with, not to mention the machine guns on swivel stands.

On the *Shobak Castle*, the government-controlled liner that had carried me from Southampton to Port Said, then to the Persian Gulf via the Suez Canal and the Red Sea . . . that three-week voyage had not been quite so relaxed an affair. The tub was well worth a torpedo, and in the Med there'd been half a dozen crew on deck with binoculars at all times.

But on the *Mantis*, opera glasses for sightseeing rather than binoculars were the order of the day. On either bank of the Tigris, green wheat grew under the burning sky, but the river being *below* the wheat, I could not make out the desert that I knew lay beyond. Occasionally, I would glimpse the roof of a reed hut or the top of a stone-built building like a windmill without sails, and these, I believed, were to do with the control of the irrigation canals — and the system evidently *worked*, for everything was besieged by the wheat.

54

The man Dixon took *The Wide World* and laid it over his face. He had an easy time of it, being batman to an amiable major called Hartley. Both were old for serving men, being somewhere around the early fifties. Hartley hadn't seen much in the way of action, but he was a brainy sort, who knew all the angles on Mesopotamia.

I would listen to him of an evening, as we all sat holding our drinks and smoking in the cramped and sweltering mess. His main topic was the Arab Revolt. Apparently this was already under way in the Ottoman territories of Syria and the Hejaz, and the War Office was all in favour of it. At least, *some* parts of it were — the parts allied to the British Intelligence Bureau in Cairo, where the plan for stirring up the Arabs had been hatched by some "fiercely clever" young British agents. (Hartley said "fiercely" in a very fierce way, spraying half his drink over me.) These British agents — the Arabists — were now bent on extending the revolt to Mesopotamia, which Hartley always called "Mespot". Not all the Arabs were keen on it, however. A few were pro-Turk, and some — perhaps the majority — just "generally incredibly bloody-minded and indifferent".

India . . . now India was not at *all* keen. Lord Chelmsford, Viceroy of India, was at loggerheads with his governors in London. He had supplied most of the troops by which Maude had taken Baghdad, and what he wanted in return was the Arabian Peninsula as a sub-colony of India. He argued further that a Mohammedan revolt so close to home might inflame those of that persuasion under Indian rule. The loyalty of Indian troops might come into question. Yet it had to be admitted these were mostly Hindu, whereas fully one-quarter of the Turkish army was Arab.

The Turks tried to play the Moslem card as a means of keeping their Arabs on side. Well, the Turks were Moslem after all — they had that going for them. But an Arab revolt would trump that card, and spell the final collapse of the Ottoman Empire. It was just about possible, Hartley suggested, over what might easily have been his fifth whisky, and his third cigar, and in response to a question from me, to imagine how a fellow might feel some sympathy for Brother Turk, as for an acquaintance down on his luck, his picturesque empire crumbling daily, practically forced, by fear of the horrible Russians, to get into bed with the even more horrible Germans. In fact, he'd heard there were a good many in the British government who were pro-Turk, and they argued the strategic benefits of suing for peace with the Turks, but mainly they were romantic types, who appreciated the exotic East. Turcophiles — that was the word for those fellows.

It was a five-day cruise from Basrah to Baghdad, I had been told by the first mate, and our present slow rate of progress meant I would arrive there on the 24th, the very day of my night-time rendezvous with Captain Boyd. We were against the current, and only making eight knots or so.

From the aft deck, I watched strange-coloured small birds skimming over the fields, fluttering their wings quickly, then ceasing to flutter and swooping low, as though in a faint from the heat, but they would always recover, and ascend again. One bird swerved off its course and came out over the river, making directly towards me, and I saw that it was *not* a bird but some giant species of dragonfly — and dragonflies could bite, especially Mesopotamian ones.

I went back under the tarpaulin, but the thing did not stop me baking, and there was the oil smell into the bargain, so I turned in at a hatchway, and retreated to my cabin, where an overhead electrical fan revolved at what I had been told — but which I did not believe — was three hundred revolutions per minute. It was not enough, anyhow.

I lay on my bunk in my undershirt, and lit a cigarette, watching what happened to the smoke when it tangled with the blades of the fan. On the table beside my bunk lay an envelope containing a cash advance of twenty pounds, a quantity of Indian rupees and Turkish lira (all or any of which could apparently be tried on the merchants of Baghdad with some hope of success), together with two copies of my letter of engagement as Assistant to Lieutenant Colonel Shepherd, who was designated a Political Officer (Railways) at the Corps HQ in Baghdad. The letter was not from Shepherd himself even though my recruitment was all his doing, but from the assistant to a Brigadier General Barnes, on behalf of Sir Percy Cox, who was the Chief Political Officer. There was a telegram on the table as well. It had been handed to me at Port Said, and came from the Deputy Chief of Staff at Corps HQ in Baghdad. It informed me that a Private Stanley Jarvis of the North Yorkshire Regiment (one of the British units of the Anglo-Indian force) had been seconded to me as batman. I would be sharing him, so to speak, for he was also one of the motor-car drivers attached to the Corps HQ. He would meet me on the quayside in Baghdad, and escort me to the HQ, which was evidently located in the Hotel Grande Bretagne, which I rather liked the sound of. All of the foregoing was, so to speak, the official side of things.

But there was a *second* envelope on the table, and this one bothered me. It had been brought into Manners's room at the War Office by the boy scout and its contents struck me as nonsensical, and dangerously so. I considered looking them over again, but in the end decided it was just too bloody hot.

I put out my cigarette, tried to sleep, and gave it up after five minutes. The fan had started to rattle and shake. I stared at it, wondering . . . is it actually unscrewing itself? I could not imagine Baghdad railway station. I could not imagine myself slinking into it at close on midnight, and I could conjure no mental image of the man Boyd, witness to the treachery of Shepherd.

On the *Mantis*, I was out from under the tarpaulin, for the sun was now setting, slowly crashing down into the desert that came and went between the orange trees to which the wheat had given way. The air was hot and soft — not unbearable. We had passed Kut, the scene of Townshend's reversal of the year before, and Maude's recent victory. It looked the place for a reversal all right — a desert compound of blockhouses with no colour in it, but plenty of mangy dogs wandering about.

At this point, with Baghdad approaching, both banks of the river seemed to be used as pleasure grounds. An Arab, fishing with a trident spear, frowned as we went past. The wake from our boat was not helping his cause. Arab men, holding hands (I'd been warned they would do that), wandered between the trees, or lay against them and smoked. Sometimes the smokers called out to the Arabs on our boat, of which there were a dozen or so, most employed to help with the horses we were taking up. They all stuck together, and were now standing at the midships, repeatedly shouting one word that I understood:

"Ingilhiz!"

And the Arabs on the bank and the Arabs on the boat would have a good laugh about that. They seemed very easy-going about having their country taken over by foreigners, and just as well too. I supposed they were used to it.

Reed huts were coming into view, and mud houses — long low buildings, bunker-like. I saw a mule tied to a windlass and drawing up a skin of water. A small boy, crouched on the river bank, waited for the water, but the moment he saw me, he stood, and addressed me in Arabic. He appeared to be asking a question, and one that required a quick response. I waved to him, and called out, "Salaam alaikum!" which meant "Peace be upon you", and at which he called out something else I didn't understand. It was impossible to say whether he was being friendly or not. As far as he was concerned, he'd asked me a perfectly normal question that required a perfectly normal answer . . . Or was the machine gun three feet away from me a consideration in the matter? As he retreated from my vision, the kid fell to talking to his mule. He didn't seem to appreciate that he lived in a strange world that was almost entirely orangey-brown, what with the oranges on the trees, the faded orange of the long shirt he wore, and the great sunset going on behind him.

. . . But now, on a kind of river-beach, stood a group of Arab women in faded *blue*. I had been told the name of the outfit that covered almost the entire face as well as the body, but couldn't recall it. Did they wear that rig all the time, being extreme in their faith? Or had they put it on especially, knowing that a boat-load of infidels would be coming along? From what I'd seen so far, most Arab women settled for headscarves, and lots of them. I waved at the party to see whether anything would happen. Nothing did, except that three of the women sat down on the sandy bank, and started what looked like a happy conversation.

Baghdad began to come and go, according to the curves of the river: palm trees with high domes and the pointed towers — minarets — above. The bunkers began to grow into proper brick buildings, and the river became dirty. I saw a floating plank, broken off a crate and stamped with the word "Leeds". We had seemed to be approaching the one bridge that traversed the wide river — a bridge of boats, with tethered black barges supporting a walkway — but now we were turning into

60

the bank. All about me on the *Mantis*, a great bustle was starting up — a clattering of boots going up and down gangways, shouted orders, and the blare of the whistle by which our captain was making our presence felt in the great city. These blasts echoed off the high buildings on the right or eastern bank. They were like so many music halls — albeit somewhat run-down-looking — with domes, arches, or castellated tops, and strange-shaped windows with balconies and verandas overhanging the river. On the western bank, the buildings were lower, and seemed overwhelmed by palm trees.

I read the words on the warehouses on the eastern side: "Lynch, Import Export"; a giant signboard built up over a warehouse read "Hanbury's", and then, stacked still higher above it, a kind of pyramid of smaller boards reading "Oranges", "Onions", "Coffee", "Cigarettes". Another sign read "British and Foreign Bible Society", and I thought: Well, this is definitely the *foreign* end of the operation. I wondered whether these signs had been kept in place throughout the war (the British in Baghdad had been allowed safe passage out of the city by the Turks at the start of the show) or whether they'd recently been refixed.

The river was packed with Arabs in circular boats in a range of sizes. They would stand up in these craft, which had no bow, keel or rudder, and were paddled by a man holding a long oar. They made a fantastical sight — as though the entire town had taken to the water in so many upturned pork-pie hats — and I knew, looking at them, that all bets were off in this place. It was too weird; anything could happen at any moment.

We were now lurching and turning in the river, causing the Arabs in their smaller boats to paddle faster to get clear of us, shouting out — not angrily, but as though to encourage our steersman into the dock.

I pushed along the gangway, against the general flow of men, and collected my pack from my cabin. The gangplanks were coming down. The quay was between two of the music-hall palaces, one of which might have been the Hotel Grande Bretagne, Corps HQ. Waiting on the quay were half a dozen mules, two motor lorries throbbing, a couple of dozen Indian soldiers (tiny fellows — sepoys, they were called), some Arab stevedores in long blue shirts. Another vessel was being unloaded alongside us. Under circling gulls, a derrick was taking bales off it while the Arab dockers chanted, "Allah, Allah, Allah, Allah".

On the quay, an English private blocked my path.

"Are you Jarvis?"

"Sah!" he said, and he snapped to attention, which was quite the right thing for him to do, but he also eyed me curiously, which was not.

"I'm Captain Stringer," I said.

"Sah!" he said again. He then became normal, and it was good to hear a Northern accent. He said, "The base is this way, sir. We're in the Hotel Grande Bretagne — Hotel Great Britain that is, sir."

"I know," I said.

He held out his two arms for my pack, and I gave it him.

The dockers were still chanting the name of their God as Jarvis said something about ". . . I hope this place will be a home-from-home for you, sir."

We joined a flow of soldiers walking up a kind of dirty sluice that rose up from one side of the quay, and this took us into a packed narrow street, the road not much wider than a footpath, where we came up against the doorway of a very compressed mosque with green lanterns burning on either side of the entrance. A loud singing rose up from somewhere, and made me start.

"Time for prayer, sir, time for prayer," said Jarvis, "always at it, they are. Five times a day, starting at dawn. If you should go in there, sir . . . take your shoes off. Don't put your hands in your pockets, and don't put your hands behind your back either, sir."

We pushed through a crowd of beggars. Jarvis was saying something to them in their own language — sounded friendly enough. Well, he was a friendly-looking chap: small, round-faced, and dead keen. "Chirpy", that was the word. As we pushed on past the beggars, he said, "It goes without saying, sir, that you don't go into a mosque in *shorts*. One of the officers did that yesterday, sir, and there was a bit of . . . well, there was a bit of a riot really." (In khaki drill, which was the cotton version of service dress, short or long trousers might equally be worn.) "See any lions on your way up, sir?" Jarvis enquired.

"No — dogs. Plenty of dogs."

"This place is full of dogs too," said Jarvis. "Yellow, they are. And starving."

I said, "Is it quite the thing to wear shorts?"

Jarvis did not, and his trouser legs looked even more sweat-soaked than mine.

"Frowned on in the officers' mess," he said.

"But a good deal cooler," I said.

"I've been thinking much the same myself, sir. Nearly put my pair on this morning. I will if you will, sir, how about that?"

I wasn't sure that was quite the sort of thing a batman should be saying to his officer. He seemed a smart customer, Jarvis, and that could be good or bad.

"Is it a long walk to the Hotel?"

"It's not a long walk to anywhere, strictly speaking. Town's about a mile and a half by a mile, sir. Three-quarters of it on this side of the river, one-quarter on the other." He paused, before adding, "It's a walled city, sir, so you know when you've come to the end of it."

I'd read something about that: Baghdad was the first fortified city of the Turks against the Persians.

"What's beyond the walls?"

"To be quite honest with you, sir," said Jarvis, ". . . graves. Then the desert."

"How far away is Johnny Turk?"

"Beaten back to about a hundred miles on all sides, sir. He's mainly to the north, sir, beyond Samarrah. Their central point is a spot called Aleppo."

"Any danger of 'em coming back?"

"Certain to try, sir, but it's a question of when. Both sides are in their summer quarters, as you might say. Our boys were chasing the old Turkey cock out at

64

Ramadi last month, sir, and it was too hot for campaigning even then."

We were now into what I first thought of as an alleyway, but which was in reality — I would soon realise — a typical street of Baghdad. The "roadway" was half broken cobbles, half mud dust. There were arches at intervals overhead, and three of these in succession boasted great storks standing one-legged upon them. Some of the walls were blank stone, with faded posters and barred windows, so that it looked like we were passing a succession of small prisons, but some held shops or places of business, and I had glimpses of Arab life in dark, hot, oil-lit rooms — grey stone relieved by colourful carpets and cushions. We came to a building enclosed in scaffolding.

"Reconstruction," said Jarvis. "That's the order of the day out here. Well, that and fatigues and parades and *waiting*, sir."

Gas lights, yet unlit and of ancient design, stuck out from the walls. We passed a man in a doorway rolling cigarettes and setting them neatly on a table top; then some sort of shop or store with what looked like beautiful but battered biscuit tins containing pastries. Next came a shop that evidently sold water — in bottles or leather skins. Jarvis turned to me, saying, "Excuse me one second, sir, if you don't mind," and I watched from the doorway as he stepped into the shop and spoke a few words of Arabic to the blokes inside, who seemed to know him of old, and grinned quite enthusiastically at him.

"Like a bloody mental ward in there, it is, sir," he said, stepping back into the street.

"What were you saying?"

"*Taze su*, you see, sir — means fresh water."

So he'd been telling them what was in their shop.

Jarvis said, "Your first camel, sir."

I looked forwards, and there it was — seemingly bowing to both sides of the street as it walked. It carried a great wooden crate on top of a saddle that looked to be made of a collection of carpets. It was being led, so to speak, from behind, by a fellow constantly flicking its rump with a stick, like a man playing the drums. From this you'd have thought the camel meant nothing to him, and yet he'd decorated the saddle with little silver bells.

Jarvis said, "Looks like it's got two left feet, doesn't it, sir? But then it's not at home in the town. Ship of the desert, sir — and it's said you do feel a little seasick when you're up on board."

The camel stalked past.

". . . Until you get the rhythm that is. *Gemel* or *jemel*, it is, sir," Jarvis ran on, "so it's an easy one to remember."

"You've a pretty good grasp on the language, Jarvis."

"Made a bit of an effort, sir, bit of an effort. When we first came here, I was thinking: Right, where's the blinking pyramids?, if you'll pardon the expression, sir. Ignorant, I was, but I've decided to make a study of the place. Mesopotamia, sir. The land between two rivers — that's what that means. There's an Arab saying:

'When the devil created hell, he saw it wasn't bad enough, so he created Mesopotamia, and added flies.'"

"I should say that's about right."

"But I *like* it, sir. I have a guidebook: *City of the Khalifs*. This was quite the place to be, sir — about a thousand years ago."

"Were you in the scrap when we took the town?"

"No, sir, but I was in the show at Kut — the first time we went in there; before the siege. September 1915 — worst month of my life, sir. Then I was at Basrah, having a fairly easy time of it. I came up here on the steamer four weeks ago."

"What were you up to in Basrah, Corporal?"

"Motor-car driver. Then I was batman to another gentleman, sir. Then I went back to driving."

There was a tap on my shoulder, I turned around, and an Arab was there, holding out a bottle of water. It was one of the blokes from the water shop. Behind him, a rather irritated voice called out, "Can you smile? He's giving you a present."

Beyond the Arab, in the crowd of the street, a man stood next to a cine camera on a tripod stand. I knew immediately what it was, even though I'd never laid eyes on one before. It resembled a thin wooden case stood on its end. The operator — he squinted into a hole at the back of it and wound a handle on the side — wore an officer's uniform but with no badges of rank. You'd have thought he was a colonel from the way he gave orders, however.

"Take the bottle and thank him!"

I took the bottle from the Arab, nodding briefly at him.

"Oh God!" said the man at the camera, who'd left off winding the thing, and was standing next to it with hands on hips, the better to let me see the great patches of sweat underneath his arms. All the Arabs at his end of the street were looking at him, and I could tell he liked that no end. "Look, do you know how scarce fresh water is in this town? We're all drawing it from wells, and putting lime in it, and boiling it and doing God knows what, and here's this chap giving you his last bottle in recognition of his liberation from the bloody Turk . . . Respond appropriately, please."

I eyed the bloke, shading my eyes against the low sun. "It's not his last bottle!" I called back to him. "He's got a bloody shopful!"

The Arab with the bottle was smiling at me, and nodding.

"Look," said the cameraman, "can you just take the bottle again, but with a bit of enthusiasm this time?"

The Arab seemed dead set on *offering* the bottle again — fancied himself an actor no doubt. Had he been put up to the whole business by the cameraman?

"Look," that bloke was now saying, "don't bother. There's no light anyway."

And slinging his camera over his shoulder, he turned on his heel, and walked the other way down the street, with his little fan club of Arabs in tow.

I turned around, and another bloody camel was loping by, and giving off such a rancid smell that I was put on the edge of a swoon, what with the persistent heat, and the strangeness of it all. I took the stopper off the bottle and drank down the water. I saw Jarvis sitting on a doorstep. He was looking down at his dusty boots.

"Jarvis," I said, and I could see he was in a bath of sweat. All of a sudden, a great strain seemed to have been thrown upon him. He too had got hold of a bottle of water, but his was full. As I looked on, he set it down in the gutter, and I did likewise with my empty one.

"Drunk the water, did you, sir?" he enquired, rising to his feet.

I nodded.

"You said it was fresh," I said.

"I was just trying out the word really, sir," he said. Suddenly, he looked all-in. And now a man leading a train of white donkeys was coming between us, trapping Jarvis against the wall.

"Who was that bloke with the camera?" I asked Jarvis over the top of a donkey.

"Wallace King that is, sir," he said, and he seemed to know the man of old, and to be bored by the idea of him. "Famous back home, he is — in the music halls. I mean the picture houses — made dozens of films. He's out here making newsreels. I should think every Tommy in the place has been filmed by him — most of the sepoys too."

Night was dropping rapidly. The air had a green-orange sort of tint to it; the temperature seemed if anything to be climbing. I put this to Jarvis, who said, "It is a bit cooler at night, but it's more humid because the moisture's not burnt off. Directly we arrive at base,

I'll fix you up with a glass of something cold sir, how about that?"

I said, "The Arabs don't drink, do they? Alcohol, I mean."

"Not really, sir, no. They do smoke though," he added, as if that made up for it. "Do you know what you'll be wanting after a week or so, sir? Tea in a cup. Tea comes in glasses here, and very small ones at that, but my advice, sir . . . get used to it."

The street widened into a square, and there was the hotel — the front of it (the rear I had already seen, overhanging the river). It had a golden dome; palm trees criss-crossed in a series of Xs in gravel beds to either side of the main entrance, two parked phaetons, two sentries looking very casual. New telegraph poles marched across the square, spoiling its appearance, and carrying wires to the top of the Hotel. Jarvis showed his identity card, muttering something about "Escorting Captain Stringer, seconded to Corps HQ." I myself was not required to show my papers. I might have been a parcel the sentries were taking delivery of.

". . . And raspberry jam," Jarvis was saying as we entered the Hotel, "there's no raspberry jam in the whole of Baghdad, and once you know that, sir, you really want it. But forget about it. Forget all about it. Honey, that's the big thing here."

The lobby was dark and it took me a while to accustom myself to the gloom. A giant noticeboard headed "PART ONE ORDERS" had been fixed to one of the wood-panelled walls. The floor was black and white tiles, with palms in wicker baskets, wicker chairs

70

and tables about the place. The reception desk was not in use. Before it stood a row of smaller desks, and behind each sat a political officer of the British Indian Army.

These were my fellows. I was a political officer too. We had left our own army units behind, soared above them, so to speak, in order to become a species of civil servant. But whilst our political, and supposedly peaceable purposes were indicated by the white tabs on our uniforms (I'd sewn mine on while sailing up on the *Mantis*), we still wore our badges of rank and most of us — including all the men at the desks — wore our guns.

White cloths were draped over the front of their desks, and Arabic and English words had been crudely painted on to these, so as to signify the business of the fellow at the desk. I read "Police", "Transport", "Agricultural", "Commercial Department", "Taxes", "Trade (Import-Export)", and there were queues of Arabs at the last three named, some sitting, some standing. They wore beautiful robes, and a couple held gnarled sticks. It was horribly hot in the lobby. I looked up: no ceiling fans, but at either end of the rows of desks, banks of free-standing electrical fans whirred and swayed.

Jarvis was saying, "Second floor, sir. The billets are all on the second floor, with the hotel rooms kept just as they were. All the other rooms are offices."

An Arab was now carrying my bag, and so the three of us climbed the wide staircase. On every step, a strip of rubber had been placed so as to save the carpet from the dusty boots of the British Indian Army.

"I think you'll find your quarters to be quite cushy, sir," said Jarvis.

"But it's only for one night, isn't it?" I said.

"That's right, sir. Your place is off Park Street."

"Where's that?"

"Over by the park, sir," he said, and we might have been talking about the streets of York. "I'm off there first thing in the morning with an orderly, and we'll set it all up for you."

On the first landing, he pointed to double doors, saying, "Officers' mess, sir, for your glass of something cool in a little while. They've got the local chaps taking ice up there on the hour every hour."

We pressed on up to the second floor, and Jarvis threw open a door . . . A smell of dusty carpet, a wide, low bed; wooden sun shutters, closed, with mosque-like shapes cut into them, through which the green evening light oozed.

"It's a bit better than the Western Front," I said.

"To say the least, sir," said Jarvis. "To say the least."

At a nod from Jarvis, the porter departed; Jarvis now began unpacking my pack, and laying the things out on my bed. He held my second tunic and trousers: "Take these away for pressing," he said, which meant he was going to go. "Will that be all, sir?" he said. "You'll find me two doors along if you need me in the night. I'll be here in the morning with coffee at eight o'clock, sir."

I looked at my watch. It had stopped.

"What's the time?" I said.

"Nearly nine, sir."

"Will it start to get cool soon?"

"About October sort of time. Even the Indian lads find it a bit . . . I don't mind telling you, I thought I was going off me dot at first. Thing is, sir, you must wear clothes to keep it off. I'll fix you up with a keffiyah — that's a sort of headscarf."

"I'm going out tonight," I said.

"You crossing the river, sir?"

I eyed him.

"Why do you ask?"

"It's not patrolled, sir, or not so much as over here. Patrols are to be stepped up over the next few days. But you'll be carrying your piece, I take it, sir?" He nodded towards the holster of my Sam Browne belt, together with the Webley .455 that it held. I nodded back; I would be carrying the Webley.

"What's over there?" I said.

"You've got the ranges — the artillery spend a good deal of time over there in the daylight hours."

"*Machine-gun* ranges?"

"Some, I think. And you've got the railway station — and the south gate of the wall."

"How's the feeling in the town — towards the British, I mean?"

"They prefer us to the Germans and the Turks, sir."

"Good."

"But that's not saying much. See, they're trying to figure us out. It's all in the balance between us and them. That's why I've taken a bit of trouble to learn a few words of the language, sir. That's why I go in the water place — hoping to build a few bridges, so to speak."

I noticed that he'd stopped calling it *fresh* water. How did I feel? All right, considering, but when Jarvis offered to fetch me a glass of cold beer before departing, I turned him down. I couldn't face beer.

"I'll just take a sluice-down," I said, which was Jarvis's cue to quit the room.

Ten minutes later, feeling better in some ways but worse in others, I looked into the officers' mess on my way out of the Hotel.

It was a luxurious room of many sofas and many carpets, but not enough electrical fans — only two of them doing their strange bowing dance. All the men in there were staff officers or political officers. The individual battalions and regiments that made up the corps would have their own quarters and their own messes around Baghdad. I couldn't see Lieutenant Colonel Shepherd in the room. I heard one man saying, "Ought we to retribute?" as though he wasn't much bothered either way. Another was saying, "Well, it's a kind of an opera." I knew I was out of my league, and was about to quit the room when a man came up and introduced himself.

I told him I had come out to work for the Political Officer (Railways). "That's Lieutenant Colonel Shepherd," I added, and the fellow looked blank for a minute before leading me over to a noticeboard, where he indicated, next to something about a smoking concert, and beneath something about a cricket match, a paper headed: TALKS ON RAILWAY TOPICS.

74

The fellow returned to the conversation from which he'd broken off a minute before, leaving me to read:

The Baghdad Railway Club. Meetings every Saturday, 7.30p.m. prompt at The Restaurant, Quiet Square (behind The Church of the Saviour's Mother). Good food and drink supplied. For further particulars contact Lieutenant Colonel Shepherd, Room 226 Corps HQ.

As I quit the mess, I heard a voice saying, "We have more railway people than would seem to be justified."

CHAPTER
FOUR

I went down to the river by a different crowded lane. A new boat was on the quay where the *Mantis* had lately been: a cranky-looking old packet, laden with boxes marked "Bully Beef", and quite unattended. It bumped and scraped against the quay, and I saw a man in a much smaller boat — a blue wooden canoe of sorts, but with decorative mouldings — who floated just beyond the stern of the bigger one, bumping and swaying in rhythm with it, occasionally extending an arm to keep himself from clashing against it. He was grinning up at me.

"You sail!" he said.

I was looking along to my right — towards the pontoon bridge at about a quarter of a mile's distance. I counted the number of black barges that made it up: twenty exactly.

"Ingilhiz!" he shouted, and it wasn't a question. "Ingilhiz, go over. Cross river. You sail."

He was paddling towards an iron ladder that went down into the water amid floating rubbish. I climbed down the ladder, and into his boat. It was like one of the swinging boats of a fairground detached from its chains.

"What's on the other side?" I said, just for something to say.

"Same town," he said, smiling but paddling hard against the current.

A white launch was bearing down on us, a group of uniformed and un-uniformed white men standing on the prow.

As it went by, and we bounced on its backwash, my companion nodded at me, saying, "Kokus," and then, trying again, ". . . Coxus."

I frowned at him.

"Coxus," he repeated, grinning. "Your friend! Coxus!"

It broke in on me that he was referring to the Chief Political Officer.

"You mean *Cox*?" I said. "Sir Percy Cox?"

He nodded briefly, having already lost interest in the matter. He was fighting the current, the sound of which was now loud in my ears. Gas lights of a pale blue glimmered on the bank we'd left behind, whereas the bank we were making towards was half enclosed in darkness. I could not tell whether its buildings were newly made and barely finished, or so old that they were crumbling away. Having passed the middle of the river, my pilot was now resting, letting the current carry us, and smiling as it did so. But a minute later, he was all action again, using his oar to steer as we ran up fast on to the opposite bank. We were on a narrow beach, lying beyond the main run of buildings. There were palm trees, two long wicker benches with shades built over.

"Baksheesh," said my pilot.

I had dreaded this moment. I fished in my pocket and handed over a single rupee, which my pilot began examining closely. Say it was worth 9d. That would be a decent, if irregular, sum to tip a station porter in London or York. But this fellow was not a station porter, and we were not in London or York. On the contrary, I was on a ghostly river-beach of black and orange sand, in rapidly fading light but with the heat still like a weight upon me. My companion was now looking at me slightly sidelong. He had found the coin acceptable, and secreted it somewhere in his robe. I was free to go.

I put my boot into two inches of brown water, as the fellow began again his struggle with the current of the Tigris.

. . . Low buildings, including some low domes with green and gold-coloured tiles that would have been beautiful were it not for the dirt . . . One shuttered place had a wooden board across the front: an Arabic word and "Koffe". Was this the place Boyd was supposed to recommend to me, the *Salon de Thé* of Baghdad station being closed? A man sat smoking in front of it. He was surrounded by a sort of display of the circular boats. He had passed the long, hot day in putting pitch on them judging by the black spatterings on his long shirt. I nodded at him, and he tipped his head back, blowing smoke rather haughtily in my direction. The broken buildings extended back not more than three or four streets, and there was very little life in them. At one junction of alleyways, I saw a knife-grinder, his grindstone on a barrow. He pedalled the stone, sharpening a long blade, and a kid sat on the broken pavement at his feet. He might have been a customer, the owner of the blade. But he looked more like the knife-grinder's disciple.

"Salaam alaikum!" I called to the pair, and they looked at me as if I was mad.

I was now at the limit of the buildings, and had begun walking over a waste of dust and rubble littered with old bricks and tiles. I made out a low sign in the fading light: "Ranges". I contemplated it for a while, hearing still the creak of the knife-grinder's wheel.

Instead of a shooting range, the sign *seemed* to indicate a sort of warehouse that had partly exploded, for there were piles of its own bricks all around it: one of the buildings blown up by the Turks before they quit town, perhaps. I'd been told there were plenty of those. Beyond the roadway was a plantation. I walked under the trees. The dates had not been picked. Presently the trees thinned out, and I saw a railway line.

I stood on the rail, and wondered which way to follow it. To left and right it went into more date palms and low, rocky embankments. Again, I had the swooning feeling. I was still sweating like a bull, the stuff coming off me faster than it had been before if anything. I'd been a fool to drink that water. I turned left and walked the line until the trees cleared again, and I came to a railway territory. There was the station; also an engine shed, some tracks meandering between the two with blockhouses and coal bunkers at intervals, a half-smashed hand-cranked turntable, and sidings going off, most out of commission, being buckled and broken. Had they been shelled? In the silence, I stood waiting for the flare of a Very light, the shriek of a five-nine or a whizz-bang, but that was the Western Front, and I was in the East. A different sort of death awaited here.

It was ten o'clock; I was an hour early for Boyd. I contemplated the tracks.

As far as I could judge, the one I'd followed here had been the one that ran up north to Samarrah and Tikrit — up towards where the Turks were. Another drifted off south-westerly, leading, as I believed, to the town of Feluja. A third — a narrow-gauge line — looked badly broken up, but I believed it led almost due south to Babylon, where the ruins were. Each would have to cut through the city walls, parts of which I could make out in the distance.

I approached first the engine shed. Double doors stood open at front and back, revealing two tracks and one crocked engine. It was a big beast: a 2-8-0 of German manufacture, and it had a name: *Elefant*. But the thing couldn't travel; its side rods were missing. In between the tracks, some bushes grew. What were they? Jasmine? Basil? I thought: *the smell of them is very loud*, and I considered — slowly — that "loud" was the wrong word. There were also rough wooden tables, a quantity of tools and papers piled upon them. The papers were smeared with oil and written in German — they related to the engine. Beyond the shed, a hundred yards off, was a water tower made of stone with a metal tank on the top of it, and as I looked on, a giant bird of some sort came and landed on the top of this tank. I hadn't bargained on any of this. The colour of the evening was now a dark green, and it was unnatural that such darkness could go with such heat. I turned about, and stumbled on the rocky ground, where I saw cartridge casings, left over from the fight for the city. As I began walking towards the companion building of the shed, namely the station, I thought back again to the water I'd drunk. I should not have had it. It had *not* been fresh. Had the fellow who'd given it me known that?

The station was a building of rough grey stone with pointed, church-like windows and a church-like bell hanging from a little arch at one end of the pitched roof. There were two platforms and two tracks running between them. There was not *enough* in the station: no ticket gates, no posters on the walls, not even any nameplate saying "Baghdad", and certainly no people. But between the tracks stood a Janus-faced clock on an iron stand. The clock said half after ten, so it was about right. The platforms were low, and dirty booths of glass and iron ran along the left-hand one, all in a line like compartments of a carriage: waiting rooms or ticket offices, and one must be the *Salon de Thé*. I recollected that I was supposed to say, "It is closed."

Well, I'd look a bloody idiot saying that. Looking again at the walls, I saw that the station name *was* indicated, in that the word "BAGHDAD" had been written on the right-hand wall in tall, shaky letters of red paint. There was a nightmare quality to the work, the long thin letters seeming to be formed of dripping blood. I began to make out through the gloom other scrawlings on the walls, in a different shade of red. I first thought these were all in a foreign language, but I made out the word "Tommy". I looked harder . . .

I heard a footfall coming from beyond the far end of the station. Through the soft, green gloom, a man approached. I believed he had stepped out of one of the blockhouses set amid the broken tracks. He wore a long black coat, and it became clear that the small hat he wore was red — a fez. I had thought all Arabs would wear a fez, but here was the first. He held a lamp, and as he came under the station roof, the swinging white light illuminated the scrawl on the walls: "One Tommy — 100 Askari", I read, and "Tommy, where is your Lon . . ." and then, some way off, ". . . don."

I tried my "Salaam alaikum" on the man as he approached. The collar of his coat was braided with gold.

"Hello, my dear," he said, which knocked me rather. He was a thin, handsome chap with a deeply lined face — but then most of the Arabs were. His coat made him look priest-like, but I thought I knew what the braid signified.

"Are you the station master?" I said.

"Of course," he said, "of course."

"When is the next train?" I said, since that was the kind of thing you asked a station master.

"Next train?" he said. "Next day."

"Who wrote this?" I said, indicating the scrawl on the walls.

"Turk, my dear," he said, and he grinned; then his grin faded rather rapidly. "Next train, next day," he repeated, "God willing."

This next train was getting less likely by the minute. "I help you?" he said.

I shook my head. "No thanks," I said, and he turned on his heel. I watched him walk along the platform, then step down into the territory of the sidings. He was a station master at arm's length from his station. He seemed to be heading back towards a certain blockhouse when the darkness enclosed him; perhaps he lived there; or perhaps he would walk beyond it and go to some other place entirely. I was glad he was gone, not so much because he would get in the way of my meeting Boyd as because I was about to be sick. I did not want to be sick in the station, however.

I was halfway back towards the engine shed when the stuff came out in a yellow fountain. Well, it missed my boots; and I immediately felt better, getting — for the first time since my arrival in Baghdad — a hint of coolness about me. I sat on the ground savouring the feeling for a while; I then pursued my way back into the engine shed and found a lamp there. I lit it, and turned up the wick. I looked at my watch — ten to eleven.

"Next train, next day . . . God willing": I revolved the words. Why *would* God will it, given that it could only be a British Army train, an organisation not over-full of Mohammedans? Or had the station master meant that God might favour the return by rail of the Turks? Was he one of the pro-Turkish Arabs? Which side, in fact, was the fellow really on?

I turned back towards the station, going by the blockhouse from which the station master seemed to have emerged. By the light of the lamp, it appeared locked and shuttered. There was no window in it. If I'd come across this sort of brick bunker in the railway lands of York, I'd have said it held lamps, lamp oil, track shoes, not a person, and certainly not a station master. The *deputy* station master at York had a chandelier in his office.

I was under the station roof again at dead on eleven, and there was unquestionably no sign of any Captain Boyd on the platforms. In the light of my lamp, the "B" of "Baghdad" danced as I closed on the glass and iron booths. The door of the first was ajar. I pushed, and saw a jumble of rubbish, iron chairs and tables, photographs with scenes of Baghdad on the walls. I held up my lamp and it revealed a counter bearing two kettles, assorted kitchen clutter, and the dusty remains of what might have been a spirit stove. A dead palm also lay on the counter, and the soil that had come out of the pot was scattered everywhere. There was a kind of sideboard against the wall. No — a shallow display cabinet of sorts, with broken glass doors. My lamp showed — pinned to cork board — photographs of engines near buildings that looked more like castles than stations, but which I knew to *be* stations. Above the photographs was pinned a blue tin strip with white lettering: "*Die grosse Berlin-Baghdad Eisenbahn*". On a shelf lay a whistle with a green and red tassel, and two copper medallions, also with tassels. I picked one up, moved it near the lamp. On one side was an engraving of a locomotive surrounded by a circle of laurel leaves; on the other was an inscription in Arabic, perhaps Turkish Arabic. The whole display was a celebration of the Berlin-Baghdad railway, but whoever had put it up had jumped the gun, for the line, as I had discovered, was incomplete north of Baghdad.

Captain Boyd was not here.

I walked towards the counter, set my lamp down there. What I thought had been soil was not soil. I licked my finger and dabbed at it: coffee. And the kettle was not a kettle either, but a coffee pot, and there were a couple more nearby. If this was the *Salon de Thé*, then where was the *Thé*?

I walked back on to the platform, and held my lamp up the next booth along, seeing in the glass only the reflection of an ill-looking British Army captain with lamp in hand. I could do with a shave. As I pushed at the door, another dead potted palm swung into my lamp beam. The place was full of flies. I heard a sudden shuffling from low down in the corner, and I thought: snake; I am in a reptile house. While transferring the lamp to my left hand, I took the Webley from its holster. I saw white-painted wicker chairs heaped at one end, iron tables at another. Cutlery was scattered over the floor. On the counter I saw several dusty spirit burners with silver kettles sitting on them with all the spouts pointing the same way — a kettle train. I moved a little way forward on the gritty floorboards. Many parchment-coloured moths danced around my lamp. They avoided the flies, but the flies did not avoid me.

I saw that there was a particular concentration of flies on the floor, and that they were all coming from or going to the same place: the mouth of a man. I turned away and then looked back, trying for a fresh start, but I had no luck: still the flies, and still the mouth. I was looking at a dead captain. The man was not dissimilar in appearance to me: regular sort of face, dark hair, dark eyes wide open with flies taking it in turns to settle upon them. I set down the lantern and closed the eyelids.

. . . Shirt and tie, with Wolseley sun helmet rolled a little way; three pips on tunic sleeve; Sam Browne belt, holster and ammunition pouch, but no gun to be seen. Beneath the belt, and below the ribcage, the man's shirt went into his body. He'd been stabbed.

The face was grey, with lavender-coloured bruising about the cheek. I touched the face. There was some stiffness, but his eyelids had closed easily, so he had come through the phase of rigor mortis. He gave off a sweet smell — a garden smell. Not too bad. The gut not yet exploded.

The captain had been dead for something in the region of twenty-four hours.

I heard again the heavy shuffling from the corner, but the snake (if snake it be) fell silent again. I hunted in the pockets of the dead man's tunic and quickly turned up identity card and paybook, both in the name of Captain C. J. Boyd. Whoever had done for him had taken his gun, but not troubled about his papers — or not thought to look for them.

86

The flies and moths were besieging me, and the shuffling was renewed in the corner. I walked fast out of the *Salon*, sat down on the edge of the platform and waited, revolver in hand, the unbreathable air closing about me. I leant forward, and the yellow stuff landed on the track gravel between my boots. I had not meant to chuck up in the station, but there was no help for it. Immediately a cool breeze seemed to come down the tracks towards me. I lit a cigarette. I had for the minute forgotten why I'd been hanging about alone in Baghdad railway station, and now I recollected. Boyd had evidence against Shepherd, evidence of the fellow being in hock to the Turks; evidence that would have seen Shepherd shot if proven. If Shepherd had somehow got to know of this . . . then it would be practically odds-on that Boyd should come a cropper. Had the body been put in this particular spot to make it look as though I had killed him? In which case the killer must have known of my arrangement to meet him. But if Manners at the War Office was to be believed, the communications between his office and Boyd were absolutely secure. Had Boyd let on to anyone he was coming here? I thought of the *other* intelligence man on the side in Baghdad, the one Boyd had been advised by Manners to contact.

. . . And who had been witness to my arrival at the station? I thought of the ferryman, the knife-grinder and his assistant or customer; I thought of the station master. He had shown not the slightest sign of knowing that his station harboured a body, still less of being responsible for the killing. I had told Jarvis I was coming to *this side of the river*, but that was all I'd said . . .

I threw my cigarette stump on to the tracks, and stood up. A minute later, I was striding fast over the flat rocky waste, under the dark trees. I came to the place where the knife-grinder had been, and entered one of the dark alleys leading back to the water. I came to the river-beach, and there was less of it than before, but quite enough for me to walk along, while inhaling the petrol smell of the river. There were quiet encampments on the flat roofs of the riverside houses: people sleeping under makeshift canopies, or no canopies at all. Not only did they sleep on top of their roofs, they also slept on top of their bed-clothes from the looks of things. After ten minutes, I came to the bridge of boats. An Indian soldier saluted as I stepped on to it — one of a guard of four men. There were half a dozen loungers on the bridge: Arab insomniacs, as I supposed — and they did look to be wearing nightshirts. They watched the black river flowing fast away, or listened to it, for it *sounded* cool at any rate. The bridge moved as I walked across it, and I saw the reflections of the city moving in the water at the same time: the dark silhouettes of the music halls dancing.

Once on the east bank, I entered the labyrinth, and — walking beneath the roof sleepers — became lost for a while, and lost in thought. If any report *should* put me in the vicinity of the murdered man, and I came clean about the mission I was on, would Manners back me up? I might say I'd been in the station to look at the trains. I was a corresponding member of the Railway

Club, after all. "But there are no trains," the answer would come. "I know that *now*," I would say. It was certain that I would now have to communicate with Manners anyway — and by the ridiculous method he had instructed me in.

I regained the Hotel by skirting the river until I came to the place where *Mantis* had docked. The lobby was nearly empty. All the cloths on which were written the names of the political departments had been rolled up scroll-wise and placed on the table tops. One new cloth was unfolded, however: it read "Boiled Water", and there were glasses and jugs. I poured one out, and drank it off, then took another two. It had been only lately boiled, but I didn't mind a bit.

From my room a minute later, I looked down into the square, and watched, in the half-light, an Arab going along one of the alleyways over opposite. At first I thought he was riding a slow and wobbly bicycle, but then he went under a giant gas lamp in which a tiny blue flame burned — just enough to see that he rode a donkey, his bare feet almost touching the ground on either side. I knew I felt better, for I wanted a bottle of beer and a sandwich, and the fact that I was on the mend outweighed the thought of Boyd, I must admit. Sluicing down in the bathroom, I wondered whether half the corps would be sleeping on top of the hotel roof. No, I thought, letting down the mosquito net that hung over my bed . . . because the roof consisted of domes. The people would slide off.

And I believe I was asleep at the moment I lay down.

CHAPTER
FIVE

I had forgotten to close the shutters after looking at the square, and the splitting sun woke me at six — or perhaps it was the closing of the door. A breakfast of coffee, flatbread, yoghurt and honey was on the table by my bed, and the coffee was hot. Jarvis had also left a neat map — drawn, I supposed, by himself — giving directions to my living quarters: Rose Court, off Park Street. It sounded a pretty enough spot, if not very Arabic. Jarvis would be waiting for me there at six o'clock in the evening with my kit.

I dressed, and walked downstairs to work. Lieutenant Colonel Shepherd's room was 226. On the door was a notice: "Railways (Strategy)". I knocked — no answer. I pushed open the door. The room was dark — sun shutters closed — and Shepherd was not in it. His empire also extended to room 227, however, and here I found a bluff, blond fellow, a Captain Mike Stevens of the Hampshire Regiment who, it appeared, was a second assistant to Shepherd. He walked out the instant I entered, saying he was going to fetch tea. The bed had been removed from room 227, and two cabinets and two desks put in; otherwise, it was similar to the room in which I'd passed the night: Persian rugs on a wooden floor, views of Baghdad on the walls, shutters with the same mosque-shaped holes cut in them. In the square, a team of Royal Engineers was working on the telegraph wires, with long ladders running up the poles. I was glad my office faced this way. A sight of the river would have reminded me of the other side of it, of the station, and Captain Boyd decaying in the *Salon de Thé*.

Stevens returned, and set out the tea things on his desk. He had a touch of the West Country in his accent and his face, which was wide and pink, and offset by straw-coloured hair. He wore shorts, and round wire glasses.

"So you're the railwayac?" he said, a "railwayac" being a railway maniac. But he said it in an offhand way; it did not promise to become a theme of his. He asked, "Do you understand book routine?" but didn't seem the least bit interested in my answer. Lieutenant Colonel Shepherd, he continued — still offhand — was not in room 226, but would be there from about lunchtime. He suggested I might like to "make a fair copy" of a map showing the railway line running north from Baghdad up to Samarrah. This would involve combining the details from two separate maps, and after handing me a small glass of tea with sugar lumps in the saucer — the whole arrangement looked tiny in his hands — he went over to one of the cabinets, and produced these maps. He directed me to some pencils and coloured inks in the second cabinet, and sat back at his own desk as I contemplated the maps. On the bottom of both was written, "Prepared in the historical

91

section of the Committee of Imperial Defence". One map left the "h" off "Samarrah". Both maps petered out a little way beyond there, although one had an arrow pointing north and reading "To Tikrit". Well, the Turks were up that way.

Both maps were hard to read, for a variety of reasons. In one, the names of the stations kept running into the blue-shaded River Tigris. According to the scale of *this* map, Samarrah lay about sixty miles north of Baghdad, whereas according to the scale on the other it was more like eighty.

I regarded Stevens, whose desk was directly opposite to mine. He was writing letters, from what I could see, and kept looking for addresses in a directory he kept at his elbow. Every so often, he'd jerk his shoulders about in a peculiar manner.

"The scale on these maps —" I said, but he cut me off.

"Just split the difference," he said. "Don't worry too much about *scale* or anything, but it's for Cox himself, so you might, you know . . . make it look pretty."

I had already determined on that. I didn't want to make "a bad start" or do anything to convince Shepherd that I was here for any reason but to help him with railway work — and that went double if he was a killer as well as a traitor.

Stevens's glasses made him look rather schoolboyish. Well, only at first. Throughout the morning, he seemed to expand, filling out his thin cotton shirt, and when he stood and walked over to one of the cabinets, at about

92

ten o'clock sort of time, I saw that he had the legs of a circus strongman.

Seeing me eyeing him, he seemed rather put out, so I made a start in earnest on the maps. The line to Samarrah ran in parallel with — and to the west of — what I had decided to call "R. Tigris", since that seemed more correct than just "Tigris". "*River* Tigris" might have been better still, but I wouldn't have been able to fit those two words into any of the innumerable bends in the river, of which I was taking an average from the two maps, and which I was tracing in a turquoise ink very far from the actual colour of the river. Towards Samarrah, I lost patience with all the bends of the river, so it tended to get a bit straighter up there. Also, drops of sweat kept falling from my brow, and threatening to smudge the river. I broke off to wipe my face with my handkerchief.

Stevens did not seem to sweat — an odd circumstance, in the case of such a big fellow. He must be in A1 condition. He was really frowning over his work, and kept reaching for the directory.

"What a rigmarole this is," he said, more or less to himself.

"What are you about?" I said. "If you don't mind my asking."

"Oh," he said, "ordering track from the Indian government. Like getting blood out of a stone it is."

Here, then, was proof of the story I'd heard all the way up the Tigris: that the British and the British in India were at loggerheads over Mesopotamian policy.

"They'll send it," said Stevens, "but they'll send it *slowly*. They make out they're having to tear up their own lines to do it, which I don't believe for a minute."

"They think we're building a railway for the Arabs at their expense," I said.

He eyed me steadily for a moment.

"Just so," he said. "But I don't think the camel jockeys are *quite* up to running their own railway, do you?"

This might have been just another offhand remark, but I thought it unlikely that any Arabist would have said that, even casually. Was Stevens, in this respect, falling in with his governor, Shepherd? If you were anti-Arab, did that make you pro-Turk? Turcophile? If you wanted to let the Turks in again through the back door, you certainly wouldn't want the formation of an Arab state.

Stevens stood up and walked over to the window.

"It's going to be hot," he said, and I don't believe it was a joke. He turned side on, and the thought broke in on me: *He's a boxer; a heavyweight.* His nose, in profile, didn't go as far out as it should have done. And there was no fat on him, for all his bulk. He walked over to my desk, and looked down at the map.

"We might be riding over that very line — on Monday."

I frowned at him, thinking of the bruises on the face of Boyd.

"Who's 'we'?"

"You, me and The Shepherd."

"What for?" I asked, and he gave a shrug. "Can't remember the word. Oh yes: reconnaissance."

"What'll we use for a locomotive?"

"The Shepherd has one lined up."

I thought of the broken-winded engine I'd seen: *Elefant*. It couldn't be *that* one.

"But . . . who'll crew it?" I said.

"You fire and I'll drive," he said. "Or the other way round, I'm easy."

"You can drive an engine?"

"After a fashion."

It went without saying — since he had public school written all over him — that he had never worked on the *footplate*, so I asked how he'd come by his driving skills.

"See . . . my old man has four hundred acres in a little spot called St Keyne."

"That's in Cornwall," I said.

He nodded. "Little railway goes right through our land."

"The Lyeskard and Looe line?"

"That's right," he said, and I could tell what he was thinking: *This bloke really is a railwayac.* "You know it?" he said.

"Read about it."

"Why would anyone write about the old L and L?"

"St Keyne was in *The Railway Magazine* — in a series called 'Notable Railway Stations'."

"Notable? What's notable about it?"

"Its smallness," I said. "As I recall, the waiting room is the station master's *front* room."

"That's right," said Stevens. "Plays war about it, he does."

"He told *The Railway Magazine* it gave him the chance to meet all sorts of fascinating people."

"Old Williams? Did he really? He's a bit of a pill actually, is that chap, but the other chaps, the drivers on the line . . . They were all right, and they'd give me rides up."

"They taught you driving?"

"Well, gave me a few pointers, you know."

"I'd have given fortunes to have cab rides on a branch line."

Silence for a space.

I asked, "How long have you known Shepherd?"

"Oh, practically for ever you know. His folks know my folks. His dad was at the University with my dad."

"And were you at the University with him? With Shepherd, I mean?"

He shook his head.

"The Shepherd's a good ten years older than me. And I wasn't *at* the University. The Shepherd was, of course."

"Oxford or Cambridge?"

"Can't recall. One or the other though, I know that."

"Why do you call him *The* Shepherd?"

"Well now . . . why do I call him The Shepherd? Always have done, I suppose." I thought that might be the end of the matter, but Stevens was really thinking about it. "It's his name, isn't it? So that's one reason, and then again he's *like* a shepherd."

"How?"

"Well, I don't mean he keeps sheep. His folks own a fair old patch of Wiltshire, you know, but I don't believe there's a sheep on it. But he's calm, and I suppose a shepherd is taken to be a calm sort of chap." He paused for a second, before adding, "Not that he doesn't pull off the craziest stunts."

I thought: *That fits the bill, if what I've been told about him is true.*

"What sort of stunts?" I said.

"Oh, I don't know."

And this time, it seemed, he really didn't.

"You're a boxer aren't you?" I said.

"Yes," he said slowly, "I am." And he eyed me shrewdly for a while. "How the deuce did you work that out?" He didn't wait for an answer, but said, "You met The Shepherd in a hotel didn't you?"

"We got to talking," I said, "and we found we had a mutual interest in railways."

He nodded. "Nuts on railways is The Shepherd. Anyhow, I'm off now."

"Where to?" I said, trying to keep a light tone, for I felt I was exceeding my limit of questions.

"Oh," said Stevens, "number eleven Clean Street."

You'd have thought the place was known to all, but I put off asking about Clean Street in favour of a flurry of quick questions that got from Stevens the following data during his progress towards the door. His battalion had been one of those that had fought at Gallipoli. (Asked whether that show had been as bad as everyone said, he replied, "Oh, you know . . .") He'd then joined the garrison force at Basrah, where he'd headed a team of PT instructors. He'd run into "The Shepherd" practically the moment that he — Shepherd — stepped off the boat. The two had renewed their old acquaintance, and Stevens had accepted Shepherd's offer to come up to Baghdad and help him run the railways. Stevens had not fought his way into Baghdad, as Shepherd had done, but come up in comfort on a steamer. As to our present work, I ought to remember — not that it really made any difference — that we were "Railways (Strategy)". When I asked what that meant, Stevens said, "Search me. I think it means we try out The Shepherd's ideas," He gave me to understand that most of the routine railway operation around Baghdad — not that there was much of that as yet — would fall to the Royal Engineers.

He quit the room, and I lit a cigarette. A moment later, I was standing at the window, watching him walk through the dazzling square, which he did with head tilted back, and face tilted up, as though to prevent his glasses falling off his nose. That was all wrong, I thought. In a place like this, you ought to look about you. But Stevens was not apparently a curious or very intelligent sort . . . which was probably just as well.

As he disappeared into one of the alleyways, my attention was caught by an Arab appearing from another one: red fez, long black coat. I instantly ducked away from the window. It was the station master, and he was approaching the Hotel at a lick. Evidently, he had discovered the secret of the *Salon de Thé*. There would now be an investigation. Would he supply a description of me? A suspicious white man seen at around the right time. If so, he might be taken to be trying to throw the blame away from his own people. Most likely the Arabs *would* be blamed. If the poor old station master himself should come under suspicion, I would have to speak out, but what would I say? A British lieutenant colonel did this because he was in the pay of Brother Turk, and Boyd knew it.

The call to prayer was coming through the window: a sort of wandering song, rather beautiful in spite of lacking any sort of tune, and which stopped every half minute and started again after a short pause, as if the singer wasn't happy with it, and meant to try again. It was Friday, and I had the idea that the Moslems did even more praying than usual on a Friday.

I had now written out in pencil all the station names up to Samarrah, and would trace over them in red ink. They were spaced at intervals of about fifteen miles. The first one was Mushahida station; then came Sumaika, Harba, Istabulat, Samarrah. Neither map gave any indication of any settlements, or anything at all, as being located near them. I passed the next half hour in decorating the "North" arrow on the map, and wondering about Stevens. He really was a rather hazy sort of bloke — perhaps he'd boxed too much and had gone "punchy".

Now the map was about finished, and it looked pretty enough. I wrote at the bottom, "Prepared by Captain James Stringer", then wafted it about to dry it, and rolled it into a scroll. I would take it through to Shepherd's office even though, or rather precisely because, I knew he would not be in there. Delivering the map would give me the chance to have a scout about.

In the corridor, an Arab was sweeping the spotless carpet with a broom. He stopped and smiled at me, and I said, "Salaam alaikum," which seemed to amuse him no end. I knocked on the door of 226; no reply. I looked back at the Arab, who was still watching me, still smiling. He said something in his native tongue, perhaps "It is perfectly in order for you to go in." Anyhow, that's what I did.

The room was just as dark as before, but hotter. A desk stood in the middle of it, but the bed remained, and Shepherd had spread some papers over it. I turned about. I had left the door ajar, and it wouldn't do to close it — that would be to claim possession of the room. I moved over to the bed, where I saw a plan of Baghdad station and environs, written half in German: "Bahnhof of Baghdad". I identified on the plan the blockhouse in which the station master apparently lived, and there was a tiny note next to this, which I could not read, and might have been handwritten on to the printed map. This map lay at the foot of the bed. Going up towards the bolster, there were documents in French, all bearing the same stamp or seal. I saw the word "Decauville" — that was a French make of light railway track. There was a pack of playing cards in their box, perfectly normal British ones; there was also a novel. I picked it up: *The Good Soldier* by a certain Ford Madox Ford. I flicked through the pages. It was not *about* soldiering.

100

There were two steel cabinets by the wall. I walked over and tried the handle of the first — locked. I tried the second, and it opened — nothing whatsoever inside. I moved towards the desk. Eight drawers in it. I looked towards the door, and tried the first. It held a service revolver. I stared down at the gun.

"Captain Stringer," said Shepherd, and I slammed the drawer and saluted.

He seemed thinner than before — browner too, of course, but still with the redness beneath. In fact our exchange of glances had sent the colour rising as fast on his cheeks as on my own.

"Excuse me, sir," I said. "I'd just come to show you this map." I waved the scroll about stupidly. "It combines two other ones. I was looking for an India rubber because there's a mistake on it." I unrolled the map, held the two ends apart on the desk.

"Very good," he said, examining the map. He looked up at me and smiled. "And what is the mistake?"

We both studied the map. There was no mistake to be seen. Out of sheer gentlemanliness, it seemed to me, Shepherd broke the silence:

"It seems to be absolutely . . ."

"It's just that I put an 'h' on 'Samarrah'," I said.

We both looked at the "h". It seemed very tiny and inconsequential, and was evidently worth no further remark for Shepherd said, "Well now, how would you like a ride up there?"

I let the map curl up again. "Captain Stevens said we might be going."

"Do you fancy the trip?"

Did I have any choice in the matter? Instead of putting that question, I enquired, "What do we use for motive power, sir?"

"An engine," he said, and this time he was embarrassed at *himself*, at the smallness of the joke. I knew that any information withheld by Shepherd, or any query deflected, would cause guiltiness in him, so that a fuller disclosure of data would follow. And so it proved. "A *DS 18*," he said, "to give the technical designation. It's a rather large German locomotive."

I nodded. "I saw . . ."

But what had I seen? I could not let on I'd been to the station. Once more, he came to my aid: "I think you'll enjoy the run, Jim. The stations along the line could hardly be more varied in their appeal. I believe one or two even have a platform."

"Will we go beyond Samarrah?"

"Oh, I hope so, a little way."

You'd think we were in for a holiday jaunt.

"But the line gives out up there," I said.

"It does," said Shepherd. "Runs into the sand."

"Will there be any Turks thereabouts, sir?"

"We might run into the odd stray patrol or two," he said, and he smiled kindly.

He was fishing in his tunic pocket, bringing out smokes. He offered me one, and I looked down at the packet: the couple walking along the beach, the four stars exactly, the unreadable script. There did seem a kind of damnable pride in his face as he offered them, a kind of defiance. But perhaps this brand was common throughout Asia Minor. Perhaps these were the

102

Woodbines of Baghdad. I took one with slightly shaking hands, and Shepherd lit it for me.

"Now tell me about your long journey," he said, perching on the desk. "What sort of a voyage did you have?"

He seemed to want all the details, and when I'd run out of them he said, "By the way, we have our own Railway Club here in Baghdad."

"I saw the notice," I said.

"Come along on Saturday. Anybody can have the floor, as long as they speak on a railway subject. You've missed my party piece by the way, luckily for you. I spoke last week."

"On what, sir?"

"Oh, a very out-of-the-way subject: the passenger railways of Turkey."

CHAPTER
SIX

I lunched alone, on a kind of stew with currants in it. I was only one of half a dozen blokes in the canteen, which was in the grand dining room of the Hotel, half of which had been given over to the storage of packing cases. Reaching into the inside pocket of my tunic, and touching a certain envelope that I'd kept close about me since my arrival, I revolved the idea of going off to the British Residency to communicate with Manners, but decided I'd better put in a full day's work beforehand.

Recrossing the lobby, I saw the police team, and I was itching to ask, "What did the station master tell you?" but discretion prevailed. I walked over to Part One Orders, and there was a new notice: officers were to wear their guns at all times.

Stevens returned to room 227 half an hour after me, and continued writing his letters to the Indian government. After his polite enquiries about my voyage, Shepherd had put me to writing a report on the very *Decauville* light rail systems he'd been reading about himself. He'd said he wanted to know how they would adapt to desert conditions. I said I didn't know desert conditions. What I knew was mud. He'd said, "You will do after Monday," and told me to make a start anyhow. It seemed to me that, for all his politeness — and on the face of it, he was about the most considerate officer I'd ever come across — he hadn't much interest in anything I might write, but that he'd brought me out here because I could drive and fire an engine. I guessed that he'd taken Stevens on for the very same reasons — unless the fellow was his partner in crime.

Shepherd had said I might knock off at about four, and when the time came, I went up to my room, and had a wash. Jarvis had already packed my things prior to our move to new quarters, but there was no sign of him, and I had two hours until our rendezvous on Park Street. After my adventure of the night before, I was all in. I went down to the mess where I put my hands on an electrical fan. The moment I got the thing started, it blew the ash off the cigar of a fellow smoking on the other side of the room. Luckily, he was only a Second Lieutenant. I put my hand up to signal an apology and he waved back as if to say, "Don't mention it, old man." Satisfied by this, I immediately went to sleep, and dreamed of what looked like rain clouds appearing over Baghdad, much to the relief of all the men on the ground. Only they were not rain clouds but dirigibles, Turkish ones, and they began dropping bombs. I was awoken by the roar of the motor on one of these dirigibles, which turned out to be the noise of the fan. I turned it off, drank down two glasses of the boiled water, moved over to the window. There was a little less dazzle to the day, and the men were working on the wires again.

I set out for the British Residency, which was the second HQ of the Corps, so to speak. Getting there was a matter of following the wires along the riverside alleyways. As I walked, alternately through dazzle and shadow, I took the envelope from my pocket. "Now as to communication, and encryption thereof," Manners of the War Office had told me, "we have decided in your own case to take the simplest possible approach."

The thin booklet I had been handed by the boy scout summoned by Manners — and which I took from its envelope as I walked now — was headed "Railway Clearing House Code Book".

"Secret code," Manners had said, keeping an absolutely straight face, but letting me know it was costing him quite an effort to do so.

"Not *very*," I had said.

I'd seen this booklet, or close variants thereof, lying about in many a railway office. Anyone sending a standard sort of railway message was supposed to make use of it, not so much for secrecy as for money-saving. It was drilled into any clerk that telegraphy was expensive, and brevity essential. But in practice the book was not much used, for the messages represented by its codes were too simple, and it was regarded as a rather comical production. Opening the book at random, I saw — under the list of code words related to "Duty" — the word "Chute". "Chute", I read, meant "Proceed to the following station for relief duty". Why did it mean that? No reason. There was seldom any obvious connection between the word and the message, although I'd always thought that railway clerks with

106

time on their hands must spend long hours trying to make one. *The bloke required for the duty at the other station would be sent down a chute to take up his position.*

The booklet contained a folded sheet of flimsy paper.

"Open it out," Manners had commanded.

I had done so in his office, and I did so now, seeing the following words in capitals, with their meanings set down alongside in lower case.

ANCHOVY — Move immediately to arrest and detention of suspect.

RUSTIC — Request prolongation of investigation.

GRUFF — Request identity of local agent.

RATIO — Impossible to proceed with investigation, request immediate return to London.

LOCOPARTS — Turkish treasure located and secured.

RELAX — Request telephonic communication.

The beauty of the cipher — according to Manners — was that the words in capitals corresponded to the ciphers in the railway code book. In that, as I knew without looking, "Anchovy" came under the heading "Missing and Tracing", and meant "Item certainly sent; have further search made, and wire result", while "Rustic" was under "Forwarding" and meant "Wire full particulars of despatch under delivery".

Now the telegraph clerk in the British Residency — a trusted man supposedly, but you never knew — would either have an understanding of the railway codes, and believe that I really was asking the Head Clerk, Department F, War Office — Manners, in other words — to wire further particulars in some railway matter. (Not completely unlikely, since I was in the railway office of Corps HQ.) Or he would just be baffled by the word "Anchovy", recognising it as some new code, separate from the standard military ciphers (with which he would be closely familiar). The third possibility was that, as a student of codes in general, the clerk might recognise "Anchovy" as belonging to the railway code, know its meaning as given in that book, but realise that in this particular communication it was being given some new meaning. In which case, as Manners had said, "So what?" For he would not know the new meaning, and could not discover it without having sight of the paper I now held in my hands.

And whatever he thought, it was the clerk's job to send the message.

Also listed on the paper were the words I might receive by way of reply:

CHRISTIAN — Will act as instructed.

CRATE — Cannot accede to your request, continue investigation.

JUMP — Terminate investigation.

I recalled that in the railway code "Christian" stood for "Nothing to indicate sender or cosignee". I could not remember the railway meanings of the other words.

I was restricted to this cipher. Therefore, I could not send "Boyd is dead. What do I do now?", much though I would have liked to.

108

Manners had considered the code a very clever dodge indeed, and amusing into the bargain. "However," he had said, "I would much prefer that you did not use it. The matter is too sensitive. Unless you wire 'Rustic' you will remain in Baghdad for a month collecting evidence and acting quite independently."

Should I need to send a wire, he had stressed, it was imperative I did so from the telegraph office of the Residency, since the strategic and diplomatic communications were sent from there rather than from the telegraph office of the Hotel. The men at the Residency were more trusted, in other words. To make use of that office, a fellow needed a document of authorisation, and I had one of these in the same envelope as the code. Most of the words on this chit were typewritten. The important ones, however, were scrawled in a shockingly bad hand that I could not read. It began, "For the Attention of", and then I couldn't make out who it was for the attention of. Then it said, "Captain J. H. Stringer is hereby authorised to despatch and receive telegraphic communications of level . . ." and the level I couldn't make out either. It was signed by an unreadable personage (it *might* have been "Manners") of "Department F, War Office".

I approached the gates of the British Residency, which was another palace on the river, this one set around a quadrangle.

"It's no go, sir," said the sentry, when I explained my business, showing all necessary credentials.

"You mean you won't let me in, Corporal?"

"By all means go *in*, sir. You'll find they're serving tea and cakes on the veranda. Only, the telegraphic office is shut."

"What is it, Corporal? Half-day closing?"

"Some wires are down, sir."

"Cut by the natives?"

"Ten-to-one on, sir. The telegraph office in the Hotel ought to be operating, sir. Why not try there?"

I shook my head. "That's out," I said. "I must send to . . ."

I looked through the gates and saw, in the quadrangle of the Residency, the man with the cine camera — bloody Wallace King. He stood by the side of the thing, for now he had an assistant to turn the handle, and the lens pointed directly at me. I turned on my heel, and the sentry called after me, "Come back tomorrow, sir! Be all fixed up by then!"

In the labyrinth once more, I reflected that Wallace King and his camera would be the death of me. The man was a liability. But at least this reverse put off the question of whether I should send "Gruff" or "Relax", the two options I'd been revolving.

I found I was wandering amid displays of dates, pastries, biscuits, breads. A sort of roof began to close over my head: wooden beams running between the houses with rushes laid over. Four sepoys came bearing down on me from the opposite direction, the second patrol I'd seen in ten minutes. This would be on account of the cut wires and — perhaps — the discovery of Boyd. I turned two more corners, and broke free of the labyrinth, finding myself walking towards the bridge of boats. Two army vans crawled across it, forcing the Arab river-watchers hard up against the rope barriers on either side . . . And the call to prayer was once more rising up from all over the town. Many Arabs were coming towards me along the river bank road, and I had a feeling of helplessness. I was outnumbered. But they began diverting to the right, towards a steeply rising terrace fringed by palms. It rose up towards a glittering mosque.

I came to a brick and timber quay: a hurly-burly of loading, men and animals. Even the gulls seemed to say "Allah! Allah!" A hot wind rose, sweeping dust off the top of a crumbling yellow brick wall that stood over the road from the quay. It enclosed a garden of palms, orange, lemon and other trees. In this garden — rising up from the river — a horse rider came and went between the trees, and I moved closer to the wall, trying to make sure of what seemed on the face of it an impossibility. The rider was a woman — a white woman. She wore jodhpurs, a white shirt, and some species of bowler hat. It was a funny sort of hat, but then everybody in this town wore a funny sort of hat, and she carried hers off particularly well. There was in general a trimness about her, and this taken together with the command of the horse . . . it all added up to a person I would like to have seen at closer quarters. But as I moved towards the wall in the fading light, an urgency came into the world, so that the wind rose, the prayer-call reached higher notes, the horse's canter became a gallop, and it was up through the trees, clear of them, over a stretch of gravelled track by flower beds, and gone from sight through the gate of a castellated wall.

I took from my pocket the map Jarvis had supplied. He'd taken a good deal of trouble over it. Some of the highlights of the eastern bank were marked: The Hotel GB, The Residency, Big Bizarre. (By which I took Jarvis to mean "Bazaar".) Some streets were drawn in, and the names given them by the Tommies were set down: Dog-Pack Square, Straight Street, Cemetry View (as Jarvis had it), Clean Street, and here number 11 — the intended destination of Stevens — was marked although no reason given as to why. The park I now faced was also marked. With my back to the river, I looked at it. To the right of it lay streets with names that seemed to take their cues from the park: Rose Lane, Jasmine Lane, Lemon Tree Grove, and the address I'd been allocated, Rose Court. Beyond the park was the Cavalry Barracks, then the North Gate of the wall, which was the principal one. If Turks came back, they'd come by that way.

I began skirting the park (where thoughtful-looking Arabs sat under trees), making for Rose Court. As Baghdad streets went, Park Street was pleasantly wide and smooth, and to demonstrate the fact, a smart phaeton came trotting along it pulled by a well-groomed horse. But it was in the nature of this place that the horse should lift its tail as I looked on, and that it should deposit on the road bricks a considerable poundage of shit, which was then scattered by the wheels of the carriage in the vicinity of one particular

112

set of open gates, beyond which I saw dark red roses. The place corresponded to Rose Court on my map.

I was half an hour early for Jarvis, but I crossed the road and passed through the gate, where I saw many rose beds, fertilised by other instances of the stuff the horse had dropped. The garden air was overcharged with the dizzying smell of roses and horse shit, and the twisting sounds of evening birdsong . . . And voices. These came from behind a thicket of palm trees, and they were very English voices — one upper-class, one not so. Something told me to retreat from them, and I backed into a second area of palms, this one enclosing a rectangular ornamental pond of very green and dead water with rose petals scattered over it, unable to sink. It was Jarvis and Shepherd who were speaking. I could not make out particular words, although Jarvis broke through with ". . . That's it, sir . . . reported by the station master . . ."

There was then a question from Shepherd — and the soft civility he'd shown to me was evident, even though here was an officer addressing a private soldier. They separated after additional muttering, and I watched Shepherd go through the gate. As he crossed the threshold, a sudden rattle of piano music from one of the apartments in the compound seemed to cause him to give a skip, and to move away down the street at the double.

I closed on Jarvis; a Ford van was parked behind him. He saluted, but did not snap to it as he had the night before.

"Number four's ours, sir," he said. "Very nice, sir, but dusty. The boy's just giving it a clean over."

We eyed each other; the music had stopped.

"Your things are already in there, sir," said Jarvis, leading off along a gravel track between low brick buildings.

"How are you acquainted with Lieutenant Colonel Shepherd, Jarvis?" I enquired as we walked. "He was leaving as I arrived."

Jarvis didn't break stride: "I'm not, sir, but I know who he is. I mean, I know he's your governor in the railway department, sir. But besides that, I know he was at the railway station when the city fell. He was there with another officer, a man I do count a friend — or did."

I was nearly but not quite so blockheaded as to say, "You mean Boyd?"

". . . Name of Captain Boyd, sir," Jarvis ran on. "The police team put the notice up in Part One Orders just after lunchtime, sir. Found dead at the railway station this morning — in the buffet."

"And you were breaking the news to the lieutenant colonel?"

"They'd seen action together. I thought it only right. Everyone knows they were the first men into this place — if you take the station to be part of Baghdad."

What would I ask if this were all new to me? I settled on "What unit was Boyd with?"

"Hundred and Eighty-Fifth Machine Gun Company, sir."

"And how did you know him?"

114

"I was batman to him down in Basrah. Before that, he'd done me a bit of a good turn, and that's how we'd got acquainted."

So I had been given as batman the very fellow who'd done the same job for the man whose murder I was investigating.

Was Shepherd behind this? Had Boyd himself been behind it?

"You said he'd done you a good turn?"

"Kut, sir . . . Saved my life, did Captain Boyd. I was very sorry when I was transferred back to driving duties after being with him three months."

"He saved your life? How?"

"He brought me a drink of water . . . So I'm a bit down now, sir."

And he did seem genuinely cut up by the death of a man he thought a lot of; I would have to get the details out of him later.

There were perhaps half a dozen small houses in the enclosure. An Arab stared at me from the doorway of one. "This is Ahmad, sir," said Jarvis. "He's the boy."

"Hello Ahmad," I said, touching my cap.

"*Ack*-mad," he corrected me.

He was about six and a half foot tall, and at least forty — a rather glowering sort of fellow in a black robe and white turban. I nodded to him and he stepped aside, saying, "You will like it here," as if to say "You'd *better* do."

It was a hot box, really, with plenty of flies in it, but quite a decent diggings all considered, being pleasantly furnished, with two wicker sofas, scattered rugs on a

115

stone floor, a divan, green-shaded oil lamps. Ahmad now upped the ante by saying, "You will *really* like it," a good deal of threat put into that word "really".

One doorway connected to a slightly more modest version of the same room: Jarvis's quarters; another led to a narrow stone room running along the side of the building — a sort of scullery. Jarvis too had a door leading into this area, which in turn had its own exterior door leading out into the compound. Ahmad, who had his own sleeping quarters elsewhere, would come and go by this.

We were back in the main room. Ahmad was pointing to the divan, saying, "You will have a piece of sleep."

He appeared to be commanding me to go to sleep there and then. It struck me that he might mean the *peace* of sleep. Jarvis, who was distributing my things about the room, said a couple of words in Arabic to Ahmad, who then went off.

"He's squared for half a dozen bottles of Bass, sir," said Jarvis; "he'll be back with them in a minute."

I said, "I hope he has them in a cool place. Do you suppose it was an Arab who did for Boyd?"

Jarvis may have nodded.

"They're starting to turn, sir. A stone was pitched through the window of the Hotel."

"They were throwing flowers when we arrived," I said.

"*Some* of them were," said Jarvis. "You see they're not all the same. There's the Sunni and the Shia. They have a disagreement about the religion. I don't know

116

the ins and outs of it, but the Sunnis have been top dogs in Baghdad under the Turks, and they're shaping up to be the same with us. They know how to toe the line, sir."

Ahmad returned with a bottle of Bass. I had a vision of him taking the cork out with his teeth — he had a good face for doing that sort of thing — but I saw it had already been removed. He handed it to me together with a small glass in a metal holder.

"Clean glass," he said, in his sinister sort of way.

"Thanks," I said, nodding, and setting bottle and glass down on the low table in the centre of the room.

"Drink," said Ahmad, eyeing me.

"Can you tell him to go?" I said to Jarvis.

Jarvis got him out of the room, more by gestures than words.

"Which do you suppose he is?" I said when he'd gone. "Sunni or Shia?"

"Shia, I think," said Jarvis.

So he was part of the awkward squad. That was a bad lookout. I took up the bottle of beer, and thought for a moment: *What if he's poisoned it?* It would have been a perfectly reasonable move on his part; I knew for a fact that no Arabs were allowed in the kitchens of the Hotel or the Residency, but I was parched so I raised it to my lips. After I'd taken a belt, I said, "You'll have one of these yourself, won't you, Jarvis?"

"I will do sir, yes. Later on."

It wouldn't really do for us to drink together, I knew that much.

Jarvis said, "I don't believe it *was* an Arab who killed Captain Boyd, sir, and I mean to find out who *did*. I've plenty of free time, sir. I mean to turn detective."

I gave this faintly alarming news the go-by, or tried to.

"You were a detective yourself, weren't you sir? On the railway force at York?"

I nodded.

"Jarvis," I said, "how was it that Lieutenant Colonel Shepherd was actually here in Rose Court?"

He was fixing the mosquito net over my bed.

"I saw him walking past the gates just as I was driving in."

Having fixed up the net, Jarvis said, "This flipping place, sir."

"I thought you liked it."

"Yes," he said. "Well, I do try."

He was much less given to chirpiness than I'd first thought. And his uniform was quite black with sweat.

CHAPTER
SEVEN

I traversed the Baghdad labyrinth. It was getting on for nine. The heat had hardly abated; the only difference was that the light had turned dark green again. Jarvis and Ahmad between them had prepared my evening meal: some species of spiced meat (Ahmad's contribution), with fried potato (Jarvis's doing). Jarvis had not eaten himself, but had gone off early to his bed with a bottle of beer. It bothered me that there was a connection between him and Shepherd. I'd now got possessed of the idea that they were in league; that Shepherd had been somehow instrumental in having Jarvis posted batman to me. But why would Jarvis have anything against a man who'd saved his life?

I must find out more about what had befallen him at Kut-al-Amara.

I turned into an alleyway, and saw a camel's head on a pole. It stuck out from the front of a shop made bright by unshaded lamps and white tiles. In it sat two Arabs conversing pleasantly amid a litter of bloody camel parts. I saw two other camels' heads further along, signifying another couple of butcheries. In fact it seemed this street was given over to the selling of camel parts just as certain quarters of any town in Blighty would be given over to the selling of motor-car parts. The heads put me in mind of one of my daughter Sylvia's toys — hobby horse. That was a *horse's* head on a stick, and it too looked pretty glum about it. I thought of the four weeks' voyage that separated me from Sylvia. That was if malaria didn't do for me, or cholera, or the ferocious Ahmad, or Shepherd and his associates (if any). In the ordinary military sense, I was safer in Mespot than I had been on the Western Front, only it was too hot here. It didn't do to dwell on the fact, but I could hardly breathe.

I saw an alleyway going off, its name neatly and newly painted on a wall: "Clean Street". Captain Stevens had come here earlier in the day — to number 11. That spot had also been marked on Jarvis's map, and I hadn't had the chance to ask him about it.

Clean Street was only clean in comparison to Dead Camel Street. I walked along the dusty, broken cobbles to the last building, which was long and low, with arched windows of dusty glass, yet it seemed as if I was seeing only the tops of the windows, as though the building had been pressed down into the ground. There were two doors, both painted with a number 11, and one of the two stood open. It gave on to a stone staircase, which took me down to a further door, and from beyond this came the sound of a rapid whipping, and a desperate groaning. I pushed at the door as a cockney voice within roared, "What's your *purpose*, John? What's your *purpose*?"

My eyes roved over a vast, echoing basement packed with boxing Tommies. Well, Tommies and sepoys both.

120

There were three boxing rings, and shirtless men in white shorts either scrapping in the rings or milling about in between, or hitting at punchballs, or skipping, which accounted for the whipping noise. I looked at one of the skippers, and he doubled his speed, commencing a kind of dance into the bargain. It took me a second to realise that a horn gramophone was playing American music — all shaking drums with a band of lunatic trumpeters trying to keep up. The walls were green tiles, shining with sweat, and hung with home-made banners. I read "51st Sikhs", "53rd Sikhs", "2nd Leicestershires". Clouds of steam somersaulted through the unbreathable air. The place was evidently connected up to a generator, for it was lit by crude electric lamps that would flash occasionally — or had I blinked twice in disbelief?

A rather faint voice behind me said, "You are to sign in first, sir," but I paid it no mind. The man who'd been roaring "What's your purpose, John?" was now down to "*Purpose*, John! Purpose!" He was an instructor at the ring closest to me. One fighter — the purposeless John, who was taking a pasting — wore leather headgear to soften the blows and save the brain. These were a new thing in boxing and my governor in the railway police, Chief Inspector Weatherill (a champion army boxer in his day), was dead against them. The other bloke, the one handing out the pasting, hadn't bothered with one.

"What are you, sir? Welterweight?" said the instructor. He wanted me in that ring — wanted to see an officer get bashed. "Get stripped off, sir, and you can go against the southpaw." As I stood stunned, he

121

roared out "Two minutes!" and the pair in the ring resumed their scrap.

A southpaw was a left-hander, I knew that much. But in the flurry of the scrap, it was the devil of a job to see which man fitted the bill. "*That* bloke'll be your mark, sir," the instructor said, seeing my difficulty, and indicating the meaner-looking of the two, the one without the helmet, "Irwin — the little machine-gunner."

At this, I started. "Machine-gunner? What company?"

"Eh?"

I indicated the ring. I was pretty sure neither fighter had yet clapped eyes on me. "The southpaw," I said, "The machine-gunner. What company?"

The answer came back slowly. It was quite a mouthful, after all:

"Irwin, sir . . . he's in the 185th Machine Gun Company. I know that, see, because I'm in the 186th."

I hadn't exactly been clutching at a straw. There wouldn't be more than a dozen or so machine-gun companies in Baghdad.

"Kit's over there, sir," said the instructor, "in that room by the little blokes."

He pointed over to some Indians, who were watching one of their fellows laying into a punchbag — only he did more prancing than punching, and his pals laughed at him for it. They were near a low archway. I ducked down through it, coming to a cooler subterranean room that was half swimming bath, half changing room, which is to say the boxing kit was tumbled about in a series of baskets placed on the stone edging of the pool.

The place was empty, crypt-like — a flooded crypt lit by candle stubs, and cooler than the gymnasium on account of the water, which was greyish, but damned inviting all the same.

I put my hands on some kit that fitted — all save for the gloves and headgear. This last was the key item. The man Irwin had not looked my way, and he never would get sight of my features as long as I wore the protector, which covered the cheeks and temples as well as the skull. I would quiz him from behind it. After all, boxers did talk in the ring; they weren't supposed to but they did. It was usually of the order of "Stand still while I clout you, you fucking rotter!" but I would ask Irwin about what if anything he'd seen at the Baghdad railway station on the night the town fell.

Glancing about, I saw two of the protectors spilled out of a canvas bag. I put one on and I thought, *I'm a fucking racehorse in blinkers*. Feeling a prize chump in baggy shorts, I found my way back to the ring and to the instructor, who was bawling at his fighters, "As you were, gentlemen, as you were!", at which they left off punching. Irwin stayed up, the other climbed down. The instructor went off somewhere, came back with gloves for me. I held out my hands, and he laced them without a word. My opponent shadow-boxed in the ring; or he was dancing to the American music. As he moved, he was in a bath of sweat.

"See your stance, sir?" said the instructor.

I put up my fists, and he immediately wheeled away, as though in disgust. But it was just that another bloke wanted his attention. This other bloke was a big bloke

123

— heavyweight — and had blood coming from his nose. It was coming down on to his chest, and every so often he'd swirl it about all over his front in a manner rather child-like; otherwise he didn't seem too bothered about it. The bloodied man tipped his head back, and the instructor watched his nose bleed for a while, then sent him away with a word I couldn't hear, but which made the other laugh. The instructor turned back to me, and made no remark on my stance, but just said, "Keep your chin down, sir. Don't hit him with this . . ." at which he nearly hit *me* with the palm of his hand.

I climbed into the ring, and the instructor shouted "Two minutes!" which was evidently the signal for "begin" as well as "stop", and Irwin the southpaw machine-gunner came over and clouted me. Whether he'd done it with his left or his right I was for the moment too dazed to say, even though the protector had somewhat lessened the force of the blow. He then started dancing again. I aimed a couple of blows at his midriff, which he defended easily. You were supposed to go for the solar plexus, but where the hell was that?

"You were at the station with Captain Boyd," I said. "On the night the city fell."

He gave me a left and right to the head.

"No talking," he said. He was a Londoner. His plimsoles squeaked furiously on the canvas.

I tried the following lie: "I was at school with him."

"You don't sound like you were. Sorry sir, are you an officer?"

"I am," I said, and he went into a faster dance, as though in celebration at having an officer to bash.

"He's been found dead," I said. "At the railway station again."

"I've heard that, sir," said Irwin, still dancing.

I said, "Did anything funny happen there? First time around, I mean?"

Irwin came for me again, and this time I defended better, or thought I did, but the instructor, looking up, said, "Box hard, box hard," as though I'd just been nancying about.

"I wouldn't know," said Irwin, "and how do you mean 'funny'?"

The instructor shouted, "As you were, as you were."

Was this the end of the bout or the end of the round? Evidently the former, for my opponent said, "Go again in a minute, eh sir?"

"Captain Boyd went into the station with another officer," I said.

He nodded, went over to his corner for a towel, came back.

"Boyd was my C.O., sir. A good man. We were in an advance party with some infantry. This other officer was with this infantry lot . . . I mean as far as I could make out. He went into the station where the Turks were. A little later, Captain Boyd went in."

"What happened then?"

"They came out."

"In what order?"

"Captain Boyd first, then the other chap, as far as I recall . . . There was a lot of smoke floating about, sir, some pretty hard scrapping in the vicinity of the station

125

. . . and the train was pulling out. It was a confused situation, sir, and there was a hell of a din."

"Two minutes!" called the bloody instructor. Then, to me, "He's a southpaw, keep left!" (Having observed my performance, he'd dropped the "sir".)

Irwin was immediately dancing again. Talk about "passed A1"; he was as fit as a flea. He walloped me a few times, and I suddenly found I hardly had the energy to lift my arms, let alone take a shot at him. We went into some close stuff, tangled arms, and I wasn't so much sweating as melting. I'd been scrapping for a little over two minutes, yet I was practically asleep on Irwin's shoulder.

"What did the other officer do when he came out?" I asked, drowsily. "Was he carrying anything?"

"Lead!" the instructor was calling, "Lead!" but it was a lost cause, and he knew it.

"He was," said Irwin.

He was at me again with fists flying.

"What?" I said, reeling back.

"Don't know. A package; a box. He held it under his arm."

I put a pretty good right on Irwin's ear.

"And what did Boyd do?" I said.

Irwin was dancing again. "He told us we were to stand by. And then . . ."

"Yes?"

The instructor was shouting again: "Time! Time!" which, thank Christ, brought an end to the bout, leaving the two of us standing in the middle of the ring

126

at rather a loose end. My head burned though. I would have to take the protector off in a minute.

"Some more artillery came up, and it was all back to — you know — confusion," said Irwin. He walked over to his corner, picked up a towel; I followed him. New fighters were climbing into the ring. I nodded at Irwin, and we touched gloves.

I asked, "What was the expression on Boyd's face when he came out of the station?"

"The *expression*?" said Irwin, evidently appalled by the question. "Well, it was the middle of a battle. So I suppose he looked *worried*. We all did."

I nodded. "The other chap?"

Irwin hesitated, and a slow grin came over his face: "Winked at me, he did, just as he was walking by. It was very fast so it might not have been a wink. But I believe it *was*."

Luckily, Irwin did not follow me to the changing room, where I pitched away the cursed protector, had a dunk in the water, and put on my uniform. With head down, I headed back through the gym towards the door, where the faint voice piped up again: "You've to sign out, sir, if you would be so kind as to do so. And I don't believe you signed *in*."

A young sepoy sat by the door, with a ledger, a pen, blotting paper and a watch on a little table before him. The kid couldn't have been more than sixteen. He spread his beautiful thin fingers over the paper, showing me where I should have signed in, giving my unit and the time, and where I ought to sign out, putting the time again. He gave me a pen, and I did what every other man did — wrote scrawl, which was a shame, everything being so beautifully presented by the boy.

"Your time in was nine twenty-five," said the boy as I scribbled. "Your time out is ten fifteen."

If you did P.T. or sports you could cut certain fatigues, and that was the reason for the ledger. My eye roved over the list of names, and the one I didn't want to see came towards the end: "Captain W. P. D. Stevens" of "Corps HQ". He had booked in at eight ten, left at nine fifty-five. In other words, he'd been in the place when I'd arrived, and left at about the time I'd completed my bout with Irwin. Well, it would only signify if (a) he was in league with Shepherd, (b) he'd seen me, and (c) he worked out that I was quizzing Irwin, and *why* I was quizzing him. But I had a pretty good notion that he *must* have seen me.

I stepped back into Clean Street hoping for cooler air, and not finding it. I turned into Dead Camel Street thinking hard, only faintly aware of the drone of a petrol motor. I'd not gone ten yards before I was blinded by a horrible glare. I raised my arm to shield my eyes, and turned away.

"That's no bloody good," said a voice.

"He's blinded, Mr King," said another. "Dazzled, he is."

The light swung away from me, so that it illuminated the camels' heads on one side of the street only, and I was able to see its source: a great searchlight attached to a generator, an entire field searchlight company standing around it, together with Wallace's King's bloody camera, Wallace King's *assistant* (who also wore

128

a uniform without badges, only his was a private's) and Wallace King himself. He held a loudhailer by his side.

"This is Dead Camel Street!" he called out. "It's full of dead camels. It's not every day you get a street full of dead camels." He raised the hailer to his lips for added emphasis: "It's *interesting*! It's a curiosity! Could you turn around and come back looking slightly less blasé about it? Just ignore the light. Go out of the street and come back in again."

I went out of it all right, and found a different route back to Rose Court.

The place was silent. No sign of Ahmad or Jarvis. I stripped off all my sweat-soaked clothes. I lit a lamp . . . and the main room was all in perfect order — there were not even any flies. But I became aware of a steady ticking. The sound froze me. I could not detect the source of it. I picked up the lamp, and carried it about the room, listening hard. The ticking was louder near the bed. It came from underneath the bed. The lamp would not fit under the bed, so I lit a match, and moved it towards the thing. It was made of wood and brass. I shook out the match, reached in again, and pulled the device a little way towards me. After further contemplation, I pulled it again.

The answer broke in on me only when I turned it upside down. The contraption was quite involved, but in summary I held a rectangular wooden block with a spindle threaded through it. The block was smeared with grease; I swiped at it with my finger and put it to my lips — Ahmad had used the fat from whatever meat he had cooked for me three hours since. The

129

mechanism periodically turned the block through a hundred and eighty degrees so that the flies that had been on the top were deposited into a mesh cage beneath. And the cage seethed with flies. I set the flytrap next to the light, and sat naked on the floor, contemplating the little prisoners. Why must they fret so? Wouldn't they be better off keeping still in this incredible heat? I put the thing back under the bed but decided, two sleepless hours later, that its tick was keeping me awake. I took it out into the rose garden, where I left it. I then thoroughly soaked my bed sheet at the creaking water pump.

I lay down again under the wet sheet, but I knew sleep to be a luxury out of the question. I was concentrating now on breathing.

CHAPTER
EIGHT

I climbed out of bed with the sun, and opened the door to Jarvis's room. He was asleep, twisted up in his one sheet, with four empty bottles of Bass lined up by his bed. One more bottle, I reckoned, and I would have had to say something, not least because I knew he had some driving duties in prospect for that day. There wasn't much else in the room, beside the bottles. He appeared to keep most of his belongings stuffed into his pack, which leant against the wall next to his rifle. There was a book open on the floor near my boot. I leant down and read the spine: *The City of the Khalifs*.

It was Ahmad who prepared the breakfast: yoghurt, figs, coffee. I ate them in the scullery as he glowered at me.

From the stone sink, he indicated Jarvis's room, saying, "He . . . trouble."

"Why?"

"Make scream," he said. He opened his mouth wide to reveal a jumble of black teeth, and raised his hands to his face, making a dumb show of screaming. It was worse than if he *had* screamed.

"In his sleep?" I said, and Ahmad nodded.

"*Really*," he said.

I asked Ahmad, "Are there Turkish cigarettes for sale in Baghdad?"

"Turkish," he said, "Turkish gone."

"But their cigarettes?"

"Many cigarettes here. Turkish gone," he said again, and he smiled. "You boot them out. You *booted*."

"I know," I said.

Silence for a space.

"Is good," he said, contemplating me.

"What?" I said, and he indicated the open door, and the rose garden beyond. "Beautiful weather."

"It's far too hot," I said.

"In London ugly weather."

"I am not from London," I said, and he folded his arms and scowled at me, repeating, "In *London*, ugly weather."

The labyrinth baked, and I baked in it as I threaded through the alleyways towards the British Residency. I would send my message to Manners before putting in my day's work with Shepherd. In fact, I hoped it would be only a half day, since it was Saturday.

A new sentry directed me to the telegraph office, and I crossed the quadrangle in the direction indicated, passing a pool where a fountain was supposed to come out of stone fruit, but did not. The Turks had stabled horses here, and that was the fragrance of the quadrangle, while in the interior the smell of hot carpet took over. The place was museum-like, with great oil paintings of desert scenes and fancy carvings around the door frames. On the second floor, one of these doors was marked "Post Room" and as I passed by, a

132

pock-marked and dishevelled-looking Tommy came out of it, with a bunch of keys in his hand. He did not salute, but eyed me with curiosity. He was not the sort of man who ought to have come out of that sort of door.

Another sentry stood at the door marked "Telegraph Office", and this showed its importance. He inspected my identity card, my chit authorising me to send from this office, and opened the door for me. Most messages from the Hotel were, I believed, sent "clear" — that is, not in any code save the Morse of all telegraphy. Here, I believed, the majority of the messages would be coded. It was a long, thin room, facing on to the river, with all shutters and windows open on that side. The river was directly below, but the sounds from it seemed to come from far off. The desks were placed crosswise at regular intervals, and each was loaded with a mix-up of equipment. But when it came down to it, every bit of kit could only either send or receive, and it was all connected by wires to a clock in a glass case on the end wall. Next to the clock, and in joint command of the room *with* the clock, sat an officer smoking a pipe, and with absolutely nothing on his desk save a leather tobacco pouch. A large safe stood on the other side of the desk from the clock.

The officer rose as I entered the room. He was a tall, dark-eyed and hairy man, although whether his head was hairy I couldn't tell, since he wore his cap. His legs, certainly, were extremely hairy. (He wore shorts — and very well-pressed ones at that.) He wore a wristwatch, the better to show off the thinness and hairiness of his

133

wrists, and I was sure this watch would be exactly keyed to the clock on the wall, for he was obviously the most orderly of men. His name, he told me, after smoking at me for a while, was Captain Bob Ferry. He had very clean fingernails, and he wore a gold signet ring on the little finger of his left hand.

"I want to send to London," I said.

He smoked on.

"War Office?" he said, with a kind of gasp. He was afflicted with a stutter, only he did *not* stutter, but waited for the word.

"Well, take . . . a pad," he said. "The man Collins will see you right."

He had twirled his pointing finger in the air before settling on Collins, who sat two desks away from where we stood. Ferry placed a small notepad in my hand. The headings were "Message", "To", "From", and "Sender Can Be Found At". There was a carbon beneath, so that a duplicate would be made of whatever was written.

Under "To", I put "The Head Clerk, Department F, War Office, London". (That was Manners.) Under "From" I wrote out — somewhat reluctantly — "Capt. Stringer, Railway Office, Corps HQ". Under "Sender Can Be Found At", I gave both Rose Court and my office number at the Hotel. That was the easy part, but what was my message? Of the choices available it must be either "GRUFF" — "Request identity of local agent", or "RELAX" — "Request telephonic communication". I wrote "GRUFF" and then, because it looked ridiculous on its own, I underlined it.

134

The clerk, Collins, was typing at a perforating keyboard, making words into Morse as he read from another of the pads. I saw on it a list of five-digit numbers: a military code. It might have been anything from "Turkish assault expected" to "Send more foot powder". I shouldn't have been looking at it either way.

Collins turned around, and said quite sharply, "Be with you in three minutes, sir." I stepped back. Captain Ferry was speaking to another of the clerks: "It is not to be sent from this office. We are not in the business of transmitting tittle- . . . tattle. It is a private matter."

"We refuse to send, then?" said the clerk.

"We do."

Ferry did not sound angry so much as rather steely. A little under two minutes later, the man Collins held out his hand to receive my pad, and I watched him as he read the word "GRUFF". He keyed it in at lightning speed and with not a flicker of expression on his face. He then made a note in a ledger referring somehow to the message sent, and took the Morse tape he had created to the man at the next desk, who fed it directly into an automatic transmitter. Collins returned the top sheet of the pad to me, but kept the duplicate copy.

As the man at the automatic transmitter sat back and closed his eyes, I imagined the word "Gruff" flying down the cable to Basrah, running under the waters of the Gulf to Bombay; then reversing, so to speak, out from Bombay to the south of the Red Sea, proceeding north to Alexandria, crossing the Med to Malta, then on to Lisbon, before embarking on the home straight: running north under the Atlantic to Cornwall, from where, as I believed, the cable followed the tracks of the Great Western Railway up to London, and the War Office. I figured the word coming out of the machine in Department F, being torn off and handed on to a runner — a boy scout, or perhaps *the* boy scout who had guided the Chief and me — and given at last into the hands of the supercilious Manners.

I went back to Collins, and enquired, "How long does it take to reach London?"

"Three minutes," he said.

It appeared those two words were about the limit of his conversation. Ferry had returned to the vicinity of his desk, where he stood smoking, and looking down at the bustle of boats on the Tigris.

"Where will the reply come to?" I asked Collins. Without looking up from his desk, he stabbed the air with his pencil, indicating the man at the desk over, opposite Captain Ferry's.

This chap commanded *two* machines. Tape was coming from both, and he was reading one of the tapes. I took up station next to him, and he gave me a narrow look before going back to reading the tape. I thought: *Is this message for me?* No, couldn't be. It had come too quickly and it was surely too long. The message was in Morse, whereas the one coming from the second, bigger machine was in actual words that seemed to flow on unread for ever. (I made out ". . . Religion has a great influence over the Arab . . .") This second machine was operated by compressed air, and made a kind of sucking noise at frequent intervals. I became aware of a similar sound closer to me, and Captain

Ferry and his pipe had come up close. The clerk tore the Morse tape from the first machine, and handed it to Ferry, who read it thoughtfully with pipe in hand, before placing his pipe in his mouth, and quickly twisting the tape with his long brown fingers into a perfect, pretty bow.

I found myself saying, "I was told to expect an immediate reply," whereas in fact I had been advised by Manners not to wire at all.

Ferry removed his pipe from his mouth. "That means", he said, ". . . tomorrow." He added, "At the earliest . . . I should think. A runner will be sent to you."

I nodded. "Much obliged," I said.

"You're in the railway section," said Ferry. "Has Lieutenant Colonel . . . Shepherd interested you in his Railway Club?"

"Yes," I said, "I'm going along tonight. Will you be there?"

A long period of smoking followed from Captain Ferry, during which time he saw that my own cigarette was coming to an end, and so fetched an ashtray for me from a window ledge.

"Yes," he said.

"Good," I said, which rather got across whatever he had wanted to say next, requiring him to smoke for a while longer as he mustered the words for a second time.

". . . I will be," he said, "although I have no particular interest in railway topics. Except perhaps for . . . railway telegraphy."

Nice, I thought. He probably knows the railway code book backwards. But then what could it matter if he thought that, by "GRUFF", I meant "Blockage on the 'up' line" or whatever might be its meaning in the railway code? (I could not just then recall it.)

"However," Ferry was saying, "the Club, as I understand it, is not really to . . . do with railways. The main concern of Lieutenant Colonel Shepherd seems to be —"

And at this the receiving clerk cut in, for the Morse printer had started up again, and the matter was evidently urgent.

"Excuse me," said Ferry, and he turned to the machine.

Being fascinated by Captain Bob Ferry, I contrived — by means of lighting another cigarette near the doorway — to delay my departure from the telegraph office. As I looked on, Ferry stood over his man, and read the tape coming from the machine. He tore it off, and quickly made another bow of it while walking to the safe that stood alongside his desk. He put both paper bows into the safe, glanced up and saw me watching him do it. He removed his pipe from his mouth, and called, "I will . . . see you this evening, Captain Stringer."

And still the words spooled unread from the second receiver.

CHAPTER
NINE

Trying to picture the Baghdad Railway Club, I had
kept thinking of the original Railway Club in Victoria
Street, London, namely a dusty room, green-papered
walls crowded with pictures of trains — something like
that, only hotter. The reality of the matter was as
follows:

The Club was housed in a three-storey building that
had once been grand. On each floor, overlooking the
small square — Quiet Square — was a window of
coloured glass and a faded red veranda. A sign
projected: "The Restaurant". The front door gave on to
a hot, dark lobby into which a spiral staircase of fancy
ironwork descended. Arab voices echoed from rooms
off. I had been told to go to the third floor and here I
smelt pipesmoke, and found Captain Bob Ferry sitting
alone at a long table, his lean, dark form strangely
decorated with geometric patterns of blue and
red-brown light from the window. His hat was off, and
he was quite bald.

I sat down opposite to him.

"You're early," I said.

"I was just around . . . the corner," he replied.

He reached into his tunic pocket.

"Your reply," he said, handing me an envelope.

"Thanks," I said. "It came quicker than expected?"

"Yes," Ferry eventually said.

Opening the envelope, I was not surprised to read the single word "CRATE". Bob Ferry manipulated his pipe with his long fingers as I did so. In the cipher that I had agreed with Manners, the word "CRATE" meant "Cannot accede to your request, continue investigation". Even so, I thanked Ferry again. He must have read the message, but at best it would have meant something like "Your shortage of coal acknowledged" or whatever was its railway code-book meaning.

Just then, Stevens entered. I introduced him to Ferry, since they did not appear to know each other.

Stevens asked me: "Are you speaking, then?"

I shook my head. "Maybe next time."

"Are *you*?" he asked Ferry.

I was embarrassed for Ferry, since now his stutter would be discovered. He had got as far as removing his pipe from his mouth when Stevens said, "*I'm* speaking. Worse luck."

He gave no outward indication of having seen me at number 11 Clean Street. He sat down, and set his great right leg bouncing. It was very irritating.

"Some Arab's going to bring up some cocktails, or something," he said, glancing over to the door. "I could do with a stiffener. Public speaking always makes me nervous. Ever since schooldays, you know. I did a talk on the National Debt and I couldn't remember anything about it. 'The first great rise in the National Debt occurred in . . .' Totally blank. The moment I apologised and sat down looking a prize idiot, it all came back to me and I've never forgotten it since."

I nodded. Stevens continued to bounce his leg.

"In the Revolution of 1688," he said, "the National Debt rose from £664,263 to over sixteen million." Turning to Ferry, he said, "Do you know what it was in 1816?"

Ferry removed his pipe from his mouth, and said, "I —"

"There's a cat over there," said Stevens. There were two long red sofas in the room, loaded with green and red cushions. Among them was a thin white cat that had just woken up. "I know *her* game," said Stevens, contemplating the cat, "she's pretending not to look at us."

I wondered whether he'd been drinking already.

A young Royal Engineer turned up just then, saying, "Did you hear about the trouble in town? An Arab was beaten to death just now."

Stevens gave a shrug. "I heard something of the sort."

I wondered: Did *he* do it? He'd certainly be up to beating a man to death, but he looked perfectly smart, carried none of the marks of a fight.

I enquired, "Do you think it was one of our boys that did it?"

"Should *think* so," said Stevens.

An Arab entered with blue glasses and silver bowls on a board. He put them on the table by the window, walked out again without a word.

"What *is* this place?" I asked Stevens.

"No idea," he said, sitting back in his chair.

"It was once a restaurant deluxe," said the Royal Engineer. "Unfortunately that was some time ago."

Turning to Ferry, who might be feeling a bit left out, I said, "What did you do on civilian street, Bob?"

"Taught," he said at length. Thinking he wouldn't be much good in a classroom with that stutter of his, I asked, "Where was that then?"

"Oxford . . . University," he said.

The sound of voices came from the staircase. In walked a chap in the mid-fifties; he wore the white tabs of a political officer, and his badge of rank was crossed swords, denoting a brigadier general. Shepherd came in behind him. The brigadier removed his cap, and we all saluted. He had thin grey hair and sleepy, kindly eyes. "All students of the railway hobby, I take it," he said, in a husky voice. "Very good, very good." He then took up where he'd left off with Shepherd, speaking in a low tone. Presently, the brigadier drifted towards the window, and Shepherd came over. I introduced him to Captain Ferry "of the telegraph office at the Residency".

The moment I said that, I thought: It must not come out that I've just sent from there.

Ferry said to Shepherd, "The fame of your club has reached as far as the . . . Annex."

"The Annex" was what some people called the Residency. Shepherd had listened politely as Ferry had spoken that delayed last word, so I wondered whether the two had met before. I doubted it, since most of the

142

telegrams sent by political staff such as Shepherd would go from the Hotel.

Shepherd said, "Oh, I assure you, it has even reached as far as the cavalry barracks." He was indicating one individual (a cavalryman, I supposed) in amongst a group of new arrivals, but I couldn't see which one. In fact, a general bustle of standing up, saluting and making of introductions was proceeding at the other end of the table, which sent the cat scampering from the room — into which confusion was added the return of the waiter, with more food and drink. Shepherd now turned his gracious attention to one of the younger officers, a Royal Engineer, who'd just passed him a paper-wrapped package — a framed painting, as it turned out. "Ah now," said Shepherd. "The halt in the desert . . . and the *locomotive*. I believe it's one of the big Krausses."

The young officer was embarrassed. "It's a 2-8-0 anyhow."

"It is," said Shepherd, "and it's a Krauss to the life. I believe you've worked from the engineering drawings, Harry."

We all clustered around the painting. It showed an encampment in the desert: soldiers illuminated by pinkish fire glow, palms behind them, and mountains, ghostly in moonlight beyond. Emerging from a mountain pass was a locomotive, and its smoke, rising up and over the mountains, spelt out the words "Baghdad Railway Club", with the small moon as the dot of the "i".

"We'll hang it for next time," said Shepherd.

"Very good painting," murmured the brigadier general, who'd wandered back over from the window.

I heard one of the R.E. men saying to Shepherd, "I gather you're having a run up to Samarrah, sir." I could not hear Shepherd's reply. The R.E. man said, "On *The Elephant*, I gather? But where did you turn up the side rods, sir?" He was talking about the giant engine at Baghdad station, but Shepherd did not answer. Instead, he called, "Gentlemen, take your seats please!"

Shepherd put the brigadier general at the head. I presumed that he took pride of place by seniority rather than knowledge of railways, unless he *owned* a railway or two. To his right sat Shepherd, chief mover of the Club. Opposite to Shepherd sat a man I'd not seen enter the room: a handsome and sunburned major with swept-back blond hair. I heard him saying to his neighbour, "Well now, isn't this jolly?" Then, a moment later, "Railways aren't really my thing. Interesting though." Aside from myself, Stevens and Ferry, there was also a collection of amiable-looking officers from the Royal Engineers. One was the amateur painter. Apparently a free chair at my end was being kept free for a "special guest" who would be appearing in due course, and whose identity was a mystery to me. The actual dinner was being laid out on the other table. It would be taken as a buffet meal after the talks were concluded.

I turned to Ferry and whispered, "Who's the guest of honour, Captain Ferry?"

He began, "I have an idea that —"

But the proceedings were starting. Shepherd was saying, "Captain Stevens will be entertaining us with a talk on 'Some Memories of the Liskeard-Looe Line'."

Stevens was tensing and untensing his shoulders in a vexing sort of way.

"That's in Cornwall by the way," added Shepherd, blushing. "But we begin with some local railway news."

This was evidently the custom of the Club. The building of the line running north from Basrah was proceeding satisfactorily. It was two miles short of Nasiriyah. "And there is now a signal box on the line," said Shepherd, at which there were polite cheers, and raised glasses. "There are not, as yet, any signals, however."

The brigadier said in his whispering tones, "Poor show," and smiled directly at me, for some reason.

The line from Kut to Baghdad was coming along more slowly.

"The wooden sleepers", said Shepherd, "are found to warp in the heat. The trouble is, they are made for the cooler climes of . . . *Bombay*." He gave his shy grin at this. "And now," he concluded, "Captain Stevens will take us to Cornwall."

With a horrible scraping of his chair, Stevens rose.

"Sorry about that," he said. From beyond the window, the call to prayer was starting up. "Oh," he said, "there they go again." While fiddling with his tunic sleeves, as though trying to perform some delicate operation with his cuff buttons that his thick fingers were not quite equal to, he said, "I *could* talk about how I won the silver cup in Bulmer's Boxing Academy at the Penzance Fair in 1910. I knocked out Dan Patterson who went on to become the West Britain Light Heavyweight Champion, but I was only a kid then. That's why I was only a *light* heavyweight, but it's not really anything to do with railways, is it? No. So I thought I'd talk about something that . . . Well, there's nothing to it really, nothing to it at all . . ."

Shepherd indicated to the waiter that another glass of wine be brought for Stevens. He drank it off in one, and embarked on a description of the Liskeard and Looe railway, which unfortunately did not do anything as simple as run from Liskeard to Looe, but rambled about over half of Cornwall, so that in Stevens's speech "Coombe Junction", "Moorswater" and "Bodmin Moor" were all confusingly mixed up with the evening call to prayer floating through the windows. Having set out the route of the line — as he thought — Stevens then described how he'd been given footplate rides on some of its tank engines in the school holidays, and how this had led him to learn the "rude implements" of firing. By that, he might have meant "rudiments" — it was shocking to think how much money had been wasted on his education. The brigadier was half asleep, what with the suffocating heat, and the droning of Stevens and the prayer call.

But then our speaker took a more promising turn.

". . . Now, see," he said, "The fellow who principally taught me the skills of a fireman was an old Cornish chap called Kit Bassett, and he'd spent most of his life running up and down the Cornish main line on goods.

146

Old Kit collected all the sheep from the halts that served the big farms, my dad's included, and he took them to the slaughterhouse at Truro. Well, the knackers' yard, not to be too polite about it. How many sheep that man carted to their deaths, it's beyond counting, beyond imagining. Thousands and thousands, and . . ."

The door opened, and the guest of honour entered — a much more decorative individual than I had expected, and of an altogether different sex. Everyone stood up, but she wouldn't have any formality, and motioned us to sit down as she moved rapidly towards the spare seat. It was the sureness of her movements that gave her away. She was the woman who had ridden through the public garden or park. As she took her place — in between Stevens and myself — she removed a wide-brimmed hat to reveal a mass of auburn curls. In the course of this, she and Ferry exchanged nods. I believed that he had not been surprised at her arrival. She also nodded at Shepherd, who grinned at her while blushing. Her arrival had certainly not surprised *him*; the lady was, after all, *his* guest. Her hair had perhaps once been held in place by a small ebony comb buried in it. After an expert bit of business with curls and comb, she was perfectly meek and still, waiting for our pink-faced speaker to continue.

". . . Thousands", Stevens resumed, "and *thousands* . . . So when Kit Bassett turned sixty-five or so, and was coming up to his superannuation, the company took him off the main line, and he worked a link that kept him always on the branch."

"The Liskeard-Looe," put in Shepherd.

147

"Correct, sir. He was put out to grass, so to say, working a stopping goods through all the villages there — well, I won't name them all again — sometimes with yours truly standing in for the fireman."

One of the Royal Engineers put his hand up like a schoolboy: "Wasn't that against regulations?"

"Oh tosh," said Shepherd, grinning and colouring up.

I glanced sidelong at the lady. She was looking down, still — what was the word? — demure.

"Well now," said Stevens, "picture old Kit on his very last run before he goes off to be given a gold Albert or carriage clock or whatever it might be, and listening to a lot of fellows saying what a grand chap he is at the railwaymen's institute at Truro, and clapping him on the back, telling him now it's time to take that garden in hand. It's Saturday early evening, and he's riding up with Timmy Rice — that's his regular fireman," Stevens added, with a half turn to the lady, as though the detail might have been of particular interest to her. "It's about five o'clock sort of time, and he's coming up to the little station at Coombe where he books off, do you see?"

"Set the scene for us, Mike," said Shepherd, "paint the picture."

He sat back, and the lady eyed him, and smiled. Meanwhile the red-faced, blond-haired man smiled at her — a hopeless kind of smile.

"Well, I wasn't there," said Stevens, "but y'know . . . a late summer's evening in Cornwall. Not much in the way of . . . A few swallows zinging about . . . Thresher

148

rattling away in the fields probably, and the chaps working on it waving to Kit as he goes by; the haze all around the machine, the sun going down, and the whole thing sort of golden."

I believed that everyone around the table *could* figure the scene, the late sunshine of Baghdad leaking in through the window seeming not so different from the gentler sunshine of Cornwall. And Stevens was still at it: ". . . The sheep grazing by the tracks running away a little as Bassett comes along, but only a little jog, because I mean they knew him just as well as everyone else . . . All save this one sheep, you see, and he doesn't run away, but he walks — calm as you like — up the embankment, and he turns, and he faces the engine head-on. By all accounts, old Kit was put into a sort of daze by the sight of it. Well, it wasn't natural. Hypnotised, was old Kit, leaning out, staring at the beast, and the bloody thing . . ."

Stevens turned to the lady, saying, "Sorry, Miss Bailey."

So he appeared to know her, too.

"The . . . well, the flipping thing is staring right back at Bassett, and he's sort of entranced by it as I say, and he makes no move for the brake. It's his mate, Timmy Rice, who claps it on, and Bassett goes flying forward, and . . . he only crowns himself on the fire-door handle doesn't he? Knocked his lights out, and that was the end of old Kit Bassett."

A beat of silence.

"The revenge", said one of the R.E. men after a while, "of the sheep."

"That's just about the size of it," said Stevens. "Well, that's my story . . . *Bit* of railway in it anyhow."

He collapsed into his seat, as the assembled party broke into applause, a sound that began to mingle with shouts and running feet from beyond the square. I heard the raised voice of a Tommy: "You fucking . . ." But the whole incident was mobile, and faded away fast.

Stevens was breathing deeply and clasping and unclasping his fists. His blue glass was empty. After his great effort, he needed another drink. I reached for the wine jug, but of course I would have to offer the lady first, since she sat between us.

"Would you care for . . ."

She turned and saw me for the first time. And she held my gaze for longer than was needful, frowning the while.

". . . wine?" I said.

She shook her head briskly, and I poured for Stevens. A moment later, she put her hand on my wrist.

"Is there water?" she said.

I reached for the other jug, and poured.

"That's very kind," she said, turning and facing me directly. "I've been in the desert all day."

"I'm Captain Stringer," I said. "I'm in the Railway Office, assisting Lieutenant Colonel Shepherd."

Again, she eyed me. Then she said, "Naturally . . . I know nothing of railways, and nor does Major Findlay."

She nodded towards the other end of the table, where Shepherd was introducing our next speaker: the fair-haired, sunburned major: Findlay by name, evidently. As he stood, I saw from his uniform that he was a cavalry officer. It was the lower half that gave it away. He would be addressing us on "Some Notes from the Indian Railways", which — he hoped we'd agree — was "a very fitting subject for an officer of the British Indian Army".

As he spoke, the lady lit a cigarette — a Woodbine, I was astonished to see — with the same practised speed as she'd employed in the arrangement of her hair. She looked sidelong at me, saying, "Where's your gun?"

"It's in my haversack," I said, shocked at the question, "under my chair." I mumbled something about webbing being too uncomfortable in the heat.

The lady sat back blowing smoke as Major Findlay began his speech. Very dull it was, too, and all directed at the lady, who after a while lowered her gaze and began looking down at her lap as Findlay droned: "The South Indian railway is preeminently a Third Class passenger-carrying line. The Third Class contributes eighty-two per cent of the numbers . . . The gross receipts of the Assam-Bengal Railway . . ."

I thought: *India's a big place. This could go on all night*. It was nothing you couldn't have got from an article in *The Railway Magazine*, and I believed Findlay had cribbed it all from some such paper. Why? More men came into the room at intervals as he spoke, and stood against the walls. The waiter offered them drinks, and as he did so there was another round of shouts and commotion from the square, which drew some of the new men over to the window — and

151

caused the brigadier to ask no one in particular, "What's the bally racket?"

Half to herself and without looking up, the lady uttered a single word: "Insurgency."

Findlay was saying, ". . . the stock being subscribed about two and a half times over by the railway's own stockholders," and sat down. Apparently, he had finished. There was a small round of applause, and it was safe for the lady to raise her head. Shepherd was saying that the formal business of the evening was concluded, and we were to help ourselves to supper. Captain Ferry remained in his seat, smoking steadily, but most others were beginning to circulate, and the atmosphere of the mess room took over. The lady turned towards me, and began a close inspection of my face, breaking off when the waiter came past. She spoke to him in fast Arabic, and he brought a couple of small plates over. One held bits of meat in a thick sauce.

"Dhansak," she said to me, "it's very good."

Most people were moving towards the table by the window for their grub. But not only did the food come to the lady, so did half the men in the room, some addressing her respectfully by name: Miss Bailey. A sort of queue was forming at her chair, with the boring major — Findlay — at the head of it. It did not include Shepherd, however. He was being charming to the brigadier, was evidently stuck with him. He had been "landed" as they say in Yorkshire.

Major Findlay had now got close to Miss Bailey. He said, "Well, I daresay you've heard enough about the railways of India to keep you going for a while." She

152

made some enquiry of him, and he said, "Oh, pretty fed up." I thought: he's trying to appeal to her feminine concern, but she turned away from him, and he was drawn into a conversation with a fellow officer, enquiring, "My dear chap, are you being attended to? We don't have quite the waiting staff we need."

"What were you doing in the desert?" I asked Miss Bailey.

"I went to see Fahad Bey ibn Hadhdhal, chief of the Anazeh tribe."

"Why?"

"To get his support in the western desert."

She spoke in a low tone, requiring me to lean close to her.

I said, "Is he in with the Turks at present?"

"How do you mean 'in with'? You might say he was *used* to the Turks."

"And what did he decide?"

She laughed. "He's thinking it over, working out his price."

"He's very powerful, is he?"

"About five thousand rifles."

The sound of another fleeting commotion rose up from the square. I heard the blond major, Findlay, say, "*Quiet* Square, that's supposed to be." One of the Royal Engineers near to Miss Bailey asked her: "What's he like? As a man."

"Fahad Bey? Well, he's *rather* beautiful," and at this she glanced over to Major Findlay, who was looking pained. "He's a quite superb horseman," Miss Bailey was saying, now addressing all the men around her.

"He's also very shrewd, and fascinated by the antics of white women. I feel like a music-hall turn every time I see him. I climb on a horse, he practically applauds. I light a cigarette; I remove my hat; I request wine." She leant closer to me. "I do try to shock him, I admit. I will contradict him . . . contradict him openly, before his men. Then there is an intake of breath — a rather sharp one, mark you, but he rallies quickly. He extends his arm, commending me to his fellows. 'The women of the Anglez!', as if to say, 'What freaks they are, but damned amusing with it!'"

She liked the sound of her own voice, but then *I* liked the sound of it, too.

"You've obviously won him over," someone said.

"Perhaps I have, perhaps I will. All the sheikhs know that I love the desert; that I speak to them as a student of their history and culture, and that I have their best interests at heart." She turned directly to me, saying, "That's pompous, isn't it? Patronising too."

From beyond the window came more fast-moving shouts. Some of our party stepped out on to the veranda, but Miss Bailey seemed unconcerned.

"Unfortunately," she said, taking another piece of meat, "the Cairo people have promised most of Iraq to Faisal."

I frowned somewhat.

She said, "You disapprove?"

"No, I just don't know who he is."

"Third son of Sharif Hussein — of the Hashemite dynasty. It's amazing how many people have been promised Iraq. The French think we're going to split it with *them*."

"What gave them that idea?"

She shrugged — a secret smile.

I asked, "Who has Cox promised it to?"

Miss Bailey had now finished her dinner — about six bites — and was lighting another Woodbine. She offered me one, by way of an afterthought.

"Coxus? He's not in it really. Most of the promising's done from Cairo. Cox wants to see Iraq annexed under India, and Ibn Saud made king."

"Faisal and Saud? They're enemies, aren't they?"

"Rivals," she said, blowing smoke.

"Who do the Turks support?"

"Another man again. Ibn Rashid."

At this she too stood, and went over to the window, and I tamely followed. All was once more quiet in Quiet Square: just a couple of sleeping palms, one stork wandering about aimlessly, criss-crossing the shadows of telegraph wires. I looked around the room. Of our host, Lieutenant Colonel Shepherd, there was no sign. The blond major — Findlay — was saying to a Royal Engineer, "You know, I don't think anything's struck me as more peculiar about this place than the women. Have you seen the ones with the thick black nets over their heads, like sort of walking corpses?" The Royal Engineer made some reply, and Findlay said, "Yes but it only makes you more curious about what they look like. You see, what I don't understand is . . ." But Miss Bailey had moved next to him, at which he seemed to sigh with pleasure, not now feeling the need to say what

155

he didn't understand. She said to him, "I'm giving my address next week, if you can believe it. Honestly, first The Shepherd charms me into coming here, then he charms me into speaking."

"What'll it be," asked Major Findlay, "the railways at Babylon?"

"That's it."

"*Are* there any railways at Babylon?" he said.

Stevens was next to me. He'd lately been eating spiced meat — by the smell of his breath.

"What's the name of our brigadier general?" I asked him.

"Barney or Barnes or something. I think it's Barnes."

Of *course*: it was his assistant who'd written to me to confirm my engagement with Shepherd. All he'd done, perhaps, was sign the letter. Barnes worked in the office of Coxus himself, and he was most likely the fellow who'd invited Shepherd out to Mespot in the first place.

"And who exactly is she?" I said, indicating the lady.

"Oh," he said. "Harriet Bailey. She's spoken for, by the way," he added, unexpectedly. "Married, I mean."

"But everyone calls her 'Miss'."

"Even so."

"Who's she married to?"

"Oh, I don't know. Professor at Oxford. Or Cambridge."

"Is he out here?"

Stevens shook his head. "He's in Oxford . . . Or Cambridge."

"Why does she talk to the Arabs?"

"Search me," he said.

Ferry was alongside us. The pipe stem now protruded from his tunic pocket. He held a plate. With his long, clean fingers he was dabbing bread into a pink paste.

"She's an . . ."

I waited.

". . . archaeologist."

"Do you know her?"

"Oh. She's . . . famous."

"One thing," said Stevens, who'd found himself some more wine, ". . . she does speak Arabic, which is a big help if you're — y'know — actually *speaking* to the bloody Arabs. I wouldn't bother myself."

"Wouldn't bother what?" I said.

"Speaking to them. I know *imshi galla* — go away — and *igri* or something — hurry up. Hurry up and go away. I don't like them myself. Deceitful people. I like *him* though," he said, nodding to our Arab waiter. "He's rather bold with the wine. I believe he thinks it's strawberry juice."

"And what about Findlay?" I said, indicating that blond-headed officer who was so obviously stuck on Harriet Bailey.

"Cavalry," said Stevens. "If you want a horse ride in the park, he's your man."

I said, "Well he plainly doesn't come here for his interest in railways."

"No," said Bob Ferry. He was cleaning the bowl of his pipe with a beautiful penknife with mother-of-pearl handle.

Shepherd came in through the door. He looked flushed. I knew what he'd been up to — he'd been in the vicinity of the square chasing Arabs. I heard him muttering something to the brigadier by way of explanation. Something about "Bit of trouble . . . Setting a few fires . . . Tried to roust them out . . ."

When Brigadier Barnes had done with Shepherd, Stevens moved in, and the two of *them* began a quiet conflab. How thick were they with each other? Perhaps they were just discussing the practicalities of the run up to Samarrah.

I watched the faces moving under the soft, coloured illumination. They were mostly young people — in the late twenties or early thirties — but made to look older by the sun, by being the conquerors of a nation; or by worry they were not up to the mark. I watched Harriet Bailey sipping wine under the gaze of Findlay. Strange that she was Shepherd's guest of honour. She was pro-Arab, after all. She spoke the language fluently and called Mesopotamia "Iraq". Well, perhaps Shepherd agreed with her. What made me think he was pro-Turkish? He had seemed to defend the Turks when at the London Railway Club; he smoked Turkish-looking cigarettes, and according to the report of Captain Boyd, he was in league with the Turks as a result of the deal supposedly done at the railway station. In addition, he seemed quite thick with Stevens, who was certainly anti-Arab.

But what did it all amount to?

I turned around and saw Bob Ferry. He inclined his head somewhat, but he'd been eyeing me carefully, no question of it. Entering the main room of my quarters, I found the oil lamp lit, and the single sheet on my bed turned down. There were four flies in the room; the flytrap — restored to its place under the bed — clicked, but there was also another sound. I walked quickly through to the scullery where I saw Ahmad setting a pitcher of water into what I thought of as the pantry — a half-underground cupboard, like a clean coal hole. One oil lamp burned. He turned and contemplated me for a while. He walked over to the stone sink.

I asked him what he was doing. He took out of the sink one of the metal cups with which the scullery was equipped. He dipped the cup into the pitcher, handed me the cup.

"You drink," he ordered.

"You put . . . lime?" I said. There was chloride of lime about the place. It was to be added to all drinking water for purification.

"It is really clean," he said.

"Not without lime it isn't."

"It *is*."

"Where is the lime?"

He turned away from me. He was readjusting the linen curtain on the pantry, and I believed he said, "I chucked it," but that can't have been right. I sipped the water, then drank it all off in an instant.

"Give," said Ahmad. I handed back the cup. He dipped it again, and I drank again.

"It is late," I said, taking a third cupful from him.

"So what?" he said. There was a swift, bitter outburst of laughter from him, as though he was amused by my inability to answer his question. "At night," he said, "very nice and cold."

"You must be bloody joking," I said.

"I must?" he said, and he frowned — it seemed a genuine question.

"There was trouble in the town tonight," I said.

"Trouble," he said, "yes," and he took the cup again, and put it in the sink, saying something very like "We boot *you* out."

CHAPTER
TEN

On Monday morning, I woke from my half doze at six when the flytrap cylinder turned over with a click. The one sheet was soaked in sweat, and located somewhere about my ankles, just as it had been on Sunday morning. That had been a day of unbearable heat, and idleness on my part. This day promised the same weather combined with hectic activity.

I kicked off the sheet, and lay in the rising heat and light until six thirty, when I heard the roar of a motor. Jarvis. He had spent the night at the Hotel, having been on driving duties until late. He would now run me to the station — "An easy motor ride", he'd called it. I heard the sound of him entering the scullery. He'd left the van motor running. Presently he came through with dates, bread, coffee, and a letter for me. It had been delivered to the Hotel. I saw from the writing that it was from the wife. It must have been posted very shortly after I'd left Britain.

"Morning, sir," said Jarvis. "A hundred and twenty, they say it'll be today. I've a spare pack for you in the van: tonic water, mineral water, quinine, two hundred rounds of ammunition." He was in one of his chirpy phases. "No hurry with the food," he added.

It was impossible to make a breakfast with the motor running outside, so I just downed the coffee and walked to the van while chewing on bread. The letter I'd put in my tunic pocket to read later.

"You'll be all right on the trip, sir," said Jarvis as we climbed up. "Lieutenant Colonel Shepherd's a pretty high class of soldier."

"Did you speak to him over the weekend?"

"Me, sir?" he said, as the van, shaking like buggery, made for the gates of Rose Court. "Why would I speak to him?"

"Well, you were speaking to him the day *before*."

He appeared to have forgotten, or did a good job of seeming to. Five minutes more in the sun, and the passenger seat would have been too hot to sit on. It was a good job I wasn't in shorts.

"I tell you who I did speak to yesterday, sir," said Jarvis, "and that was the police team at the Hotel."

"Have they got any further with their investigation? Regarding Captain Boyd, I mean."

"Nowhere at all, sir."

That was good. It surely meant that the station master had not provided a description of me. Or perhaps that his description had not been understood. We were waiting at the gates of Rose Court. A wagon loaded with furniture approached along Park Road, the Arab driver smoking thoughtfully. "All we need now", Jarvis said, "is a camel." And he drummed his fingers on the steering wheel. "After speaking to the police, sir, I went to Captain Boyd's billet to see what I could find out for myself."

162

"Where's that?" I said.

The Arab had smoked his way past and the road was clear, yet we hadn't pulled out. Jarvis was revolving some idea. "Tell you what, sir, we've got a few minutes in hand, I'll take you there."

So instead of turning left, which led to the river, he turned right, then quickly right again, taking us, with much revving of the engine, into the heart of the labyrinth. Numerous Arabs in numerous alleys had to press themselves practically flat up against the walls for us to pass, and one poor fellow had to dismantle the whole front of his shop in half a minute flat. Our motor creaked like an old bed on the broken cobbles. As he drove, Jarvis told me he'd "bumped into" Captain Boyd twice in the fortnight before he died.

"And how did he seem?"

"He seemed a bit down if you ask me, sir, but I'd got to know him a little and that was his nature — a rather melancholic sort. The second time I saw him he was walking alone by the river, and that did bother me."

"Why?"

"Because I didn't know what he might do."

"You mean he might chuck himself in?"

"He was a man who came into his own on the battlefield; the rest of the time he was up or down really, not much in between."

We'd come to a square with a mosque in it. Market stalls were being set up, with canopies of brightly coloured stripes. Jarvis indicated a gate in a wall, with a low building behind palms. This had been Boyd's digs.

Jarvis stopped the van but once again kept the engine running.

Jarvis said, "I talked to his man —"

"You mean his batman?" I cut in, "the one who took over from you?"

Jarvis shook his head. "He didn't have another batman. He said he didn't want one in Baghdad."

(Well, an officer could choose to go without, and probably would do, if he had secrets to keep. I did not believe that either Shepherd or Stevens had one either.)

"When I say his 'man'," Jarvis continued, "I mean his *boy* — the Arab servant. He has hardly a word of English. Got nothing out of him at all — not even using the dictionary in this." So saying, he half lifted a book from his tunic pocket: *City of the Khalifs*.

"We'll come back later," I said, and Jarvis looked surprised at me. It was the first time I'd indicated that I had an interest in finding out about Boyd. "We'll bring Ahmad with us."

"That's a clever notion is that, sir," said Jarvis.

I couldn't tell what he really thought, however, for he was now making a great deal of a palaver about reversing in the square, to the amusement of some Arabs and the irritation of others. Two minutes later we were running along the river — a smoother road, where the engine ran cleaner so that the petrol smell that had filled the cab began to fade. But it was replaced by another: a penetrating, sweet smell coming from Jarvis.

"Samarrah," he said. "It means a joy for all to see."

"Mmm . . ." I said.

"Just think if a day dawned like this in Scarborough," he went on, as we contemplated the boats of the river. "You'd be overjoyed, wouldn't you, sir?"

"I think I'd be quite alarmed," I said.

"Think on, sir," said Jarvis, "old Giordano, who has the ice-cream concession on the South Bay ... He moved house from a little tumbledown cottage in the Old Town to a big place near the station on the strength of one scorching hot summer — 1911, sir, as you'll remember. But a summer like this ... why, he'd be on the Esplanade: one of those white mansions up from the Spa! And he'd have Tom Jackson, who does the donkey rides, for a neighbour!"

Yes, I thought, and after three months of 120-degree heat, the town undertakers would be up there with them. We came to the bridge of boats, and showed our papers to a sentry. There was now a proper guard post with barrier. The van bounced crazily on the bridge.

"Have you heard of Harriet Bailey, Jarvis?" I said.

He said brightly, "She's about the only white woman here, apart from a few of the officers' wives."

"She was at this meeting I went to on Saturday," I said.

"I believe she came up here about the same time as me."

"Where from?"

"Basrah."

"So she didn't come up directly after the city fell?"

"No, no, a few weeks after. She's just the ticket isn't she, sir? Very pretty — and clever with it. Terrifying combination in a woman really, sir. She's quoted a lot in here," he said, indicating again *The City of the Khalifs*. "A lot of letters after her name. By the way, sir, did you see those shades on the market stall? Green, red and white stripes. Before I came here, sir, I thought all the Arabs would be togged up like that, and all with the shoes curled up at the toes."

I merely gave a grunt, and Jarvis fell silent on the rubble roads leading to the station. On the tracks round about there now stood a fair quantity of locos, some animal wagons, flatbed wagons, a steam crane. *The Elephant* had been shunted into the station, and pointed in the direction of Samarrah — and she was in steam. This I discovered when Jarvis put me out by the tracks at the station mouth. As I climbed down from the van, he looked me over.

"Revolver, sir?" he said.

"It's in here," I said, and I took it out of the haversack.

"The Webley," he said, studying it. "Captain Boyd favoured the Colt — the single-action."

I said, "That's rather old-fashioned — and slow."

(With a single-action piece, you'd to cock the gun manually before firing.)

"He liked the balance of it," said Jarvis. "And for rapid firing . . . well, he had his machine guns."

To test Jarvis out, I said, "Do you want to come and look at the station? We could try and see where Boyd was found?"

"No fear," he said, "I'm going to have a *jolly* day today. Good luck in the desert, sir. They say a pint of water every half hour."

166

As he saluted from the driver's seat, and roared off in the van, I thought: that bloke's been on a large quantity of some liquid himself, and it's not water.

In the station, a number of Royal Engineers were making the engine ready, one touring the lubrication points with an oil can. They were at the far end of the platform. Immediately before me, squatting on his haunches on the platform and stroking a thin cat, was the station master. He held out his long thin fingers, and the cat would move through them back and forth, like a little bull charging the cape of the bullfighter.

"Hello, my dear," he said to me.

I nodded and looked away. Did his greeting mean he'd recognised me? It was hard to tell. The *Salon de Thé* was on the opposite platform, and I could not help but glance over. The door of the place now stood open, and it looked in worse order than before, sunk in dust and dirt.

"Bad," said the station master, seeing where I was looking. He then pointed up, and repeated the word. I saw a great hole in the station roof.

A voice said, "Just as well it's not raining," and Shepherd was alongside me, also looking up.

Setting down two huge brown canvas bags, he glanced sidelong at me and smiled. He appeared calm, but my own thoughts were racing in a circus. Where had he come slinking up from? What was in the bags? The station master was still sitting six feet away, playing with the bloody cat. He looked between me and Shepherd, apparently revolving a further remark. What was the Arabic for "Go away"? Stevens had known. But a few seconds later, the fellow did it of his own accord.

Shepherd wore shorts, and carried a thin haversack, but there was an identity between the tanned, skinny man before me now and the reserved figure in a good suit that I'd first seen in London, a sort of enviable style to the man. I heard the bark of an engine, which then became a rhythmical snuffling and chuffing. A filthy carriage was being shunted towards us. It was a period piece all right, with verandas at front and rear.

"Is it German, sir?" I enquired.

"Turkish," said Shepherd, and it seemed to me that he said it proudly. The thing was greenish in colour, with faded white scribble of Turkish Arabic on the side. What did it say? First Class? Third Class? There were curtains at the dusty windows.

The tank engine smashed it up hard against our engine's tender, and a private of the Royal Engineers began coupling up.

"Doesn't *look* much, does it?" said Shepherd.

I had to agree.

". . . But it was the personal saloon of General von der Goltz."

I'd heard of him; he was commander of the German forces in Mespot. I'd seen a photograph of the fellow. Being German, he was fat and wore a monocle.

"Where's he these days, sir?"

"Dead," said Shepherd. ". . . Cholera."

If a general could die of it, then anybody could. We wandered forwards towards the engine. It was a big beast was *The Elephant*. And the tender was nearly as

168

long again. Well, it *had* to be for desert running. I mentioned this.

"Four thousand gallons," said Shepherd, and I thought: If it comes to it, we can drink it. The stuff would come ready-boiled, too.

I suddenly realised: the engine had got its side rods back; and I recalled that Shepherd had been asked about this at the Club meeting. Indicating them, I asked Shepherd: "Where *did* you find them, sir?"

"Oh, they were buried nearby," he said, and he coloured slightly, but for once didn't follow up with additional data.

Stevens now approached, wearing pack, haversack and rifle. He too wore shorts, and as he stood by the locomotive I thought: You're the *real* elephant. With a nod of apology to me, Shepherd walked forward to meet Stevens, and they began speaking out of my earshot. They *would* keep doing that.

Shading my eyes, I put my face towards the window of the green carriage. All I could make out in the gloom was a sort of old-fashioned-looking sofa with a bundle of rifles laid on it, all strapped together with webbing. Why so many? And who would they be aimed at?

The Elephant was blowing off, impatient to be away. Royal Engineers who'd been attending to the engine were now flowing towards the carriage and boarding it by the veranda at the engine end. Hold on . . . It seemed they would be riding with us! I would not be alone with Shepherd, the possible traitor, and Stevens, his partner in crime as might well be. One of the R.E. men made to take my pack and haversack, saying,

"You're at the sharp end, aren't you? You won't want these if so." I let him have the pack, but kept hold of the haversack, for that held the soda water, cigarettes and the Webley. (The Webley was heavier than the Colts with which most men were issued. In the heat of Baghdad, it was easier to carry it and the ammo pouch in the haversack than the holster — and it was just about within regulations to do so.)

I mounted the footplate of *The Elephant*. Stevens and Shepherd — and Shepherd's two brown canvas bags — were already up there.

I asked Stevens, "Who's going to drive and who's going to fire?"

"Toss you for it, if you like."

He took out a coin of some kind and made ready to toss it, but it was evidently foreign, perhaps one of the Turkish ones still acceptable in Baghdad. He turned it over, frowning. "It's got tails on both sides," he said.

"Then I'll drive," I said.

"Good man," Lieutenant Colonel Shepherd put in. He evidently thought little of the fact that I'd never stood on a foreign footplate before, but that was the public-school product all over. He'd have confidence in himself and confidence in others, often misplaced in both cases. The driver's controls were all on the right-hand side, which was the *wrong* side, but the steam injectors looked familiar, as did the braking system: steam brake for the engine, vacuum for the train. I turned to Stevens, saying, "Let's have a look at the fire, Mike," and he casually pushed the handle of the fire door with the blade of his shovel, which looked

170

a very flimsy thing in his hands. The fire was thin, but the colour was right: namely a dazzling white. Its own heat, added to the heat of the day, meant I couldn't breathe as I stood exposed to it.

Turning away from the fire, I checked the injectors. Stevens wasn't shovelling, but holding his arms out from his body and repeatedly bracing them — here were more of his funny "exercises". "Steam pressure," I said, "it's low." He nodded, and set to with the shovel. He could pitch the coal to the back of the box — he could *swing the shovel*, I mean — but he was a very lackadaisical fireman. For one thing, he hadn't thought to break up any coal. He was putting lumps on that were as big as his own head. Trying to give a hint, I booted one of the bigger specimens, but Stevens just caught it up with its shovel, and put it in.

I looked at Shepherd, and he gave a grin. Then he grabbed the pick from the tool locker, scrambled up on to the tender and started hacking up the lumps. Stevens, shovelling like an automaton, seemed hardly to notice that here was a lieutenant colonel doing hard labour on his behalf. Our joint efforts brought the needle on the pressure gauge to a hundred pounds per square inch.

"We all set, then?" I said.

For form's sake, I looked back along the platform, half expecting to see the station master holding a green flag, but he was long gone. I yanked too hard on the regulator, and made the wheels slip as we started away. That was embarrassing, with all those engineers riding up behind. We came out of the station room, and into

171

the white glare, which was like steaming into our own fire. Baghdad was to the side of us, then it was behind. When we'd got clear of the town, I saw some of our boys digging earthworks near the river. The sun would stop that game before long. A mile or so later, and civilisation had evidently run out of ideas. We moved steadily on over white rubble, through white dust. If I put my head out of the side, there was no wind at all, just a different sort of heat.

Our steam pressure kept slacking off, and I had to keep telling Stevens to put more on. Shepherd stuck up for Stevens, saying, "I believe our fireman's trying to keep the smoke down, Jim."

"Why?" I shouted over the engine roar.

"Arabs!" Shepherd said, and he gave a boyish grin. "Insurgents!"

He leant closer to me, saying, "I ought to tell you what we're about."

Very decent of you, I'm sure, I thought.

And he held out his packet of Turkish cigarettes towards me.

CHAPTER
ELEVEN

The plan was that we were to run our carriage full of Royal Engineers up to Mushahida, where Bedouin Arabs had twice shot the water tank there full of holes, and had cut the telegraph wires fore and aft. We were to drop the blokes there, and they would form a garrison.

We were meant to control the line from Baghdad to Samarrah, and if we were to move troops north when the fighting season restarted, we must make our presence felt. Shepherd, Stevens and I were then to make for Samarrah itself, and beyond. It was not what I wanted to hear.

When Shepherd had finished his briefing, I took the cork out of my second bottle of soda water and drank it down. I was having to fight the desert, which is to say that I'd twice seen engines steaming towards us from the opposite direction. It would have been a serious matter if they'd been real, since they came on fast, and this was single-line working. But they were altogether too rubbery; blended in too well with the wavering air.

As we rattled along at a steady twenty miles an hour, I took the wife's letter from my pocket. It was typewritten.

Dearest Jim,

What is it like out there? That is the question of the hour in your family. I know you're not to say exactly why you are out there, but just as to the scenery and people and so on, and by people I do not mean the British Army. Sylvia said it must be like the film of "Ali Baba and the Forty Thieves" that we all went to see. Harry said, "Don't be daft, that's nothing more than a fairy tale. It'll be nothing remotely like that."

So Sylvia has an idea (which of course Harry says is another daft one) for how to settle the point. Is it really like "Ali Baba and the Forty Thieves" or not? You're to write either "yes" or "no". Harry said this was "a ridiculous oversimplification" (and if that boy doesn't get into the grammar school, then I'd like to know who does). Sylvia said, "I daresay it is but I don't mind."

And so I leave this poser with you in the full confidence that you will provide an answer leaving honour satisfied on both sides. Do write, anyway. I know the letters take four weeks, so you'd better get on with it.

We Co-Operative ladies are concentrating on margarine, of which there is not enough, and which is threatening to create a war-within-a-war in York. All the margarine entering the city now comes to the Guildhall, from where we distribute it not only to Co-Operative Society members but to all holders of one of two registration certificates.

174

Oh, I can't be bothered to explain, and it's not as if margarine is even nice.

What else have I got to say? Amazingly little, it seems. Oh, I know. A wonderful development in our office. We have a new typewriter, to use her official title, but I call her a "typist" otherwise she sounds like a machine. She is called Margaret Lawson, and will be typing this letter for me. (You may have noticed how beautifully presented it is.) Now Margaret — and she doesn't mind a bit my saying this — has been since birth quite deaf, which gave rise to a curious incident on her first day here.

Mrs Howells from the Food Control Committee came in, and we had an argument (me and Mrs Howells I mean). It was about, guess what, margarine. I do not care very much for Mrs Howells, partly I admit for no better reason than that her husband sits for the Conservatives on York Council. As she walked — stalked, rather — out of the office, I said in an under-breath, "Confound that woman," at which I saw our lovely new typist look up and smile. Well, she could not possibly have heard me, being (a) quite deaf, and (b) on the other side of what is quite a large office room. You will have guessed the secret already: she can see speech, or to put it another way, she knows "lip-reading". In fact Margaret is a demon at it, and we pass the time very merrily by my speaking — inaudibly — quotations from the Bible, or Shakespeare, or saying what I will be buying at the market that day, while Margaret looks on, watching my lips. She then types what I have said, and it is always and without fail correct. I have asked her to teach me.

Tom Sutherland, Mrs Sutherland's son, is home from France for good after a severe shell wound to the arm. I asked him about his experiences and he said, "You are just jellified, shaking with fear all the time." He said it can't be true that fear sends your hair white, otherwise his would be. He said he couldn't stand to be in the same place for any length of time, because something bad would be bound to happen in that place before too long. Therefore he was going to buy a motor car, and have it adapted so that it can be driven by a one-armed man. He will then spend the rest of his life racing about the country. I told him you were out in Mesopotamia, and he said, "You should wear cologne. It will keep the mosquitoes off. It will also make you smell nice!"

Do write soon,
Your loving
Lydia.

The wife had always rather fancied Tom Sutherland, and as for the typist, Miss Lawson, the Co-Operative movement was well known for employing crocks of one sort or another.

Repocketing the letter, I saw that a new shimmering something had appeared by the side of the line, and I had a pretty shrewd idea that this was real, and that it must be Mushahida station. Other, smaller disturbances in the vicinity became by degrees a high water tower, a motor van, soldiers waiting. But my thoughts were on what lay still further ahead: Samarrah and beyond.

What *did* lie beyond Samarrah? Surely the Turkish lines? After his customary hesitation, Shepherd had said that Brother Turk was most likely out of the picture. One hundred miles north of Samarrah was Tikrit, and he was north of *there*, building his railway line — a continuation of the one we were currently upon — with the aid of the poor Tommies captured at Kut.

The territory between Samarrah and Tikrit could be regarded as a no man's land. It was ours really, but a little more doubtfully so than anywhere south of Samarrah. It was unlikely that we'd come across even the smallest Turkish patrol. Arabs, yes. There might be Bedouins, and they might or might not be hostile. They or the Turks might have blocked or otherwise interrupted the line, and it would be useful to *know*. It was also possible that we'd find rolling stock taken from Baghdad by the Turks in their flight from the city. This happened to be their own rolling stock of course — theirs or the Germans' — but we would bring back any worth having.

I had asked Shepherd why we weren't taking more troops with us on our forward patrol. That *had* been suggested to him, he had admitted, but three men and a single engine might draw Bedouin fire in a way that a whole train-load of Tommies wouldn't. We'd have a chance of flushing out the troublesome tribes — which seemed another way of saying we were going to make sacrifices of ourselves.

We came to Mushahida station. Amid swirling steam we unhooked our carriage. One of the blokes from inside it passed our kit bags up on to the footplate, and we left him and his fellows in the middle of nothingness while we chuffed our way forwards into more of the same.

Frazzling heat . . . one hundred and thirty pounds of steam pressure . . . the rhythmical rocking of *The Elephant* . . .

Shepherd stood behind Stevens and me as we worked. Sometimes he consulted a paper from his tunic pocket. When we were about twenty miles beyond Mushahida, I saw that he held a map, but not the one I'd made for him. Why had I been put to making that map? I believed his own map told him the stretches of bad rail, for sometimes he would tap me on the shoulder, saying, "We crawl along this section, Jim," and these would be the places where *The Elephant* would start to shake, the rails being loose in their sleepers. We had with us a crate holding plates, bolts and screws for repairs, but these goods were not touched, although we would pull to a stop for long intervals while Shepherd inspected the rails and made notes.

An hour or more after Mushahida, I turned about to collect a rag from the locker, for I could not bear the regulator on my hand. Shepherd was now gazing out of the left side through field glasses. I looked a question at him, and he lowered the glasses, leaning out, pointing

178

forwards and saying, "Sumaika" — and there, small in the distance and shaking in the heat like a fever vision, was the next station on the line . . . Or rather a little shanty of board and galvanised iron, an empty siding, a water tower with a wooden wheel on top — a windmill pump. The station was there because of the well below. The town itself was a low shimmer five hundred yards off — all brown stone, and no building higher than the palm trees that stood in its midst. As we passed the station and the line took us closer to the place, I saw small collections of Arabs, some with goats and donkeys, mostly sitting down, and ringed around the town rather than in it, as if to say, "Yes, this is our town but we don't care for it very much. Feel free to go and live there yourself."

I watched the simmer of steam over the safety valve. There was no need to watch the white desert. The whiteness just came on and on; we might have been standing still, and it rolling under us. After my Turkish cigarette, I carried on with Woodbines, in an effort to keep the flies off. The back of my regulator hand was thoroughly bitten by them, and they were all over Stevens's Wolseley hat, so I knew mine would be black with them too.

We'd swung closer to the river now, but it was invisible beyond some ancient-looking earthworks. I turned around, and Shepherd had his field glasses upraised again.

"Have you made a study of Turkey and the Turks, sir?" I said.

He lowered the glasses. "That puts the case too high," he said.

I eyed him until he added, "I wandered about there a bit shortly after my university days." He raised the field glasses to his eyes again. "Irrigation ditches," he said.

Stevens, closing the fire door, did something unusual for him. He asked a question of his own:

"Why does the river flood, sir?"

"The ice melts," said Shepherd.

"Oh," said Stevens. But after a while, he was forced to ask another question: "What ice?"

"In the Anatolian Mountains."

Stevens made do with that, and I knew that I would have to make do with what Shepherd had told me of his Turkish interest.

The spot called Istabulat came up — a tiny, perfect fort — and finally Samarrah station and its small garrison of Tommies and sepoys. I saw a radio car in a ring of palms, horses under a canopy, and proper sidings with a quantity of rolling stock, mostly of English breed (half of it marked "Gloucester Carriage and Wagon Co."); also one tank engine — an o-6-o goods loco of the London and South Western Railway, but its brown paint was covered in thousands of tiny scratches, as though someone had tried to scribble it out. Perhaps it wasn't fit to be sent north, and that's why *we* were going. It did seem that working engines were at a premium hereabouts. As I looked on, a corporal passed me up a bottle of something that turned out to be lime cordial. He said, "If summer has its delights, it also has its dangers, right sir?" It was a slogan for some kind of skin cream, remembered from Blighty. I must have looked a fright. I pointed to the engine.

"Does she go?" I asked, and the corporal shook his head. "Not on your life, sir. Sand in the motions." His accent — Birmingham sort of way — clashed with the brownness of his skin.

Shepherd stood on what would have been the platform of Samarrah station, if it had had a platform. He was handing some papers over to a captain of the Royal Engineers — details of our run. There was a good deal of official toing and froing, and we were stopped for over an hour. Eventually, we took on water for the engine, and a parcel of hard biscuits and bully beef. The grub was to be consumed immediately, wouldn't last a minute in the sun. As we pulled away from the station, we had a view of the town beyond. It was the usual low brick boxes, but with two features out of the common: the first was a structure resembling a giant wedding cake. I had heard of this: the Great Mosque. Another had a golden dome. "The Al-Askari Mosque," said Shepherd. "Ninth-century." It looked like the sun, fallen from the sky.

Three-quarters of an hour later, I noticed Stevens pulling faces. He was standing four-square in front of the fire door and twisting his head in all directions, which involved a fearful rolling of the eyes. When he saw me watching him, he left off, only to commence with another sort of "exercise" involving a violent bulging of his socks. Then he stopped doing that, and began looking left, towards the bare and barren plain.

"Boats," he said, in a toneless and uninterested sort of voice.

I scrambled over to his side and looked forwards, and there were boats — six of them, upside down on flat wagons parked in a siding a hundred yards off.

Shepherd was laughing. "I've been looking out on the other side," he said. "Pull up will you, Jim?"

I applied the brakes. Jumping down, Shepherd said, "It might be a trap," and set off eagerly towards the boats.

He's like a jockey, I thought: small, trim, somewhat bow-legged. He carried his rifle and haversack, and wore no hat. But he had a length of white cloth around his neck, which he now caught up, and wound about his head while walking. A keffiyah. I worked the injector, since the water was low in the gauge, not that Stevens had mentioned the fact. He was sitting on the sandbox and eyeing me, with his back to his master.

When I next looked towards Shepherd, he was small in the distance, climbing on to the last of the flat-bed wagons, inspecting the launch tethered on to it, then the bogies beneath. The giant sun hovered about three feet over his head. It was finally taking its bow after another spectacular performance. I could vaguely make out white lettering painted on the side of the launches. It was Turkish Arabic, but the characters looked like a series of numbers, and I thought of the pleasure boats on the River Nidd at Knaresborough. When your number was called out from the boathouse, you had to return your boat — a shaming moment somehow, tantamount to an accusation of theft. I could almost hear the swishing of the river as it ran fast between the pillars of the railway bridge; I thought of the penny licks that Harry and Sylvia would always insist on having when we returned the boat — compensation for giving it up. I was going far away, levitating out of the desert. I brought myself back to reality by running my finger over my cracked lips. I licked them, and they were dry again in an instant. It seemed to me in fact that they'd been dry before I'd finished licking them. I glanced towards Shepherd, just as he was leaping down from the wagon. I believed he'd given up on the launches; their motors would be clogged with sand, just as the tank engine at Samarrah had been. In other words, there'd be no point us reversing along the siding, hooking up to them, and taking them back. I hoped not anyhow, for I lacked the energy to do anything but keep *The Elephant* rolling forwards on its present track.

As I turned away, I heard the crack of a gunshot.

I looked back, and saw Shepherd with his rifle raised. Was he firing, or being fired upon? Another crack — and this time I saw Shepherd firing.

I asked Stevens, "What's he shooting at?"

Stevens, half turning towards the scene of the action, said, "Arabs, I suppose . . . Or Turks."

If Shepherd was shooting at Turks, then surely he couldn't be in the *pay* of the Turks. I took the Webley out of my haversack, and jumped down. Shepherd loosed off a third bullet, and this time I saw his mark: two gazelles running fast away.

Our whole camp came out of Shepherd's two brown canvas bags: three collapsible beds and chairs. The single tent was just a blanket supported by sticks. Shepherd rigged it in a minute under a ring of palms close by the railway line while *The Elephant* fumed with a low fire. She was in good order. On climbing down, I'd had a feel around the axles, side rods and big ends — all stone-cold. We had nothing hooked up to the tender. Shepherd had decreed the boats — evidently six petrol motor launches built by the Mayer company of Dortmund — to be completely shot.

"Why would they leave them in the middle of the desert?" I'd asked him.

"Abandoned on the way north?" he'd replied. "Or I suppose they're handily placed to be picked up and taken back to Baghdad. If they hadn't been wrecked."

The sun continued his descent, but too slowly for my liking, since the palms gave only about as much shade as an umbrella with the silk off. Stevens had started a campfire using a paraffined rag, our good Cardiff coal and the dead branches of a thorn bush — he was better at making a fire *out* of a locomotive than in — and we had a meal of rusks, rice and roast sand grouse (bagged by Shepherd in lieu of gazelle).

Shepherd then passed out Turkish cigarettes. As I took one, a mosquito landed on my left wrist. It bit it. I then began picking away bits of what I believed to be cigarette paper from my lip, but which turned out to be bits of skin. Shepherd stood and went off to his canvas bags, returning with a jar of petroleum jelly. I thanked him and applied it, watched by Stevens. At length, he said, "Chuck it over, will you?" He caught the jar, asking Shepherd, "Mind if I take it off over there?"

"Not in the least," said Shepherd, with a half smile.

When Stevens had disappeared from view over what was not so much a dune — a *dune* I imagined to be beautiful — as a ridge of sand and stone, I asked Shepherd, "What's he up to?"

"Doesn't bear thinking about," said Shepherd. "How did you like his talk at the Club?"

"I thought he came up trumps after a shaky start."

Shepherd nodded, smiling. "Next week we have the lady speaking on 'The Railway at Babylon'."

"Knows a lot about it, does she?"

Shepherd shook his head. "I fancy there'll be more about Nebuchadnezzar's palace than there will about six-coupled side tanks. She's bringing a man who'll be showing a film."

"Of what?"

"Of the railway at Babylon. And her, of course."

"Hold on, sir . . . Do you mean Wallace King?"

"Correct — the King of the Bioscope, as I believe he's known."

It seemed the right moment to ask, "You were talking to my man, Jarvis, sir?"

No emotion was betrayed as he said, "He was telling me about the discovery of the body at the station. You heard about it, I suppose — Captain Boyd. He and I had been in a forward patrol on the night the city fell."

Was he too modest to give the details? Or too guilty?

185

Stevens was descending from the dune, but instead of returning to our camp, he crossed to *The Elephant*, and heaved himself up on to the footplate. A moment later, I saw him illuminated there. He had the fire door open and was contemplating the flames. I couldn't see why we hadn't dropped the fire. Surely it couldn't be the plan to keep the engine in steam all night? But Stevens was now shovelling, and black clouds rolled upwards from the chimney into the violet night. Turning towards Shepherd, I heard the juddering noise that told me Stevens was working the injector — and being very clumsy about it.

"Are we taking off somewhere, sir?" I asked Shepherd.

He shook his head, blowing smoke.

"I want to keep steam up."

I eyed him.

"Precautionary measure," he said.

Stevens returned to his seat. After a while, he fell to clasping and unclasping the arms of it, in an agitated way. I pitched away the end of my cigarette. If the engine were to be kept in steam somebody would have to be at the fire and water every forty minutes or so.

Stevens tipped his head violently back, and contemplated the stars. "Bloody hundreds of them," he complained.

Shepherd said, "You want to take the first sleep, Jim?" I half nodded back, thinking: *Not likely — not so that you and Stevens can see me off with a bullet, then reverse* The Elephant *to Samarrah.*

Silence for a space, then Shepherd caught up his rifle and commenced walking towards the railway line. When he'd fallen in with it, he kept going — heading north across the desert, which had been turned grey by the moonlight, like a great carpet of dust.

"Where's he gone?" I asked Stevens, who shrugged, saying, "A little five-mile scamper."

"Has a lot of pep, doesn't he?"

"He has the right idea," said Stevens. "You get mouldy from lack of exercise."

"But he's been on the go since six — in this killing heat . . ."

Stevens contemplated me with more attention, and more intelligence, than usual.

"First rule of boxing," he said. "Keep your chin down."

My visit to number 11 Clean Street: he'd finally got round to mentioning it.

"I daresay," I said. "Why bring it up now?"

". . . But I suppose if you're going to put the gloves on to have a *conversation*," he continued, "then that goes by the board."

"I went up for a bit of a spar . . . Turned out I had a friend in common with the chap. Know him yourself, do you? The southpaw?"

Stevens — looking sidelong, perhaps scanning the horizon for Shepherd — made no answer at all.

"He's a machine-gunner," I said.

"Well, I hope he's better with the Emma Gee than he is with his fists," said Stevens, and that somehow blocked any further enquiry.

I made a show of getting ready for bed — by going over to the engine, pissing behind it, and having a sluice-down with the water from the slacker pipe. I picked up a bottle of water and carried it and my revolver over to the tent-without-sides. I lay down — and that was my mistake, for I was immediately asleep.

I awoke in a panic to see Shepherd moving about at the limit of my vision. Stevens's boots were about three feet from my head. How could these two men be acting in concert when one was five hundred yards off? Then Shepherd was running pell-mell along the tracks, and Stevens was rapidly kicking over the fire. I came out from under the tent, and Shepherd had made the footplate of the engine. He held a small handgun — a gun made of gold; no of course not, it must be brass. He was slowly raising the thing, thinking hard about what he was doing, and it was for a moment pointed in my direction, but he continued raising it so that it ended high over his head, like the pistol of the man who starts a running race. He fired, and the whole desert jolted, so that I saw it for a second seemingly tilted and illuminated by a green light. Shepherd had fired a flare — it showed on the horizon three advancing parties of men with guns. As the light of the flare burnt out, their black robes became grey in the moonlight, but still they came on. Arab raiders.

Shepherd was roaring at me from the engine, and it seemed he'd been doing so for a while. Stevens was racing for the engine. I began to follow; Stevens made his leap, and was up and on the engine, but I was checked by a droning noise, and a puff of sand six inches from my boot — a perfect little dandelion rising and falling in a second. I lay down flat. I was about fifty yards from *The Elephant*. That drone had meant a Martini bullet, and there now came two fizzes — Mausers. Another drone came, then a deep booming — a fucking blunderbuss, by the sound of it. The Arab shootists were like a choir, each with his own voice, but any one of those guns could do for me. I tried to press myself into the sand, and another dandelion rose and fell two feet from my head. On the engine, Shepherd had the reverser right back. I could see Stevens behind him, shovelling coal in a half crouch. But then Stevens flung down the shovel, and took up his rifle. He leant out and fired towards the Arabs. I turned my head, imagining I could see the bullet as it flew . . . and one of the Arabs was down. I refixed my gaze on the engine, where Shepherd had now replaced Stevens — he was the one leaning out, I mean, and he was loosing off revolver bullets at the rag-tag Arab army. I now had one of them in my own sights; I fired, and . . . nothing. I stood and raced for the engine. A drone, then two fizzes as I leapt — and I was on to the footplate.

Stevens said, at the moment of my arrival, "I got one of the filthy devils," and Shepherd, still hanging out shooting, said, "Don't crow, Stevens. He's a man just like you are." He turned to me: "Regulator's yours, Jim," he said.

Well, he was having a grand time of it, and I fancied this was exactly what he'd come for. Shepherd had already set back the reverser, so I gave a pull on the regulator — too hard again, and we shook on the spot, but did not move an inch. Fucking wheelslip. I pulled the lever to release sand from the sandbox . . . I was putting sand into the desert — a crazy notion — but it gave us the friction we needed. Shepherd held the flare pistol once again, and again he turned night into a garish, green sort of day. The number of oncoming Arabs had about tripled, and a chant or battle cry rose up from them. Some were on horseback, but the riders kept pace with the walkers, and every man was firing in a steady, calm sort of way. Stevens was at the whistle. He pulled and *held*, producing a constant, deafening scream, but I could still hear the bullets clanging against the side.

"Leave off!" I roared at Stevens. "We'll lose pressure!"

He shouted back at me — something more about "The devils!"

Shepherd, swinging back in, yelled, "He's trying to spook them. He thinks they're scared of railway engines!"

Well, they didn't *seem* to be, for they came on still, and I could now hear their chanting over the whistle-scream — something like "Allah illulah! Allah illulah!" It put me in mind of a Salvation Army meeting.

The grey desert went forwards as we went backwards, but not fast enough; I notched up the reverser, and still the whistle screamed, with Shepherd roaring at Stevens, "Look here . . . it's *aeroplanes* they're afraid of."

Stevens, finally letting go of the whistle, said, "What?"

"Aeroplanes," said Shepherd. "They take flight at the sight of an —"

A fizz and a drone came together.

". . . aeroplane."

Stevens was down.

"Oh, fucking hell," said Shepherd, and, pulling the keffiyah from around his neck, he knelt in the coal dust of the footplate, and applied it to the spurting blood of Stevens's chest.

"*Head*," I said, pulling the reverser back to its fullest extent, "he's hit in the head as well."

So Shepherd put the cloth to the spurting blood of Stevens's head, and I believe that I heard Stevens muttering faintly. The keffiyah went back again to the chest, then once more to the head, until the thing was saturated in blood, at which Shepherd sat back and gave it up.

We were flying backwards at full speed, and shaking like buggery, but we were clear of the Arabs. I told Shepherd so, and still squatting in the coal dust, he looked sidelong, nodding to himself. "The Shammar tribe," he said presently, "Rashidi . . ."

"You mean Ibn Rashid?"

Harriet Bailey had told me he was one of the pro-Turkish Arabs.

"They're a bit out of their way if so, but I think it was them."

"What was Stevens saying, sir?"

"He was saying he'd be bloody glad to be out of this heap of sand."

I drove and Shepherd fired (he was a better hand at it than Stevens), the controls illuminated by the thin ray of our footplate lantern. Stevens we wrapped in a tarpaulin and put on the coal in the tender. I had swabbed the blood off the footplate with the slacker pipe. *The Elephant* was a difficult engine to run tender-first, the tender being so big. But we kept rolling through the soft black darkness, with coal dust now flying into faces as well as sand. Shepherd and I hardly spoke, but worked well together — in harmony. He always knew when the injector was needed, or where the fire was thin. After we'd put Stevens on the tender, Shepherd said, "I'll write to his people." A little while later, he said, "The worst of it is they thought he'd be safe out here — away from the real war."

The real war was in France, Mespot being a sideshow; but if you were killed in a sideshow, you were still dead. After a further long interval, I said, "When you put the flare up, sir, it reminded me of the Somme district. In that sort of unreal light, you know anything can happen — anything bad, that is. It's like a theatre."

"I wanted to get a clear sight of the enemy. I knew there were too many for us to take on, but . . . I suppose it was a morbid fascination."

"To my way of thinking, we were trespassers rather than, you know . . . combatants. The real enemy's Brother Turk, isn't he, sir?"

"Tell that to Stevens," he said.

192

Having brought up the subject of France, I decided to try on Shepherd what I'd heard of his reputation.

"When you were in the trenches, sir, you had a taste for going on raids, I believe."

Shovelling coal, he seemed to give a half smile. "It seemed a good way of getting a Blighty."

He meant a wound that would take him home. It was not the truth.

On the left, the dark, sleeping town of Samarrah came up. Three dim lights signalled the station, where we took on more water, and the commander of the garrison — a clever-looking major in thin wire spectacles — was roused from his bed to talk to Shepherd. By way of breaking the bad news, Shepherd showed the fellow Stevens's body. It was agreed above all that he couldn't be left lying on coal, so two privates were summoned to carry him down, and set him on the platform. The head of the garrison explained that one of his men had died the week before of malaria, and Stevens might as well be put to rest next to him, so Shepherd took Stevens's papers out of his pockets. The major offered us a bed for the night, and Shepherd ran this offer past me. I did not believe that the quarters at Samarrah would be very comfortable, and I did not want the fag of relighting the fire in *The Elephant*. I indicated accordingly. "Then hot coffee and biscuits might be more the thing," said Shepherd, and these were brought before we pulled away from the garrison and the still-sleeping town.

At Baghdad station (and Shepherd had kept silence for almost the whole of the way there), a team of Royal

Engineers waited to stable *The Elephant*. They'd been alerted by telegram from Samarrah, as had Jarvis, who was on the dark platform, looking through the window of the *Salon de Thé*, with hurricane lamp upraised.

"I thought you meant to avoid that place," I said as, a few moments later, he, Shepherd and I walked towards the van. He made no audible reply — evidently in one of his glooms again.

"Locked, was it?" said Shepherd, sounding not very interested. Well, it was five o'clock in the morning and he hadn't slept for nearly twenty-four hours.

"It was, sir," said Jarvis.

"Preserve the evidence, I suppose," said Shepherd.

Jarvis indicated the Ford van, waiting on the rubble beyond the station mouth with the dawn breaking strangely all around it, which is to say that the sky was attempting unnatural colours, leaving the van looking as though badly hand-tinted, like the film of *Ali Baba*. Jarvis started the engine — making a good deal of black smoke — and after we'd been going a minute, he said, "Did you put the other fellow off on the way, sir?"

"Yes," said Shepherd grimly.

Well, Jarvis didn't know Stevens as far as I was aware, and this wasn't going to be one of his jolly days anyway, so I just said, "We came under fire from Arabs — he's dead."

Jarvis made no reaction, but as we crossed the bridge of boats, he said, "Two sepoys were killed here last night. We're all warned off the bazaar — that's where it happened. Stabbed in the back they were — only young lads."

194

I thought: Jarvis is breaking down under the climate; he ought to be on sick leave. The light was rising fast over Baghdad; the call to prayer was going up at the same time, so that a newcomer might have taken this for a city of sun-worshippers.

As we came off the bridge, Jarvis swung down an unfamiliar street near the park. "I'm opposite to the cavalry barracks," Shepherd said. But it seemed to me that Jarvis did not need to be told where Shepherd lived. Well, perhaps he had given him a lift before. Shepherd's place was in a garden compound much like my own, except that his had two storeys and a veranda.

"You'll forget about the office, Jim," he said, climbing down. "A good sleep is the order of the day."

But at Rose Court, my room was filled with sunlight and flies — looked as though it had been abandoned this past hundred years.

Jarvis said, "The flytrap has stopped working, sir."

"Evidently. Where's Ahmad?"

"He's gone —"

"To join the insurgency?"

"To the bazaar. I've asked him to get a new one."

The marketing at the bazaar started a little after the dawn call to prayer — for those allowed to go there. I slung my pack on to the bed. As I moved, my boots grated on the floor. Everything was coated in a fine covering of sand.

"A wind got up yesterday, sir," said Jarvis. "The whole city was covered in this sort of golden cloud. I walked to the hotel and back, and it was like the streets were full of bandits."

"Well, they are," I said, "we know that."

"I mean they *looked* like bandits. Every man had a keffiyah round his face: sepoys, Tommies, Arabs all alike. The worst of it is I think I've got some of it on my chest."

I was rather tiring of Jarvis. I asked him, fairly shortly, to prepare some sweet tea, and this he went off to do. Whilst he was in the scullery, I opened the connecting door and looked into his quarters. Two ranks of beer bottles now stood by the bed. This room too fizzed with flies, and these, I saw, were concentrated on an earthenware bowl near the end of the bed. I walked towards it, and it was full of scraps of greyish meat. Was this some kind of makeshift flytrap? He had told me that milk and formaldehyde could be used, but not poisoned meat. I picked up a scrap of the meat, so making myself a focus for all the flies. I sniffed. There was no particular smell — it was not yet on the turn.

I retreated back into my own quarters, where the light seemed to have redoubled. I sank down on my bed, and contemplated the flies in wonderment. It was their room now, not mine. I lay on the bed watching them, too tired to strip off. A moment later, I heard fast footsteps on the gravel beyond. The door was thrown open, and Ahmad entered. He carried a string bag with food in it, and a brown paper parcel. He stared at me challengingly.

"Salaam," I said at length, since it was obvious that he would not say it. He nodded, not so much to return the greeting as to confirm his victory. He looked with satisfaction at the flies.

196

"A really, really poor show," he said.

His English was excellent — I had to give him that. You'd think he'd spent years in the saloon bars of London; or the dining rooms, since he didn't drink. He said something very rapidly, which might very well have been: "The other *kafir*. Where's he got to?", in which case I ought to have stood him down on the spot, but that would have taken more energy than I possessed just then, and in any case I couldn't be sure. He moved rapidly towards me, and leant over me, so as to emphasise his hawkish features.

"Effendi Jarvis . . ." and he flashed a look towards the scullery. He knew Jarvis was in there. ". . . he is crack-ing?"

He had made a question of it; but he shook his head furiously, as though to erase the word he had spoken. He leant into me again. "He is crack-ers." This time he nodded in satisfaction, pleased at having found the right expression, but I considered that either would serve, as it happened. Speaking very slowly and carefully, Ahmad said, "What do you want to do about it?"

"Nothing," I said, "I want to sleep."

He was unwrapping the parcel — a new flytrap. He walked around to the other side of the bed, and picked up the old one. "This", he said, holding it up, "bust." He put the new one down, and wound it up. He leant over to me again (as the representative of the imperial power, I really ought to have been the one standing up), saying in an under-breath, "In night . . . he . . . really big *racket*. He . . ."

And with his mouth six inches from my ear, he let out a fearful scream.

"Out!" I said, badly shaken up. "Get out! I'm going to sleep."

And presently — if only for a very short while — I actually did.

CHAPTER
TWELVE

"Jarvis," I said, "you've a bowl of meat on the floor in your room."

"Yes, sir, it shouldn't be there. It's for the dogs."

"What dogs?"

"The pi-dogs that are all over town sir. It's short for *pariah*, which is an Indian word meaning 'outsider'."

"And you feed them?"

"We're British, sir; we can't just let all the dogs die."

Giving that rum observation the go-by, I said, "Now . . . You were in the show at Kut . . ."

"The battle, sir — the first one. Not the siege, when the Turks came back at us. I was out of it by then."

He took a pull on his beer. I was in for the whole story, I knew. It was four o'clock on the day after my return from Samarrah, and Jarvis and I sat under the palms in the rose garden. I had decided to get on terms with the man, so I'd asked what had been agitating him, and he had told me, "This *place*, sir. Also what happened to Captain Boyd — I can't stand not knowing. Apart from that, it's memories, sir — and not of the best."

As to Boyd, we had resolved to visit his former quarters and speak to his Arab servant in company with

Ahmad, who would translate. Meanwhile, I was in for the memories.

"September 1915, sir," said Jarvis, "and we were steaming up the Tigris. General Townshend's Regatta, it was called. Barges lashed port and starboard of the steamers. I was on a barge, sir, and I knew it was a bad lookout. Every morning when the sun was full up, the captain of the steamer would call out the temperature — a hundred and seventeen degrees . . . a hundred and eighteen degrees. I didn't care for that man at all, sir. It was just as though he was in league with the sun. There'd be Arabs on the bank sir, fishing from smashed-up jetties, and dressed in rags, but they were laughing at us. Well, they could see the field ambulances driving up the bank alongside us, so they knew we were for it.

"We came up to the camp at a spot called Ah Gharbi. Eleven thousand men — only there were tents for twice that number."

I was meant to ask why, so I did.

"Put the wind up Johnny Turk, sir. That was General Townshend for you. He had the reputation for being tactically brilliant."

Jarvis, I thought, didn't quite share that opinion.

"We started on the march, sir. Five miles — didn't fire a shot — and we were on pretty short commons, I don't mind telling you. A few biscuits here and there, and not nearly enough water. I was thinking about water all the time, sir, and I believe I started to get ill on that walk. Anyhow, we camped at Abu Rummanah, with the Turks dug in at Essinn, about eight miles north, and just south of Kut. And they were dug in *hard*, sir: trenches and redoubts . . . And they straddled the river."

"How?"

"Why sir — by a bridge of boats."

It was the Mesopotamian speciality, it seemed.

"What was the Turkish strength?"

"Getting on for ten thousand regulars, and about four thousand Arabs. Well, we were ten days at Abu Rummanah, waiting for a howitzer battery to come upriver, and all that time, the place was spinning — in my mind, I mean. Brown dirt on the ground, brown-dirt flat-roofed houses: a city of mud tilting and turning as I walked about the place. I was coming down with something but I couldn't say what. When the battery came, our company was sent on another rather long walk, sir: twenty-five miles. At first, I thought: Well, this is a bit of all right. We're going away from the Turks — out into the desert. Only . . . well, we were going round the *back* of them, sir, rolling up the left flank, so we came up behind the Turks firing on the section of our force that was advancing on their front."

"Hold on," I said. "Wouldn't that mean you were under fire from your own side?"

"You've put your finger on the flaw in the plan, sir. Anyway, it came to a fearful scrap in the Turkish trenches, and I was in amongst it for a bit, but I don't mind admitting, I wandered away after a while. I was looking for water. You see, sir, all the way on the march I'd not had a single drop."

"What about your canteen?"

"I drained that before we set out. I thought I'd get some more on the way, but they didn't stop that march for anything. There was no cigarette pause, because the lights might have given us away. We were not to talk or make any sound, and there was no distribution of water because — well, it would have been too *noisy*. Some of the men were drinking their own urine, sir. I'll tell you for nothing, I tried it myself — took my hat off and made water into it . . ."

I couldn't help but eye his sun helmet.

"It was a different one to the one I have on now, sir. I came upon some water in the end, sir, when I'd gone away from the trench fighting. It was in a kind of marsh about a quarter mile from the river, or should I say the leftovers of a marsh that was sinking back into the desert. It was black, sir, and brackish, and I believe I drank about three pints of it."

"I see."

"So I got cholera."

I took a belt on my beer.

"Well," I said, "you would do."

"I was on my back in the sand for hours, sir. Couldn't stand, and I couldn't stop the . . . Well, you know how cholera takes a man . . . And all the time, the bloody sun roasting me. I thought I was for the big ride, sir, I really did, when this fellow came up, and he had this bloody great sub-machine gun under his arm and a belt of bullets over his shoulder. He looked down at me, and he said nothing. I was covered with the black flies at this point, sir, and I thought: well, that's it, he's left me for dead. But a minute later he came back, still with the gun, but with two canteens of clear water into the bargain. A few seconds after, the field ambulance came up, and I believe *that* was his doing as well. He went off then, and I had no idea who he was — just this Good Samaritan with a machine gun. But he took a bullet in the leg not long after and ended up in the field hospital back at Basrah, and that's when I discovered his name. It was Captain Boyd, sir, and when I heard he was looking out for a batman, I put in for the transfer."

Later that afternoon, we walked through the labyrinth with Ahmad in the lead. He led us past sellers of Persian carpets, professional cigarette-rollers, doorstep smokers of the narghile or hubble-bubble, past women veiled and unveiled. His long black robe flowed out behind him not because there was any breeze but because he walked fast. I fancied that he'd been glad to be asked to translate for us, but he wasn't showing it.

From two paces behind him, I said, "Ahmad, what do you recommend for sleeping in this place? Should I lie down on the roof?"

"You will sleep if God wills it," he said.

We were going by a mosque — green lamps burning in the dazzle of the day.

"There are a hundred mosques in Baghdad, I believe," I said.

"More," said Ahmad, striding on.

"A hundred and twenty?" I said. "What do you think?"

"More."

"Really?"

"Really." After an interval he turned and gave me a half smile, saying very carefully, "The more the merrier."

Jarvis looked at me and gave something approaching a grin. He was a little better, I thought, for having spoken of his experience at Kut. I had asked him if he would like to come along to the next meeting of the Baghdad Railway Club. He might help the Arab who served us there. There'd be some decent grub on the go, and he'd see a film show into the bargain. Well, he'd leapt at the idea.

We now came to the square that Jarvis had driven me to in his Ford van. This time there was no market and no sentry either. Instead, a collection of Arabs kicked their heels at the gates of the compound. It was dustier than our own, and bleached of colour. Half the flowers were dead; there was a single palm tree, like a star on a stick. An oil-daubed corporal who was playing about with a petrol generator directed us to what had been the apartment of Captain Boyd. "You'll find his servant there," he said, and so it proved. The servant's name was Farhan, and he occupied a wide, dusty, dark room. He had apparently been doing absolutely nothing when we arrived; he was, perhaps, bored to tears. Anyhow, he seemed very glad of some company, and brought through from another room a spirit stove and assorted tea things. After the formalities had been completed, with much laughter on the part of Farhan — who almost sang as he spoke — and none at all from our man, Ahmad, the interrogation could begin.

204

I said to Ahmad, "Ask him about Captain Boyd's movements around the city. Where did he like to go? Who did he visit?"

Ahmad spoke to the man, who seemed nervous but anxious to please. Presently Ahmad reported, "He went often to the home of the British."

"The home of the British is Britain," said Jarvis, sounding like a man coming out of a dream.

"Not necessarily," I said. "Does he mean the British Residency?"

So Ahmad tried that on the fellow, but apparently there was no advance on "the home of the British".

I said, "Ask him whether Captain Boyd had any visitors in his last days."

After an interval of Arab conversation, or what looked a lot like Arab *argument*, Ahmad reported, "A man came the day before the last day of Boy Captain." (Which was what Farhan called Boyd.)

"What was his name?"

The question was put; Ahmad turned back. "He doesn't know. He has not a *notion*."

This was not the time for Ahmad to be trying out his English phrases. I said, "Then what did he look like? He was a soldier I suppose. What sort? Tommy? Sepoy? Officer?"

The argument was renewed; it ended with Farhan smiling and gesturing to his chest.

Ahmad faced me again. "The man was a British soldier, a man who truly has religion here — in his heart."

"What does that mean?" I asked Ahmad, and I thought, since it was the kind of poetic thing an Arab would be likely to say, that he would know. But he didn't. He shook his head.

Jarvis was frowning. "*What* religion?" he said. "Christian?"

The question was put.

"Christian religion," confirmed Ahmad.

"We *all* have the Christian religion in our hearts," I said. "Well, we *don't* ... But we're all *supposed* to. Ninety per cent of the Tommies would call themselves Christian."

Farhan was now distributing glasses of tea, talking ten to the dozen, and very politely as I believed, but unfortunately in Arabic. After nodding and smiling at him for a while, I tried a different line of questioning via Ahmad, asking whether there were any evidences of Boyd left about in the place, but the empty room was not promising, and Ahmad got from Farhan the information that the room had been cleared out by "the many men who came".

I asked, "Was the man with religion in his heart one of those?" and it seemed that he was not. He had come before the "many" who, I was pretty sure — after further talk — had been a body of men no more sinister than the investigating red caps, the military police team based at the Hotel.

"He makes nice tea," Jarvis said at length, and it was true, the syrupy stuff was delicious. I said to Ahmad, "Can you tell him the tea tastes excellent?"

But Ahmad had no intention of doing any such thing.

"Arabian people clever," he said, scowling at me.

"Yes," I said, wondering what the hell he was driving at, "you're all very clever."

"Not *all*," said Ahmad, and he indicated Farhan, who was now beaming at us, and holding out a wooden board on which lay sugar-dusted sweetmeats. "Not him. He is not clever."

"Oh," I said. "You mean he's simple."

Ahmad nodded. "*Really*," he said.

CHAPTER
THIRTEEN

That night, God willed that I did sleep — for about three hours — and I dreamed of Miss Harriet Bailey. We were riding horses in the park, galloping fast through a grove of lemon trees. In spite of the great speed, I could hear her perfectly clearly as she said, "Shall we make love, darling?"

I said, "How will we go about it?" meaning *where*.

"Oh, in the traditional manner," she said, and then her horse was gone, and she was sitting on the dusty ground, helpless with laughter at her own joke. I did not know what to think, and still did not when I woke up. I recollected the dream throughout the following morning as I worked — alone now — in the office I had shared with Stevens.

Lieutenant Colonel Shepherd had stepped through briefly from his own office in the morning, bringing rough drafts of two letters, outlining requirements of flat-bed wagons suitable for the carrying of shells. The letters were for a Mr Halder of Bombay and a Mr Jindal of Karachi, both of the International Office of the Great Indian Peninsula Railway, Shipping Department. I was to make fair copies of the letters. I was then to make arrangements with the Deputy Chief of Staff to accommodate a Mr Singh of the same company, who would be arriving on the steamer from Basrah the day after tomorrow and staying for a week. He was a strict vegetarian and so special arrangements would have to be made there too. In addition I was given a bundle of maps, charts and tables relating to the line between Baghdad and the town of Feluja — a line that had been broken up by the Turks at certain points indicated on the charts. The question was whether it would be better to rebuild the line in the existing gauge — the broad gauge — or build a new one in the two-foot gauge, bearing in mind that a garrison of a size indicated by a further document was to be set up at Feluja. This had seemed rather a weighty responsibility, but Shepherd had assured me that I was merely expected to sketch out some initial thoughts on the matter. And so again, I wondered whether this was real work or not.

Before departing he told me that another trip to Samarrah had been fixed for the following Monday, and did I fancy it? I said I did (although I did not), and I asked the reason. This time a proper survey would be made of the line, and of the telegraphic wires alongside; a team of Royal Engineers would be riding with us. There would be an attempt to go further north, a little closer towards the enemy territory of Tikrit in search of rolling stock removed from Baghdad. After he'd quit the room I wondered about Shepherd: you'd have thought he'd want to stay out of the desert after what had just happened.

I made the fair copies of the letters, then turned to the bundle about the Feluja line. I started in on a document comparing the costs of the two-foot gauge with standard gauge. In rails, the saving was thirty per cent; in track ties, forty-eight per cent; in ballast, forty-four per cent. But then there were all the disadvantages of the small gauge. I decided I needed some sweet tea, and a bite to eat. I would walk down to the canteen, but first I moved across to one of the two cabinets in the room and opened the doors. This cabinet held bookshelves, and I surveyed the titles: *Superheated Locomotives, Glossary of Steam Locomotive Terms, Dining Saloons of the London and North Western Railway*. (Who had thought to load *that* on to a steamer, and send it up the Tigris to Baghdad?) There was also *A Geology of Mesopotamia, The Arab and His Ways*, and a book in French: *Chemin de Fer Impérial Ottoman de Baghdad*. I then spied a grey pamphlet: *Railway Clearing House Code Book*, and my heart sank even as I told myself that the book was everywhere where there were railways and railwaymen.

I first looked up the word I had sent to Manners: "GRUFF". In the gloss on the railway code put forward by Manners of the War Office it had meant "Request identity of local agent". I found its true meaning on the last but one page of the pamphlet: "Snowstorm cleared".

Well, I very nearly laughed.

The midday call to prayer was rising from beyond the window. I took the pamphlet back to my desk, where I looked up the true meaning of "CRATE", the reply I had received from Manners. It was there in the middle pages: "Expect circus train on Sunday". Anyone

210

in the telegraph office who knew the railway codes must have thought I was playing a very queer game.

I went down to the lobby, where the Baghdadis queued at the desks of the political officers, or the assistants thereof. A dozen fans whirred and rocked, yet still the sweat streamed down the faces of those officers. One ("Agriculture") had a white towel around his neck to keep the stuff off his shirt collar. I saw the red caps — the army coppers — still at their post, and a medical orderly was there too, bandaging the forearm of a sepoy, who was at the same time making a statement. I asked the red cap who was not taking down the statement what had happened:

"Another stabbing, sir."

"Native job, was it?"

"They all are," he said.

The sepoy gave me a sheepish smile. It was rough luck on those boys. Because we'd taken over their country some time ago, they had to help us take over someone else's — this latest acquisition being the one place on earth more infernally hot than their own land.

Just then the door behind the man opened; it gave on to a room that was also part of the red caps' set-up in the hotel. A military police sergeant came out of it, together with a rather seedy-looking fellow that I recognised. It was the pock-marked man I'd seen coming out of the post room in the Residency when I'd telegrammed to Manners. Evidently, he was being taken in charge for some misdemeanour. No, wait. He was being let go — didn't look too pleased about it though, and he gave a glare at the red caps before making towards the main doors of the lobby. He'd been let off with a warning, I decided.

I followed the man out into the glare. He turned sharp left, then left again; he was into a short street leading down to the quays, and here he was pushing at the door of the place known as The Oasis. Officially this was Wet Canteen Number Two, but somebody had painted an oasis on walls with three beautiful women lying about in it wearing white summer dresses. I followed him in. The place had electricity; perhaps not enough of it though, for the central ceiling fan turned too slowly, and the bright lights flickered. The place (being close to the river) smelt of sewage, and was horribly hot. There was a makeshift bar at the far end with a tea urn on it, some very British-looking cakes under glass, and beer bottles, still in their crates. The pock-marked man was after beer, and the orderly was turning him down flat.

"Not while five o'clock," he was saying — a bloody-minded Yorkshireman, by the sound of him. The pock-marked man was unexpectedly Irish, and with a high, fluttery voice. He said, "What a depressing outlook this is: I've a choice of mouldy rock cake and a cup of stewed tea or *nothing*." He ought not to have been talking to me, since I was an officer and I hadn't talked to him, but he *was* doing.

I said, "Are you going to salute?" and he did after a fashion, saying, "Sorry about that, sir, I'm not right in myself. I'm a sickbay case, I think."

I said, "You've been in with the monkeys," and that pulled him up sharp, as it did the orderly standing

212

behind him. An officer shouldn't speak of His Majesty's Military Mounted Police in that fashion. I had a pocketful of rupees and I put some on the counter, saying, "I want to have a talk with this man on Corps business, and we'd both like a bottle of beer."

The bottles were given over, and I sat the Irishman down at the furthest table from the orderly, who continued to eye us from his post during the following.

The Irishman was Private Lennon. He'd been born in Ireland but lived in London. At least he did when there wasn't a war on. After I'd got this out of him, he said, "What's this about, sir?"

"A confidential matter," I said.

He was eyeing my white tabs.

I meant to ask him something about methods of communication from the Residency. I didn't know quite what, but I kept thinking of the bunch of keys he'd been jangling.

I said, "They were putting the screws to you. Do you want to tell me why?"

"Are you Intelligence, sir?"

"Correct," I said immediately. Well, I could always deny it. Anything claimed by a man like Lennon could be denied.

"Do you really not know?" he said.

I gave that one the go-by, since he evidently believed I *did* know what he had been questioned about, or that I would be able to find out with no trouble.

"See, sir," he said, "I work in the Residency, second floor —"

"As what?"

He shrugged: "General knockabout — mainly in the post room. We're all trusted men in the post room — have to be. But those coppers don't trust me, sir."

"That's a shame," I said, "why ever not?"

He took a belt on his beer, weighing me up; I took a belt on mine.

"They think I'm sending ordinary mails by the bag."

"The bag?"

"The diplomatic bag."

"Ordinary mails," I said, "you mean ordinary *blokes'* mails?"

"That's correct sir. That's what they think."

It would be a way for your average Tommy Atkins to avoid having his letter read over by an officer. But I didn't see quite how it would work. I said, "The diplomatic mail only goes to government offices, or the offices of our allies."

"Well there you are, sir. That's just what I told the gent with the red cap on."

"You couldn't use the diplomatic bag to send a letter to Mrs Jones of Sycamore Avenue."

"Exactly right, sir. I rest my case."

He drained his glass.

I took from my pocket . . . not rupees this time, but a one-pound note. I set it on the table before us. A pound note went a long way in Baghdad.

"I notice that you haven't exactly denied the charge. Only told me why there'd be no point doing it."

"No point at all, sir."

I picked up the note, and made to replace it in my pocket book.

"Of course," said Lennon, "it might be different if your brother worked in the bag room of the War Office in London."

I set the note back on the table, and pushed it a little way towards Lennon.

"Now if I pick that up," he said, "you'll arrest me on a charge of taking bribes."

"Try me," I said.

"You're the only officer who's ever bought me a drink, sir."

"Just so," I said.

He swiftly pocketed the note, and I said, "I will now arrest you on a charge of taking a bribe unless you help me out with my special duty."

"You're very bad for my nerves, sir, do you know that?"

"Do you want another glass of beer?"

He nodded and I got two more. When I returned to the table, he said, "I've decided it's official business you're on sir, although of a secret sort. And the money I take to be fair wages."

We both nodded for a while. I was thinking of the letter sent by Boyd to Manners at the War Office. That had gone via the diplomatic bag. Had its contents been somehow leaked? What exactly *were* its contents? I had not had sight of it, but I knew that in it Boyd had told what he'd seen at the station, and set out the case against Shepherd. I asked Lennon, "Are you aware of anybody trying to find out the content of letters sent in the diplomatic bag?"

"No."

"But that does not mean you haven't put other letters into it — ordinary letters."

"It doesn't in itself mean that sir, no."

"If for instance a fellow wanted to send a mucky letter to my wife."

"Now *that* doesn't sound like secret service business," he said.

It seemed to me — weighing the fellow up — that Lennon *had* added letters to the diplomatic bag, but had probably *not* taken from it, since that would be too big a proposition . . . In which case I was thrown back on the question of the *telegrams*. According to Manners, the ones sent by Boyd (both before and after the sending of his *letter*) had not disclosed any names, either of people or places. But it would be worth trying to make sure of that; and to find out about any other wires sent by Boyd. Since a copy was kept of all messages, it would be possible to do this given access to the records. Sitting back in my seat, so as to appear relaxed, I said to Lennon, "Do you have the keys to the telegraphic office at the Residency?"

"Now there'd be no point having those keys," he said. "A sentry is posted outside at all times, and in any case the place never closes."

"I need to find out what was sent by a certain man and where to."

"When?"

I thought back. When would Boyd have been sending? He had first wired to the War Office the day after the fall of the city, which meant March 13th. The wires arranging the rendezvous at Baghdad station, or

216

the "safe place" (which turned out to be no such thing), were sent the third week of April. That was the end of his communication with the War Office. But Boyd might then have sent any number of other telegrams to other people up to the day I found his body: May 24th, Thursday last.

I said, "Between the fall of the city and last Thursday?"

"Then you don't need the telegraphic office."

"No?"

"You need the strongboxes in the room around the corner. That's the archive. Everything sent up to the end of last week will be in there."

"Can you get me in there and can you get those boxes open?"

"For a pound?" he said.

"For your freedom from arrest."

"And another quid when the job's done, sir?"

The man was incorrigible.

"We'll see about that," I said.

At ten that night, I presented my identity card to the sentry at the Residency, and passed into the quadrangle. The horse smell, the heat, the falling darkness, the puttering of a generator, one or two whispered conversations proceeding on the overhanging verandas . . . The man Lennon waited by the fountain. It still did not work. He had been trailing his hand in the green water, but he stood up snappily enough when I approached, and he very nearly saluted.

We ascended the main staircase under flickering electric light; ordinary bulbs and black cable were tangled amid the candle chandeliers. Our boots made no sound on the thick and dusty carpet. On the first landing, I heard the sound of a closing door — an official in civilian clothes locking up for the night. Approaching the second floor, Lennon took out his own bunch of keys. We walked fast down the long corridor, passing an open door, through which I glimpsed another civilian: a man with well-oiled hair calmly reading a newspaper — one of the few fat men I'd clapped eyes on in Baghdad. He was perhaps the consul himself: The Resident.

We now approached the telegraphic office — with its sentry outside the door. I had been worried about the position of the telegram archive in relation to this sentry but we continued a fair way past him, and made a left turn with the corridor. As we stood before the unmarked door of the archive we were out of the sentry's eye line. Private Lennon opened the door of what turned out to be no more than a glorified cupboard.

"One minute, mind," he said, and I was in.

He called after me: "Anyone comes along, I shut the door on you, sir, all right?"

Given that this cubbyhole was part of Captain Ferry's empire, I'd thought it would be neater. The room held three sizes of box. The smallest ones accorded to the size of the sending form I'd filled in when communicating with the War Office, so I started on the stack of those. Each box had a paper label pasted on, and some had more than one — and on the label was just a mix-up of letters and numbers. Lennon stood guard some way beyond the half-open door. He commanded the right angle of the corridor, so he would have early sight of an approach from either direction.

I pulled the lid off the first box that came to hand. It held the carbon copies of the forms all right. The first I saw was sent by a Second Lieutenant Foster of "Div. 4 Mobile Vet. Section" to a man called Knight in Basrah, but many were not so clear. Where the handwriting had been decent, the carbon was invariably poor, or vice versa. I flicked through and came to a Captain Windust of what might have been the 26th Punjabis. He'd sent on March 25th; I couldn't make out the message. The next fellow was somebody Battacharjee. He'd sent on March 25th also, and the message was readable, and had been sent clear: "Operation completed satisfactorily." Then came messages of March 26th . . . But the papers would take an eternity to rifle through.

In hopes of I-don't-know-what, I reached for the next box, and took off the lid. But I froze when, from beyond the half-open door, I heard a tread on the corridor carpet. Somebody was addressing Lennon, a whispered enquiry. Lennon said, "Fuck off, Sinclair," and the footsteps retreated. Evidently another Tommy, some pal of Lennon's, had come up. The bloke no doubt worked a few dodges of his own.

Now Lennon stepped into the storeroom.

"You'll have to get cracking, sir. We'll both be in lumber if the wrong bloke finds us in here."

"It's hopeless," I said. "I give it up."

"Another half minute," he said, and he stepped back.

He was earning his extra quid. I began leafing through the second box, picked up a form and read the date: March 17th. So this box was earlier. I glanced at another form: Jackson of the . . . couldn't read the rest. I glanced down at the message, and it was just four clusters of numbers: some military code. Lennon was closer to the door, becoming agitated. I tried to think of the offence we were committing — offences, more like. Trespass . . . Conspiracy . . . Injuries to the Telegraph. No, that was pulling down telegraph poles. Interfering with the mails — that was more like it. But it went beyond that: a charge of espionage might be preferred, and with only Laughing Jack himself — Manners of the War Office — between me and the firing squad.

I plucked out another form, and . . .

"Ferry!" called Lennon.

I stuffed the paper in my hand back into the box, replaced the lid and turned out of the room with fast-beating heart. Lennon had the door locked and we were walking fast away the moment Ferry turned the corner. Had he seen us? Impossible to tell; and uppermost in my thoughts was the image of the last paper I'd held. The name Boyd had been at the top, alongside a number I assumed must have been 185, denoting his machine-gun company. I had not had time to make out the date, the message, or the name of the person to whom it had been sent, all of which had been faint, but there had been something odd about the slip: *a diagonal line had been drawn clear through it.*

220

CHAPTER
FOURTEEN

Come Saturday, I went again to the Baghdad Railway Club.

As before, Bob Ferry was already present in the club room, smoking alone under the dark colours made by the stained glass when I arrived with Jarvis. He was beautifully turned out in recently pressed khaki. I said, "I do believe this weather suits you."

Ferry smiled. "It's a case of mind . . . over matter."

There was no sign of his having seen me raiding his archive.

Jarvis was getting acquainted with our Arab waiter whose name, evidently, was Layth or something of the kind.

"Your name means lion," Jarvis said.

Layth, who had a few words of English, asked, "Stanley . . . what mean?" and I could see the question had knocked Jarvis. What *did* Stanley mean?

As other club members began to arrive and take their places around the table, I asked Ferry how things were going on at the telegraphic office of the Residency.

". . . Overwhelmed," he said at length.

I heard from the other end of the table, "Ah, a glass of fizzle."

It was the cavalryman, Major Findlay; Jarvis poured champagne for him. We had not run to that at the previous meeting, and I wondered who was paying for it. No doubt Shepherd himself. His parents owned half of . . . what was it? Worcestershire? Why would a wealthy man like that risk his life taking Turkish backhanders?

Miss Bailey arrived, and I stood together with all the other men. She wore a sort of Chinese coat. Now that I studied her again, I could see that her skin had been a little roughened by the desert sun; and she was perhaps a few years older than I'd thought. Findlay looked on very sadly as she took her place, for she was seated at the opposite end of the table to him.

The meeting began, and in spite of the champagne, it did so sombrely, with a speech from Shepherd about the passing of Stevens — evidently a marvellous pugilist, and a bluff fellow who took some knowing but whose behaviour would occasionally (*very* occasionally, it seemed to me) disclose a heart of gold. Shepherd mentioned the forthcoming return to Samarrah, and the brigadier muttered, "Tomfoolery. You're sure to get into another scrape," but he did so affectionately. "If anyone would care to come, let me know," said Shepherd. I thought this might be a joke, but evidently not. "It's a fascinating stretch of line," he was saying. "I can offer you a fine 2-8-0 engine, albeit of German make, a carriage that was formerly the personal saloon of General von der Goltz . . . the golden dome of the mosque at Samarrah . . ."

He was making a general invitation of it: come and be fired on by Arabs or Turks. It did not seem an attractive prospect, but I observed Captain Ferry take out a gold pen and make a careful note in his pocket book. Miss Bailey said, "Might make a diverting day or two," at which Findlay immediately said, "I'll come. It's the Seventh Cavalry up there — I do know they're short of saddles. I'll take a load up for them. And I suppose one ought to see the Mosque of the Golden Dome."

"It's called the Al-Askari Mosque," said Miss Bailey, rather coldly.

He looked put-out, but rallied quickly.

"Sounds good anyway," he said, "and I'm all for seeing it."

Shepherd now gave me the floor, and — very much doubting that the cavalrymen of Samarrah were short of saddles — I rose to my feet. I'd had in mind a quick rundown of the police set-up at York station, the extent of our jurisdiction, the tremendous size of the railway lands around York, but as I faced my audience, I realised I had not given enough thought to the matter.

"I'm Captain Stringer," I said, and the brigadier looked at me sharply, as if he'd only just realised my identity. (I'd thought by now that everyone in the club would know my name.) "Before coming out here," I continued, "I was with the Seventeenth Northumberlands on the light railways in France — the railway pals, as they're known, and a first-rate group of lads . . ."

I was being not only dull, but also — as the wife would say — common.

223

". . . But that's not for tonight," I said. I looked down at my hand; it was shaking. "Tonight I mean to talk to you about my work as a detective — plain-clothes — on the railway force at York. Now the police office is on platform four at York station, which is the main 'up' and anyone heading London-way on a Tuesday morning about eleven o'clock sort of time would have seen the full police strength parading outside. That was before the war, I mean . . ."

I lifted my glass of champagne, drank it all off, and everyone around the table watched me do it. "However . . ." I heard myself saying, and I didn't know why. Brigadier General Barnes was eyeing me carefully. Major Findlay — redder than the previous week — was looking at the ceiling. Miss Bailey kept adjusting the position of her glass of champagne, and I reckoned I had about five seconds before she dismissed me out of hand as a dullard and a blockhead. I was making a worse fist of this than Stevens had in his early stages, and *he'd* eventually become interesting. How had he done it? By yarning — by telling a tale.

"However," I was apparently saying again, "I'm in rather a tight corner here because . . ."

"Give us one of your cases, Jim," said Shepherd. "What's the *queerest* thing that ever happened on a train near York?"

Almost without thinking, I answered, "It was the affair of the already clipped tickets."

"Sounds worthy of Conan Doyle himself," said Shepherd.

"Not quite, sir, but it was a bit of a facer at the time."

224

"And what time *was* it?"

"Late on in 'thirteen, sir. December. The matter first came up on a bright but cold day as I recall, with just a riming of snow on the streets of old York . . ."

Somebody said, "Ah, the thought of it," and all of a sudden the whole shining, sweating company was leaning forward. Shepherd nodded to Jarvis, who set down another glass of champagne for me, but I didn't need it now. I was away.

"It was Friday morning, and I'd been in the middle of town questioning a suspect . . ."

(I had in fact been buying cigars for the Chief but I left that out.)

". . . As I stepped under the station portico I saw that two fellows from the maintenance department were putting up the Christmas tree . . . and they had these coloured lights on a cable. They were untangling them, and Harold Spencer — who was a ticket inspector 'A' grade, which meant he worked the main line — came haring round the corner from the ticket gate, tripped over the cable and went flying. This was a turn-up because Spencer was knocking on — probably sixty or so — and had never been known to run before. Well, he was a lay preacher and a Chief Ticket Inspector — not the sort of man who needs a sudden turn of speed. When he got up, he had a nasty graze on his cheek, but he paid it no mind at all, which was also a shock because he was normally very careful of his appearance. He just said, 'I've been looking for you. I've got the rummest tale to tell you.'

225

"Evidently he'd just come in off a London train that was heading for Newcastle and had stopped twice before York — at Peterborough and Doncaster. He'd got on at Doncaster and started checking the tickets, only to find that every one given up to him had already been checked and clipped with the regulation North Eastern Railway hole punch, which cuts a crescent-moon shape out of the tickets — other companies have diamonds or squares or what have you. He'd gone through four carriages and it was the same story in every one — some other fellow had beaten him to it. Now Spencer seemed completely floored by this, said he thought he was going nuts, but I said, 'It's not so much of a mystery is it?' He said, 'How do you make that out?' I said, 'It's obviously the work of another ticket inspector.' He said, 'It can't be. If an inspector boards a train, he tells the guard on doing so, and a note is made in the guard's log. No such note had been made.' I said, 'How about this: he got on the train without telling the guard?'"

. . . At which Shepherd spoke up again, observing to the meeting at large: "You see the calibre of men we have in our railway office."

A good deal of laughter at that, and I fancied I heard in amongst it some shouting from beyond the window, apparently a repetition of the disruption overheard at the previous meeting. I suddenly had cause to think about the Webley. It wasn't in the haversack; I'd left it at Rose Court. I'd given it to Jarvis for cleaning; he'd handed it back to me, and I'd put it on the bed. The trouble was that I'd been carrying it sometimes in the holster and at times in my haversack — that was how I'd come to forget. The noises had faded anyhow.

Where had I got to?

". . . When I put my theory to Spencer," I continued, "he said, 'You're saying he wasn't a real ticket inspector. Why? Why would anyone pretend to be a ticket collector?' I said, 'To charge excess fares and pocket the money,' and at this Spencer became thoughtful. He *had* asked the passengers if they'd been charged excess, and one woman had said she had been. She'd not been able to find a seat in third, so she'd been sitting in second with a Third Class ticket. It was only a matter of a bob or so. But a second woman, found by Spencer at Doncaster to only have a ticket as far as Peterborough, said that the previous fellow *hadn't* charged her, but just said, 'Don't trouble about it, only think on next time.' Very nice about it he was, the woman had said. As to his appearance, he was described as a middle-aged man of middling height with darkish hair — and he did have the long black coat with gold-braided collar of the ticket inspector.

"Over the next week, other inspectors on the staff found a similar thing happening to them. The tickets would be properly clipped, some excesses asked for, some not. I reckoned that if this chap wasn't taking all the excesses, then he wasn't in it for the money — and the reason he took some cash now and again was to keep up the front, keep up his credibility. In other words it was more important for him to check tickets than it was to make money out of it, and that put me on the track of thinking he might be a man who'd once been turned down for the job of ticket inspector . . ."

"A ticket inspector *manqué*," said Harriet Bailey — and I had one of her smiles all to myself, even if I didn't quite take her meaning.

"Ticket inspectors are employed by the traffic department," I said. "So I went there and looked over all the records of men shortlisted for ticket-collecting positions but not taken on, or stood down from them. There were plenty. More of the first than the second of course, but dozens all told. The men who'd resigned or been sacked had to hand over their ticket clippers, and the records showed that they always did. There was not a single pair of clippers unaccounted for, and there never had been. But I was curious about the resignations, of which there were quite a few. It was a steady sort of job, and decently paid. Why would a man chuck it up? I was told the main reason was that they didn't care for the rostering patterns. Every man had to start early or finish late because that's when most of the fare-dodgers operate — first thing or last thing in the day. It broke in on me then that our phantom ticket-checker did all his work in the morning, so might he not be using the clippers of a man who worked afternoons and evenings?"

Thoughtful nods from around the table. I seemed to have Bob Ferry quite mesmerised. Not Major Findlay, however. It would take more than a tale of petty crime on the line to distract him from Miss Bailey. I could hear no noise from the square just then.

"I asked for the names and addresses of all ticket inspectors of the York district who worked late. I then picked out the ones who lived with other men — those who lived in digs in other words. There were three that fitted the bill, and I struck lucky with the first: a fellow called Hughes. He lived in a big lodging house in the middle of York — a place not too particular about its tenants. Every night Hughes knocked off late from work, downed a few more pints of ale than were good for him and in the small hours of the morning he put his coat in the hallway, leaving the clippers in the pocket. He put the coat on again when he set off for work at one o'clock the next afternoon.

"Now there were some ruffians in that house, but it was a quiet chap who caught my eye when I went round the landings knocking on the doors. He was medium build with dark hair, and I could see he was a railway nut because he had *The Railway Magazine* and *The Railway Gazette* on his table top."

This caused quite a stir. Shepherd — a *Railway Magazine* man himself, of course — was laughing, and one of the R.E. chaps was quite indignant: "I'll have you know that I subscribe to both. Does that make me a railway nut?"

"Technically, it does," said Harriet Bailey, and she gave me another of her lovely smiles, thus increasing the anxiety written on the face of Findlay.

"The quiet fellow's name was Randall — Bartholomew Randall. We had him in for questioning, and he came clean. We asked him what he'd done with the money he'd taken for excess fares, and he took us to the collection box for the Railway Mission that stands on platform five of York station. It was all in there. He'd been putting cash in there for weeks in fact, and only a few days earlier, I'd been talking to Father Cunningham who runs the Railway Mission, and he'd said he'd detected what he called 'a real access of the Christmas spirit in the city of York' — this on account of the donations in the box. In November, the donations had amounted to four shillings and thruppence or so, along with the usual admixture of foreign coins and amusement-machine tokens. Up to the third week of December fifty-seven pounds ten had been found in the box. But even though he hadn't kept the money, Randall was charged with theft as well as personating a company officer and travelling on a train without a ticket, since he himself had not *had* a ticket. Of course, the peculiar feature of the whole case was the motive: he'd gone about inspecting tickets *just for the love of doing it*."

"A crime of passion," said Harriet Bailey.

"What became of the fellow?" someone else asked, which I'd hoped they would not, since Bartholomew Randall had hanged himself in the lodging house the day before he was due to appear in the police court, confirming too late the doubts I'd had about proceeding against him, and never put strongly enough to the prosecuting solicitor.

But the question of Randall was lost amid the applause for my talk, and the noisy arrival of Wallace King and his assistant. As this fellow struggled with a mass of equipment, King cut off the applause for my speech with a raised hand. "I am Wallace King," he said. (Somebody said, "We know.") "I will tonight exhibit a film of the famous archaeologist Miss Bailey . . ."

She nodded her head graciously.

". . . on a visit to Babylon. Rest assured, there is footage of the railway. My assistant also took some still photographs of the visit, and these will be passed around."

The assistant — he and Jarvis were wrestling with the tripod stand of the projection machine — was never named, I noticed.

"My assistant and I," King continued, "will attempt to set up our equipment with the minimum of fuss and inconvenience to yourselves, so please do carry on with the next business of the meeting. However, I must warn you all that both the film stock and the gas used by the projection machine are highly flammable, and there is a real danger of an explosion. Once the projection machine is started, I must insist that all cigarettes be extinguished — and all pipes," he added, with a glance at Captain Ferry.

The next business of the meeting was a talk by one of the Royal Engineers on the subject of Euston station in its early days. He was mainly concerned with the *sidings* of Euston station, and almost all of his talk went by the board anyhow, what with King, the assistant, Jarvis and Layth clattering about with the projection machine, testing the flow of gas from canisters in haversacks to the light box attached behind the projector, and the hanging of the picture sheet — an ordinary white bed sheet as far as I could see — on to the wall opposite.

The end of the talk on Euston coincided with the dramatic climax of the preparations, namely the hanging of black cloth over the stained-glass window (which left the hot air coloured a murky blue and gold), and the lighting of the lime in the light box. Miss Bailey put out her Woodbine. There was now a white light on the picture sheet, black scratches flying through that light, which suddenly gave way to words, "WALLACE KING BRINGS THE WORLD TO YOU".

"Just a bit of header left over from my theatrical presentations," said King. "In the picture houses back home, by the way, it would cost you one and six to see this film."

He wasn't joking either. The desert now appeared on the screen. Well, two palm trees against a pile of stones, perhaps with the river flowing behind — it would have been the Euphrates rather than the Tigris. The next minute we were looking at the sky, and many black scratches were flying through *it* too — but there was also a great black flying crow in the picture. It was immediately obvious to me that the projection machine was redoubling the already stifling heat of the room. I moved my fingertips across my forehead, and sweat ran freely down the back of my hand.

"It was very hard to get this shot," Wallace King was saying, and I thought: *Who's giving this talk? You or Harriet Bailey?* We were now looking at the bird from a different angle. "It's just a bit of scene-setting," said Wallace King, "bit of atmosphere."

232

Harriet Bailey smiled and rolled her eyes in the direction of Shepherd, who gave a boyish grin back.

"This was a month ago," said King, "when Miss Bailey went to Babylon to look at the, er . . . antiquities. It was not Miss Bailey's first visit, by the way. I believe she went there many times before the war. That right, Miss Bailey?"

Miss Bailey nodded.

"She went to see what sort of mess the Germans have made of the place . . ." said King.

"It was ruined *before*, Mr King," said Harriet Bailey. "In fact, the German team there did some excellent work of preservation."

"Tommyrot," said one of the Royal Engineers.

Now the view had changed: there was a small tank engine on two-foot-gauge track, steam flowing away rapidly from it.

"Ah," said Miss Bailey. "This is what you've all come to see — a train."

"It's a *locomotive* actually," said Shepherd, grinning and colouring up.

In the film, Miss Bailey walked up to the engine, and faced the camera. She was smoking. Three Royal Engineers took up position beside her. After a while, all their smiles ran out, and with an effort they all renewed them. "It's not exactly the Orient Express, is it?" said Miss Bailey. "Perhaps Colonel Shepherd will put us in the picture."

". . . A pannier tank of German manufacture . . . Note the low-set boiler and short chimney for maximum stability on the narrow, rough-laid track. The line is of two-foot gauge. It was put in by the Germans five years or so ago, and runs from the ruins at Babylon just a little way south to a spot called Hillah on the Euphrates. It *was* connected to Baghdad but the Turks blew that stretch up a couple of miles outside the town. We mean to restore the connection."

On the screen, Miss Bailey now stood alongside a wooden hut. She was holding on to her straw hat in what appeared to be a sandstorm.

"This shows the station," she said. "It's gone now, I believe?" she added.

"A patrol reported it missing a fortnight ago," said Shepherd.

At this, Findlay spoke up rather timidly. "Missing? You can't very well lose a railway station can you?"

"It was stolen," said Shepherd. Findlay looked perplexed, and Shepherd blushed as he added, "We assume it was dismantled and taken by natives — for firewood."

We now saw the station from side on, minus Harriet Bailey.

Brigadier General Barnes said to Shepherd, "You mean to replace it, I hope?"

"A new one will be built . . . of bricks," said Shepherd.

"Reminds me of the three pigs," said Harriet Bailey. "What are you going to call it? Babylon Junction? I'm not sure I approve."

Somebody called out, "Change here for the Tower!" It was Findlay, and there was some laughter.

There now appeared on the picture sheet a worn-down city amid grey sand.

234

"Ah," said Miss Bailey, "the kingdom of Nebuchadnezzar."

We'd seen the last of the railway, it appeared, and Harriet Bailey began explaining the ruins. It went over my head, and I had a pretty good notion it was going over the head of Wallace King as well, who sat by the projector, occasionally whispering to his assistant. I could tell he was itching to interrupt Harriet Bailey though, and as she said, "This is the east side of the palace," he stood and pointed to Captain Ferry. "That man," he said, "is your pipe out?"

"It . . ."

The assistant continued to turn the projector handle; he seemed to be counting in his head.

". . . will be soon," Ferry concluded, and something about the long pause, and the steadiness of the stare he gave back intimidated King, who sat down without a further word. It was his assistant who then said, "End of the first reel of Babylon." Somebody pulled aside the black window cloth, and the hot light poured in. A window was opened, and I walked over to get a breath of what passed for air in Baghdad. Down in Quiet Square, an Arab paced. He was being quiet all right, but there was something funny about him.

At the table, King's assistant was handing around the still photographs he'd taken.

The man in the square was treading the shadow of the telegraph wire, like a tightrope-walker. I had thought for a moment that he held a cane as he walked, for the Arabs often did. It wasn't a cane, however, it was a rifle. At the table, somebody was making a joke,

235

"By the waters of Babylon, we sat down and wept." The photographs evidently showed Miss Bailey and her party at the ruins.

The Arab bothered me; I meant to say something to the party at the table, where I saw Wallace King's assistant giving a handful of photographs to Major Findlay. Findlay, evidently, was meant to look at the photographs and then to circulate them. He looked at the first of the pictures, gave a half smile and passed it to the Royal Engineer sitting next to him.

I looked down at the square: still the Arab paced.

At the table, Findlay inspected another photograph. And he suddenly froze. The look he then gave Harriet Bailey, and the look on the face of Jarvis — who stood behind Findlay while pouring champagne, and who could plainly see the photograph — made me move rapidly to where Jarvis stood. But Findlay placed the photograph face down, like a man folding his hand at poker. He glanced left and right, to see if anyone else had seen it. Jarvis, standing behind him, was left out of account: I believed that Findlay had not noticed him. All of the following happened in a moment. The steady ticking of the projection machine started up again. This was not the showing of the second reel but only preparatory to it, for the black cloth was not over the window. King was in conference with his assistant as the words "WALLACE KING BRINGS THE WORLD TO YOU" appeared once again on the picture sheet, but this time paler, seeming more inconsequential, the room being light. More of the Babylonian ruins — also paler — appeared on the picture sheet. I made out the great statue of a lion as Major Findlay picked up the photograph that had caused such a reaction in both him and Jarvis, and began raising it towards his top tunic pocket.

The photograph did not get there however, for the stained-glass window burst; there was a splash of red on that tunic pocket of Findlay's; the lion tilted and disappeared. The machine was over, hit by a bullet. Everybody was over. The projection machine was aflame in a confusion of shouts and sharp zinging sounds as further bullets flew into the room. Shepherd was at the window, shooting his revolver into the square. Every other man was down, although I didn't believe anyone had taken a bullet. I had an image of Harriet Bailey, sitting on the floor, anxiously touching her beautiful curls. Findlay was moving towards her — explaining that the splash of red on his tunic was only red wine. The table was over, and the photograph had spilled to the floor . . .

A Royal Engineer had flung the door wide, and the room emptied in a moment. There was almost laughter from some — what with all the excitement — as we clattered down the shaking iron staircase. Major Findlay seemed to run with his right arm around the shoulder of Miss Bailey. Well, she tolerated it, all right. I thought: She is the one white woman in Baghdad; she must be protected. But of course there was more to it than that.

Major Findlay had not brought away the photograph that had concerned both him and Jarvis. Immediately before quitting the room I had looked at it on the floor, and I had seen . . . not Miss Bailey and friends amid the ruins of Babylon, but Miss Bailey in Basrah (I recognised the waterway, the type of the square house with battered veranda behind), and not alone there either. My first thought had been that I was looking at a picture of myself kissing the lady, but I had never done any such thing, not even in my dream. It had been Captain Boyd that I saw. I recognised him from the floor of the *Salon de Thé* even though his face in the picture had been in profile. It had been not more than two inches away from Miss Bailey's, who had looked very glad to have it so close.

As our party descended into the dark lobby of the building, with the double doors closed in front of us, it was evident that nobody knew what the next move ought to be, and since there were still gunshots from the square, our lives might depend upon it. But I was still thinking of the photograph, and cursing myself for having left it in the room.

CHAPTER
FIFTEEN

When we all judged that the Arabs in the square had left off firing, or perhaps somewhat in advance of that moment, Lieutenant Colonel Shepherd opened one of the double doors. The light had begun to fall; one yellow pi-dog wandered through the square. The bells of the Church of the Saviour's Mother set up a furious clattering — this by way of a belated alarm. The sound only served to point up the emptiness and quietness of Quiet Square.

We bolted into it in chaotic fashion nonetheless. Everybody took off down the different alleyways. I had my own eye on Harriet Bailey and Major Findlay, who both went together towards the narrowest alleyway, heads kept low.

Lieutenant Colonel Shepherd hesitated in the square, a few yards from me. Seconds before, Jarvis had been there with him. I glanced up at the veranda of the room we'd just quit: black smoke tumbled upwards from the shattered windows. Major Findlay whisked Miss Bailey off along the narrow alley, and I saw Shepherd, revolver still in hand, going the same way a moment later. How did things stand between those three? In the meetings of the club, Miss Bailey had seemed keener on Shepherd than Findlay, but that might only have meant that Findlay was really the favoured one, for that sort of game was always a deep one, with many a double bluff involved.

I meant to give chase, but the three had disappeared from the alley by the time I reached the entrance. They might have taken any one of a dozen passageways leading off, and the light was now fading fast. I returned to the middle of the square, where in my uncertainty I made one complete revolution before haring off along the alleyway opposite to the one just mentioned. The direction I'd decided on would take me back to Rose Court. I must put my hands on my own revolver; and I would find Jarvis and quiz him about the meaning of the photograph.

But Jarvis was not at Rose Court, neither was Ahmad, and neither was the Webley. I made a quick search of all rooms. I turned Jarvis's pack upside down, and found nothing out of the way. There was a picture postcard in there, addressed to Jarvis. The view was of the harbour at Scarborough, and the writer had been mad on exclamation marks. "Stan! Billy is back from France! He has bought The Ship Inn with his Blighty Money! He says the loss of three fingers is nothing! He says The Ship will soon be back on an even keel! He says Arras will be the breakthrough on the Western Front! He says you will be wearing your nightshirt all day when you come back, like the Arabs! (But what does Billy know? And we would all now like to hear your own tales, since he is beginning to repeat his.

You've knocked over the blooming Turks. What's keeping you?)"

I doubled back rapidly into the labyrinth.

I was looking for Jarvis, Findlay, Shepherd, Miss Bailey — and I wanted to know what had become of the club building. As I ran, I came into a gaslit part of the labyrinth, and it seemed I was seeing things illuminated for a reason — to show me that time itself had gone wrong: a camel reversing down an alleyway, an Arab glimpsed in a doorway, sitting cross-legged on the floor writing with an ink pot balanced on his knee. He seemed to be recording slowly events that were happening fast. The sight of the man distracted me, and I took a wrong turn. I stood in a blank, black alleyway, listening hard, and sure enough I heard a shot. I didn't know which way to move in order to go away from it or towards. I froze for a moment, then bolted towards an archway that framed a leaning palm. The palm, I saw when I came through the arch, stood alone in a gravelled square made up of three blank walls, and the front — the front *only* — of a dead-looking red-brick fortification behind which lay a mass of smashed bricks. A man lay along the bottom of this façade, so close up against it that I had not at first noticed him. It was Jarvis, and he was on his back, his face tilted towards the base of the wall, as though inspecting it. But he couldn't have been inspecting anything, because there was a hole in the back of his head. In his right hand, which lay over his chest, he held the Webley. There was a discolouration on the upper part of his uniform that I turned away from, something thicker, whiter, worse than blood. I heard a footfall on the gravel, turned and Shepherd came pell-mell into the square, gun in hand.

But he could not have killed Jarvis. I had entered the square only seconds after hearing the gunshot, and Shepherd hadn't been there then, as far as I had seen. As he spoke to me — which he did while kneeling next to Jarvis — I looked all around the square. There were three alleyways leading off. For Shepherd to have shot Jarvis from some way along any one of these . . . his bullet would have had to go around a corner.

Shepherd was saying, "I believe it's your piece."

He took it gently from Jarvis, and handed me back the revolver. He seemed to think nothing of doing so.

"He'd been cleaning it," I said.

Shepherd was carefully moving Jarvis's right arm.

"I'm going to look in his pockets," he said. He was cool as usual.

"Why?" I said.

"He went back into the club to fetch something."

"A photograph?" I said.

Shepherd eyed me, and for the first time in our acquaintance, it was a sharp look that he gave me.

"You saw it?" he said.

I said, "It showed Boyd with Harriet Bailey."

Shepherd resumed his inspection of Jarvis's shirt pockets.

"Hold on a minute," I said, "the place was on fire."

Having searched through the first of Jarvis's pockets, Shepherd had now started on the second. He was shaking his head: "Just a lot of smoke," he said.

"Did *you* see the photograph, sir?"

242

He hadn't had sight of it in the clubhouse, as far as I could recall.

He said, "No, but I knew there was something queer about it from the way Findlay reacted to it. I quizzed Jarvis after we came out of the building, and we agreed it could have a bearing on the murder of Boyd. I kept them talking while he went back. They would have gone straight in themselves after it otherwise."

By "them", he meant Major Findlay and Harriet Bailey.

"It's not there," he said, and he sat back on the gravel, holding Jarvis's paybook and pocket book. He sat with ankles crossed, knees upraised, arms around knees — like a boy. He had re-holstered his Colt revolver. He said, "I know Jarvis told you all about Captain Boyd. He was found stabbed to death at the station. We believed it might *not* have been Arabs that killed him."

"You think Findlay killed Boyd over Miss Bailey?"

He nodded.

"Jarvis believed there was an attachment between the lady and Captain Boyd. He had reason to believe Boyd had been wiring her from here when she was in Basrah — before she came up."

Was Jarvis also acquainted with the amenable Private Lennon at the Residency? Had he had sight of the same telegram forms as me?

"In the photograph," I said, "they're practically kissing."

Shepherd nodded. "Which is why Findlay would have wanted to get hold of it as well."

"Did he also do for Jarvis?" I said, turning again to the body. "Surely Jarvis made away with *himself?*"

"I'd say it's a certainty," said Shepherd. And he could see that I wanted to know *why* that was the case. "There's no sign of a struggle, and he wasn't shot from a distance." With a tilt of the head, he indicated Jarvis, and I looked the same way. "He shot himself through the mouth — powder marks all round the lips."

I knew he was right.

"Why would he shoot himself?"

"I got to know him a little bit," said Shepherd. "It was obvious enough he didn't care for this place."

He looked all around the empty square: what was horrible about it was that it didn't look as though it belonged to Baghdad. It was just an all-purpose nightmare setting. "He was what I believe is called depressive," said Shepherd.

"He told me *Boyd* was that."

"Boyd was a machine-gunner," said Shepherd, a trace of the sharpness returning. "They're not usually very reflective types. Jarvis was describing himself."

"Then do you mean Findlay has come by, discovered the body, and taken the photograph?" I answered my own question. "No, because I got here pretty sharpish after hearing the shot. I mean, there was no time, was there?"

Shepherd gave a half shrug, saying, "I believe Findlay *would* have gone after the picture himself. Returned to the club, I mean — after he got clear of me. He'd have discovered Jarvis had beaten him to it, in which case he'd have been looking for Jarvis."

244

"How would he know Jarvis had been in?"

"He might have seen him coming out . . . Or from Layth. He does have some English, and he never left the building."

Shepherd rose to his feet.

I said, "*When* did Jarvis go in after the photograph?"

"About three-quarters of an hour ago. I've been charging about looking for him."

"How did you disentangle yourself from Major Findlay and Harriet Bailey, sir?"

"They disentangled themselves from *me*," he said, with a ghost of the old smile. "Findlay made it perfectly clear he wanted rid of me."

"Where was this?"

"Some alleyway between here and the club premises."

Silence in the square.

Shepherd was holding his Turkish cigarettes out to me. I reached out, but he dropped the packet, and put his hand to his revolver. We heard a footfall, echoing in the square. I raised my own revolver. A patrol entered the square: a British sergeant and three sepoys. Shepherd went to them, giving over Jarvis's paybook and papers, which he had taken from his pockets while searching for the photograph. He explained that the dead man had been my batman. Of the circumstances of Jarvis's death, he told the sergeant nothing more than that we'd found the man shot — that it was very likely suicide. The man had been in a rather low state of health recently; he was oppressed by the heat, and the three of us had been under attacks from insurgents earlier in the evening; we'd all had a very narrow shave, and Jarvis had been badly knocked by the experience.

The sergeant asked: "Killed himself? With what, sir?" His voice echoed in the dead square.

I came forward and showed him the Webley. "It's my piece," I said; "Private Jarvis took it for cleaning." The matter could have been awkward for me, but the sweat and the agitation on the sergeant's face was all down to the great humidity of the evening, and not at all to do with perplexity over the death of Jarvis. He was taking a note of our explanation, but made no attempt to claim the Webley as evidence. It was very obvious to all of us that it was easier to kill yourself with an officer's revolver than with the rifle of the private — it was just another privilege of rank. As the sergeant made his note, I looked over to Jarvis, lying with his face turned away, as though in distaste for us all.

"But might not *Harriet Bailey* have killed Boyd?" I said.

"No."

"Why not?"

"Well," said Shepherd, "she's too small."

"She's tough though, practically lives in the desert from what I can gather."

We were on Park Street, closing fast on the cavalry barracks. We'd come this way via Quiet Square, where Shepherd had discovered from Layth that Jarvis had indeed returned and gone up alone to the empty club room. After he'd left, Findlay had turned up with Harriet Bailey. They too had gone up to the room — and it appeared that Layth *had* told Findlay that Jarvis

246

had been there first. It had taken the best part of a quarter of an hour to get this out of the Arab, who spoke of Jarvis as "Mr Stanley", Findlay as "Effendi Fine Lay", and Harriet Bailey as "El Khatun", meaning "The Lady".

At eleven o'clock at night, nothing less than a gymkhana had seemed to be in progress on the dusty gaslit field in front of the cavalry buildings. Late night and early morning were I believed the busiest times for exercising the horses — away from the heat of the day. Cavalry officers on their mounts criss-crossed the field; orderlies on fodder fatigue carted straw bales about the place; in the stable courts, men swabbed horses from buckets of water. Shepherd and I saw it all from the main gate, where Shepherd addressed a sentry: "Captain Stringer and Lieutenant Colonel Shepherd to see Major Findlay of the Ninth Hussars."

Major Findlay, the sentry was telling Shepherd, had signed back in half an hour ago.

"Where will we find him?" said Shepherd.

"In Dunn's." (Or it might have been "Dun's" or "duns".)

"What's that?" said Shepherd. He was running out of charm, fast.

"That side of the house," said the sentry, indicating the right-hand side of the main barracks building, which was another of the Baghdad music halls: all domes and turrets, like something dreamt rather than built.

As we made towards it, the sentry called out, "He might be in the bath if he's any sense."

Shepherd called back, "Why?"

"Because it's bath time."

For all its fantastical front, the inside of the building smelt of dubbin, and was Spartan in the extreme. The bathhouse, we discovered, was in the basement: a white-painted room with ranks of partitions created by red velvet curtains. The officers were in tin baths behind the curtains. It was a peaceful scene. The gas burnt low; smoke rose up from behind a couple of the curtains but no steam. These were cold baths. Most of the men in them were silent, save for the occasional grunt and splash, but two of the bathers, in adjacent enclosures, were conversing, their voices echoing.

One said, "Apparently, the Kaiser has become a Moslem so as to impress the Arabs."

"Utter *rot*," said the other.

Shepherd and I patrolled the gangway between the booths. I knew what he was looking for. Perfectly ordinary dining room chairs stood in this gangway, set at various angles, each one bedecked with the uniform of a bathing cavalry officer. Shepherd had stopped by one of the chairs. He indicated the tunic to me: a red wine stain. He too had seen the accident that had befallen Findlay when the bullets had started flying.

From behind the adjacent curtain there came no sound. Shepherd reached for the inside pocket of the tunic. He brought out an identity card and a photograph, displaying them to me silently like a conjurer doing a trick. One of the two conversing bathers spoke up again.

"Do you know what I saw the other day? A fellow sleeping on a walking camel."

The identity card held by Shepherd was Major Findlay's; the photograph was of Harriet Bailey and the late Captain Boyd nearly kissing. From beyond the curtain there came the sound of a great waterfall. Findlay had risen to his feet in the bath. Shepherd eyed me, the beginnings of a smile on his face. Did he mean to confront Findlay? There came another waterfall: Findlay *stepping* from the bath. Shepherd slid the papers and the picture back into the pocket of the tunic. We walked fast from the bathhouse and barracks.

Lieutenant Colonel Shepherd and I sat in the same vis-à-vis as during our first proper talk: that is to say, we faced each other over a low table, with glasses of brandy before us. Only now there were revolvers — his Colt, my Webley — by the glasses, and whereas it had been the guests of the Midland Grand Hotel who had slept all around us on that occasion, it was now the residents of Baghdad who slept. Well, mostly. Distant shouts would come through the opened windows at the veranda. I had heard three wild cries of "Allahu Akhbar!" from perhaps half a mile away as Shepherd had poured the drinks.

He'd suggested we go back to his place for a nightcap. We drank in his main upper room, which had the same general set-up as my own: little furniture and all of it low, including a carved wooden chest by the wall. He had no flytrap, and so the room fairly swarmed with them, but Shepherd didn't seem to mind, or notice. Indicating his gun, I said, "Mind if I . . .?"

He nodded, and I picked up the piece. It was a double-action, like most of the Colts in Baghdad. I said, "Jarvis told me Boyd favoured the *single*-action." I eyed Shepherd and he gave a half smile. "It's a lovely weapon, the single. If I could lay my hands on one, I would do. A chap out on a desert patrol in the first week . . . he wandered away from the other fellows, and got held up by an Arab who took his gun off him: a single-action. The Arab was about to shoot the poor fellow, but he couldn't understand the mechanism — didn't know you had to cock it. Eventually, he gave up in disgust, and threw it back." Shepherd hesitated, blushed. "So of course our chap shot *him*."

A long beat of silence; then Shepherd said, "I ought to have gone after the picture myself."

Over my glass, I looked a question at him.

". . . Can't have done anything for his state of mind," said Shepherd. "The photograph amounted to proof of adultery on both sides, and Boyd was quite a figure in Jarvis's eyes. He wrote to the wife, you know, after the body was turned up."

The same wife who'd wanted me to pass on her love.

I said, "Assuming we're right about Findlay, what do you reckon Miss Bailey thinks?"

"That woman is a closed book to me," said Shepherd.

"You and she seem to hit it off pretty well, sir."

"Well," he said, "as to *that* . . ." and he coloured up and trailed off.

"Maybe he was making himself a nuisance," I said.

"My suspicion is that she has some idea of what's happened but doesn't know the full picture, and doesn't want to. It stretches credibility to think she's completely ignorant. She's incredibly clever you know." He refilled our glasses from the brandy bottle and put his feet on the table. "She has a first-class degree from Oxford — only it's informal."

"Why?"

"Because she's a woman. They can't formally be degree-holders."

"Do you have a first-class degree sir?"

He grinned. "I have what's called a Gentleman's Degree."

"Really, sir? Stevens made out you were practically a professor."

"Well, from his particular *perspective* . . ."

I didn't believe he had been particularly set back by the deaths of either of Stevens or Jarvis. He had enjoyed the game of going to Samarrah, which had done for the one, and he'd enjoyed the game of searching out the picture, which had done for the other, albeit by a wound self-inflicted.

"My degree attests that I had a thoroughly good time in my three years at Cambridge, nothing more."

"I thought all Oxbridge types were highly academic."

"They're all *well off*, Jim," he said, "all well off."

The voice of Manners had been echoing in my head: I must show *discretion*. But Shepherd and I had become quite confidential, and Manners could go hang. I would not let slip that I was on a secret job for the government, but I must step a little way into the open.

I said, "There's a damn silly rumour about yourself, sir . . ." I ought not to have said "damn silly". That was me like a man trying to sound like an army captain. Anyhow I'd got Shepherd's attention.

"It says that when you were part of the vanguard, on the night the city fell . . . that you went into the railway station, and you met with a Turkish officer . . ."

Shepherd had set down both cigarette and glass; he did not take his eyes from me. He was indicating that he knew I was more nervous than him.

". . . That you met with a Turkish officer," I said again, "and that . . ."

"And that what?" said Shepherd. "It's true enough so far."

I was thinking I should never have started in on this, and that if it hadn't been for the brandy, I never *would* have done.

"It's that you went into the station and received from the Turk a quantity of . . ."

"What?"

"Treasure."

"A bribe?"

"I suppose so."

Shepherd now did the following. He caught up his revolver; he stood; he holstered his revolver. He turned on his heel and quit the room. I believed he'd gone downstairs, and I eyed the chest against the wall. I moved rapidly towards it, lifted the lid. It was one of the emptiest chests I'd ever seen. I sat back down, and

252

a moment later, Shepherd re-entered the room holding a tin box about a foot square. It was pretty; lavender-coloured with swirling Arabic script on it — Turkish Arabic, perhaps. Shepherd set it on the table, sat down.

"Turkish delight," he said, pouring two more brandies. "Perhaps you'd like to come in with me, Jim?"

Pouring two more brandies, Shepherd said, "I must say, the fellow was extremely courteous; spoke beautiful French and said that even though we were at war, he hoped there would be no unpleasantness between us. He said he would like to reach an accommodation with me. He was in charge of the last train of the Turkish retreat. It was in steam and we walked the length of the platform looking through the windows by the light of his lantern: three passenger carriages and one goods van. It was full of wounded Turks, but there was a quantity of ordnance in the goods van. He meant to take the train out. He said we'll have a scrap over it if you want, and some more men will die, and if you manage to stop us leaving you'll have a hundred Turkish wounded on your hands — or words to that effect. I said, 'You can go if you uncouple the weapons.' He agreed to that, and while the job was being done, he said in jocular fashion, 'We'll be back to reclaim Baghdad shortly, in the meantime please keep it in good order for us' — which was a *bit* rich, since he and his pals had spent the past twenty-four hours blowing the place up. He asked me whether I'd heard of the great railway from Berlin to Baghdad that his people were building. I said I'd attended a lecture on the subject just a few weeks before. He said, 'You have a passion for railways.' I didn't contradict him. He took me into the station buffet, or one of them — what was left of it after the Turks had ripped the place up. Not the *tea* place, where I believe Boyd was found on the Friday before last. Not the tea place at all. It was the *coffee* place next door."

Well, I'd been in there myself, but I had decided against any further declarations.

Shepherd reached forward and opened the tin. He took out a handful of what appeared to be coins, passed one to me. I saw the Arabic inscription on one side, the image of the locomotive on the other, and the eyehole on the top, so that a green and red ribbon might be threaded through. It was covered in white powder.

"There's a display to do with the Berlin-Baghdad line in the coffee place," said Shepherd. "These are, or were, a feature of it. Copper medals minted by the Turkish government for small investors in the line." He eyed me, smiling. "I have *not* invested in the Berlin-Baghdad railway, Jim. The extent of my treachery is that I accepted the half dozen of these medals that he put in this tin, which was lying about on the floor, and handed to me. They're quite worthless, I assure you."

I nodded. "What's the white powder?"

"Lick it," he said.

It was sugar.

"This tin once held Turkish delight. I suppose that when I walked away from the station holding it, the medallions inside must have . . . rattled about rather. Who started this rumour about me, Jim?"

"I don't know," I said. I was in bother now, for of course there'd be no rumour, just the allegation of Boyd, which might or might not have been leaked.

"Jarvis," I said, since Jarvis was dead.

"Jarvis?" said Shepherd, and he looked sidelong for a while. "I'd almost counted him a friend."

"He didn't believe it for a minute, sir," I added hastily. "He said it was a shame you didn't know about it yourself. Then you'd be able to nail it."

"But where did the rumour *come* from?" said Shepherd. "Where did it originate?"

We both drank our brandies; I was lost for any reply.

"Wait a bit," said Shepherd. "Did it come from Boyd? Because he was on the spot; he saw me in the station, saw me coming out."

I could see that this must be a terrible idea to him: that the man whose murder he was trying to solve should be the source of an evil rumour about him. I shook my head. My shirt was entirely sodden.

"I really couldn't say, sir," I said.

"Because if it was known that Boyd was saying those kinds of things about me, and if it *was* Findlay who did for him, then he might have felt that he could act with impunity."

I nodded.

"Since the blame would fall . . . on me."

He gave a half smile, and a look of wonderment, as though he admired the cleverness of the idea.

CHAPTER
SIXTEEN

The sun was orange, then red — then it merged with the whiteness of the sky, and set about doing its damage in earnest. I watched it through the window from my bed. It seemed to shake slightly, with the intensity of its hatred of the world.

The night before, I had once again neglected to close the sun shutters. At seven or so, Ahmad had come in with sweet tea, and questions concerning the whereabouts of Jarvis. I had waved him away from behind the mosquito net, and felt bad about it.

I lay in a half doze, and at mid-morning I reached for my bed sheet, and pulled it over. I was shivering — or shaking anyhow — at the same time as sweating. I had got properly ill, and it was almost a relief. I could not think exactly *why* I was ill, but it was what was meant to happen in Baghdad. I would put myself under the doctor — there were plenty of them at the Hotel, and in the hospital by the cavalry barracks — and then there would be someone else making the decisions in my case.

With an effort, I rose from my bed, and closed the sun shutters. Having been almost cold, I was now back to roasting. I lay down again. Was cholera the trouble? I did not think so, since I did not have the runs. I pictured Captain Boyd and Major Findlay at the station. They would have met, judging by the condition of Boyd's body, on the day before I turned up in Baghdad . . . met at Boyd's favoured "safe place", the place in which he'd also set up the meeting with me. Well, it was out of the way and yet within easy reach of the ranges where, as a gunner, Boyd might have spent a good deal of his time. In the tea place, there would have been some conflab: "You keep away from her, you understand?" It being impossible to reach agreement, they had started a fight.

I thought of Jarvis. I would write to his parents. "I am very sorry to have to tell you . . ." Ought I to state that he had made away with himself? A man born into the officer class would know that sort of thing automatically. What *was* the form? Perhaps the adjutant would write in the first place, stating the truth as per the coroners' courts — that he took his own life while the balance of his mind was disturbed. I would then follow up saying that he had come under great strain from the climate while performing his duties in exemplary fashion. If I myself died before I could write it . . . then at least I wouldn't have to.

At five, I crawled from under the mosquito net, ate two ginger biscuits and boiled water for tea. I returned to the bed, and rolled up the mosquito net, thinking it was a very ridiculous article. In this town, you might as well try to keep the air off as the mosquitoes.

When the sun began to drop, I dressed, and slowly pursued my way back to the cavalry barracks. I wore

257

my gun. On arrival at the gate, I saw that another gymkhana was in progress. I held out my identity card to the sentry, saying, "I want to see Major . . ."

I had meant to confront Findlay, but I knew I wasn't up to it.

The sentry appeared to be scowling. A horse had broken away from the general criss-crossing of the field, a woman on it. When Miss Bailey saw me beside the gate, she still came on, but with less enthusiasm. I took my cap off.

"Captain Stringer," she said, and the sentry seemed amazed that I knew her. He was probably amazed that I knew *anyone*, given the state of me. The two of us — three if you included Miss Bailey's horse, from which she did not descend — moved a little way from the sentry, but it was clear that ours was going to be a short talk. The horse was bucking about, kept wanting to start off towards its gallop in the park, and Miss Bailey gave every indication of wanting it to do just that. Neither horse nor rider was still for a minute, as I said, "Are you quite all right, after last night, I mean?"

"Quite all right, but how are you? And I was very sorry to hear about your man."

Well, there were any number of ways she could have found out about Jarvis. It wore me out to think of them.

"I suppose it was all too much of a strain for him," she said. "Are you quite all right, Captain Stringer? because you don't look it."

I said, "I'm curious about Captain Boyd."

258

"Captain Boyd? Captain Boyd is dead," she said, with no change in the agitation of herself and the horse. "He was killed at the railway station."

"I know — that's why."

"What do you mean?"

I could say everything or nothing, except I didn't have the energy for the former. I recalled what I'd said to the southpaw at number 11 Clean Street. "I was at school with him," I said.

"You were *not*," she said. "If you're going to go to the lengths of lying about it, I suppose you must have a good reason for wanting to find out about him."

"Well," I said, "I do."

"But I can't help you, I'm afraid."

And she was off.

"Are you coming up to Samarrah?" I called after her, and whilst galloping away and holding down her bowler, she shook her head.

CHAPTER
SEVENTEEN

Another driver from Corps HQ took me to Baghdad station, and this time I arrived to find a great sense of stir: Tommies on long ladders repainting the place; the repair of both the tea and coffee salons was being taken in hand. In the railway territory beyond, work gangs were fettling three new locomotives; a vacuum engine was being fitted to the turntable. And once again *The Elephant* stood ready and facing Samarrah.

It was seven in the morning, and I was feeling a little better, but still not right. Major Findlay, swathed in cavalryman's clobber, was standing beside the tender and speaking to one of the Royal Engineer officers who would be riding with us, together with a couple of their own batmen. Besides the holstered revolver, a .303 short-magazine Lee Enfield rifle was held by a strap over Findlay's shoulder. About his neck were three bandoliers of ammunition, a haversack and a canvas water bag. He carried a rolled groundsheet, and wore cord riding breeches and long boots. All in all, he could have done with a horse, and indeed he was saying, "Strange to be unmounted, though. Do you know, I very nearly brought a bag of oats!"

He *had* brought a dozen saddles for delivery to Samarrah, and these had been loaded into the Turkish veranda carriage that was again coupled up to *The Elephant*. Stacked alongside them were some other Samarrah-bound crates, but our mission was to do with looking over the railway lines rather than provisioning the garrison, which received most of its supplies by river or by motor from Baghdad.

The Royal Engineer now moved away from Findlay, who was left looking handsome but too red-faced on the platform, and above all sad. For one thing, he must now have discovered that Miss Harriet Bailey would not be riding with us. But he himself could not back out of the trip; it would not be honourable.

I tried to imagine his movements after the break-up of the club meeting.

The important photograph had shown the former sweetheart of his own sweetheart (it was all these silly, romantic-story terms that came to mind when I thought of the matter). If Findlay *had* killed his rival in love, namely Boyd, then he would have gone all out to get back the picture. If he had *not* killed Boyd, then he would still — being a gentleman — have gone after it, to save Miss Bailey's honour and spare her blushes (as the papers read by the mill girls had it). My guess was that he had got it back by finding Jarvis and ordering him to hand it over. Perhaps he'd given him a terrible slanging into the bargain, threatening who knew what punishments for making away with the private property of another person, and a lady at that. On the face of it, Findlay seemed mild enough, but the behaviour of an

261

officer in company with his fellows was no guide to his behaviour with other ranks, and having seen that picture he wouldn't be in a good mood.

On top of this, Findlay must now suspect that he was being thought the likely killer of Boyd, since he knew that other parties were interested in the photograph that incriminated him. He knew Jarvis had gone after the photograph, but who did he think had sent Jarvis? Or did he think Jarvis was acting alone? It all depended what Jarvis had told him in his last moments. It occurred to me for the first time that Findlay might have thought *I'd* sent Jarvis in after the photograph. Jarvis was my batman, after all.

Findlay looked along the platform and saw me. After a moment's hesitation on either side we saluted, and he climbed up into the carriage. I would have to confront him before long. As far as I could recall, I had not yet spoken a word to the man. From the other end of the platform, Lieutenant Colonel Shepherd had watched Findlay climb up. He came towards me.

"Did you speak to him about the picture, sir?" I said, indicating the carriage and Findlay within it.

Shepherd smiled, shook his head, in his bashful sort of way. "But we'll force the issue one way or another," he said. So perhaps Shepherd would do the confronting. He carried his pack, wore his haversack over his shoulder. There didn't seem to be anything much *in* the haversack, but his Colt revolver was in his holster, and he carried a spare Sam Browne belt with spare ammo pouch.

Shepherd was evidently convinced that Findlay had put Captain Boyd's lights out. That would be enough to set him against Findlay, but I had fanned the flames by speaking of the "rumour" of Shepherd's treachery, and raising the possibility that Findlay had known of it. Shepherd climbed up, and I watched through the dusty window as he and Findlay saluted one another. The smiles that followed were somewhat reserved, but cordial relations were being preserved for the moment. I heard a loud chuffing, and was for a moment back in the marshalling yards of York station, where I would wander on quiet days in the police office, just to watch the engines working. As a result of whatever ailed me, I found I was inclined to float in and out of myself.

The chuffing came from the tank engine that did duty as the Baghdad shunter, and it was bringing up a flat-bed wagon on which sat two radio cars held down by strong ropes. Captain Bob Ferry walked along the platform with his pack on his back, keeping pace with the wagon in a proprietorial sort of way, for they were *his* radio cars that sat upon it. My understanding was that he would be taking them to Samarrah and staying there a while with them, demonstrating their use to the men of the garrison — that he would not be entering the no man's land, in other words. Ferry wore shorts, and they had recently been ironed. His whole *person* had been ironed, it seemed to me, and he'd polished his Sam Browne belt. You were supposed to polish the belt, but nobody did. His revolver was a Webley, like my own. It too was highly polished, and looked deadlier as a result. We watched as the wagon was coupled up.

Ferry said, "When's the . . . off?"

"Five minutes," I said.

The radio cars looked like grocers' delivery vans with the rear sliced away, and wooden boxes covered with switches and dials stuffed in. Long wires stuck up from them, but the wonder of it was that these wires weren't connected to anything. It was all wire*less*. I said, "It's the latest thing in field communications, I believe."

"In their present state of development," said Ferry, "machines such as these are less efficient than . . ."

I waited. On the opposite platform, an Arab in a fez was staring at me: the bloody Baghdad station master. I had to get out of his line of sight, which meant I had to get away from Ferry. I would have to hurry him. "Less efficient than the telegraph?"

"Than the . . ."

"Telephone?"

". . . carrier pigeon."

I moved along the platform, so as to put the carriage between me and the station master. Ferry came with me. He climbed up, and I watched through the window as he took his seat at the opposite end of the saloon to Shepherd and Findlay. There was a small plaque fixed to the window where he sat. It might have read whatever was Turkish-Arabic for "No Smoking", or it might have read "Smoking". Either way, Ferry took from his pack the leathern wallet that held his pipes.

I walked forwards to the engine, and climbed on to the footplate where my fireman, a Royal Engineer, was fettling the fire. He was a pleasant sort; he'd said he was "rotten at firing" but he knew his way around an engine all right.

I was about to start oiling round when I heard a voice from along the platform. "Where can I put Mr King's champagne?"

I jumped down, and the whole station reeled. I shouldn't have done that. Wallace King's assistant was on the platform with the cine camera over his shoulder, a pack on his back, and a canvas bag in his hand. He was addressing an R.E., who leant from the carriage window. King himself was bringing up the rear, and carrying nothing. He overtook his assistant and came up to me, saying, "Can't seem to get any sense from anyone about how to keep the champagne chilled in the desert."

"No?" I said. I had still not stabilised after my leap.

"I mean, I take it there *is* ice?"

"In the restaurant car," I said.

"Oh," he said. "Fine. And where's that?"

Silence for a space. He eyed the one carriage and the flat-bed wagon.

"Are you taking the mickey?" he said.

I regained the footplate a moment later. A Royal Engineer who was acting as platform guard came up and said, "You can take it I've blown my whistle."

As I pulled the regulator, The Elephant seemed to go down as well as forwards. I watched my fireman breaking up the coal; I watched him *shovelling* coal. I could not have done that, and I found that I was clinging on to the regulator for support. As we cleared Baghdad, I looked to the right: more activity at the earthworks by the Tigris. Steam cranes and steam shovels were now in view, but still the scene looked Biblical.

And then we were into the desert proper.

The regulator was too hot for my hand already. I turned about to fetch a rag from the locker, and my fireman said, "Are you all right there?"

I nodded.

"She's a good steamer," said my fireman.

I nodded again.

Our black smoke seemed an affront to the desert. We ought not to be *bringing* smoke into a place like this. I leant out. Presently, the flame-like shimmer that would turn into Mushahida station was ignited on the horizon. It was a bigger shimmer than before, since the population had swelled: same number of Arabs but more Tommies. On our previous run I hadn't needed the regulator rag until after Mushahida, but we were now in June, the hottest month in Mesopotamia, as I had learnt from someone or other. I drank down half a bottle of tonic water, pitched the bottle into the desert. It annoyed me that it did not smash; I turned back to look at it as we raced away, thinking it might smash *later*. I took out my Woodbines. My colleague didn't smoke, and once I'd lit my own, I couldn't face it, so I pitched that away as well. Then I recommenced shivering. As I peered forward through the spectacle glass, it was important for me not to see the swoop and rise of the telegraph wires, for they made me sick, just as though *I'd* been swooping and rising.

266

My fireman said, "Are you *quite* sure you're all right?" and this time he answered his own question, saying, "I don't think you're in any fit condition to drive."

So he sat me down on the sandbox, and applied the brakes, bringing the engine to a perfect stop, right in the middle of nowhere. He held my arm as I climbed down, just as though I'd been about a hundred years old. Some of our party had climbed out of the carriage. Others leant out of the windows. They wanted to know why we'd stopped. My fireman provided the explanation.

In the carriage were a series of couches and armchairs. The armchairs at one end (where Ferry sat alone) were arranged in regular train-carriage formation, but at the other end of the carriage, the seats were jumbled anyhow. I was told to lie down on a dusty couch. A pillow was made of a groundsheet. Shepherd sat before me. He was reaching into his pack. He passed me a bottle of water and a biggish tablet.

"Take this," he said. "Just bite it once before swallowing."

I did so, and he gave a half smile.

"It's bitter," he said.

It was *so* bitter that I couldn't untwist my face after swallowing.

"Quinine," said Shepherd. "Only a precaution."

Quinine meant I had malaria. Of the dozens of mosquitoes that must have bitten me since my arrival, I had a fixed idea of the culprit: the one that had done me on the wrist while I was sitting before the campfire on the previous run. I indicated the mark to Shepherd, and we exchanged weak smiles. There were faces all around him. Bob Ferry looked on, calmly smoking. I thought: you should put that fucking thing out in the presence of an invalid. Major Findlay was saying, "Quinine . . . that's the ticket." Wallace King's assistant frowned alongside Findlay, with arms folded. He seemed on the point of speech when his master called to him from the opposite end of the carriage, saying, "We might as well take advantage of this delay." He already had the camera pointed through the window. He said, "I thought I saw something on the horizon just now. If they turn out to be Bedouins, we might try and get them to wave or something."

I slept. But I was somehow aware that Shepherd had gone forward to fire *The Elephant* while the Royal Engineer who'd been my mate was promoted to driver. I heard Major Findlay saying to one of the Royal Engineers, "Care for a barley sugar?" I couldn't make out the reply. Findlay said, "I like to see the telegraph poles. They're reassuring, somehow. But we don't have any signals, do we?" Again, I couldn't hear the answer. A little while later, I heard a sigh from Major Findlay. Was that the sigh of a killer? It was the sigh of a man in love, at any rate.

Later again, I heard the voice of Wallace King's assistant. "Mr King wants to start making features."

A voice I didn't recognise said, "How do you mean?"

"Feature *films*," said the assistant, "*story* films. He wants to make a film of the Battle of Trafalgar."

"Wouldn't that require a lot of . . ."

It was Ferry who had spoken.

"Money?" said the assistant, at length.

". . . ships?" said Ferry.

"You'd need *one*," said the assistant.

"There were a lot more ships at the Battle of Trafalgar than . . . one," said Ferry.

"The rest would be models," said the assistant. "He thinks he can bring it in for less than five hundred pounds. History, that's what people want to see in the picture halls. Just look at Tyrone Gould. He really hit the jackpot with *The Charge of the Light Brigade*, and it wasn't up to all that much."

"It was quite *shocking*, Wilson," said the voice of Wallace King, "and don't you forget it."

So I had finally learnt the name of the assistant. He might lead a dog's life at the hands of King, but I was jealous of him since he did not have malaria.

I was aware that we were making short stops — the Royal Engineers inspecting the line. When I awoke properly, we seemed to have been stopped for a longer time. I sat up. I was soaked in sweat, but felt better for my sleep. In the carriage, dazzle and gloom did battle. Every window was open. I heard voices from beyond. We were at Samarrah station, and I was the only man left in the carriage; the saddles were gone too. Shepherd was speaking to the clever, bespectacled major who was the head of the Samarrah garrison. I believed that Shepherd was saying something about me, for the major said, "Do you want to leave him here? Collect him on your way back? The devil of it is that our doctor's flat on his back with something." He then said, "Nothing for it but quinine. It usually works."

That was a relief, but not to any great degree. Everything was out of my hands, and I wanted to go to beyond Samarrah, where everything was out of *everyone's* hands, and we would all be on an equal footing. There, Shepherd would confront Findlay, and the truth would finally emerge.

Shepherd and Findlay walked into the station shack. At the far end of the platform, Captain Bob Ferry was talking to some Royal Engineers. Presently, they left him on his own, looking at the radio cars. I called to him: "Are we setting those down here?" There was a siding all ready and waiting for them.

Ferry turned and contemplated me. "We're . . . not," he said.

"You're staying with us then?"

". . . Yes," he said at length.

I had been rather hoping we would get rid of him.

We had made camp perhaps ten miles beyond the spot at which Stevens, Shepherd and I had come under attack. Viewing the desert glare from the carriage, I believe I had identified the remains of the fire we had lit, but of our single-fly tent and folding chairs there had been no sign. They must have been taken as booty by the Arabs. We had stopped a little while before passing that place — near the siding that held the motor launches. Shepherd and some of the Royal Engineers had walked to the wagons and looked them over for a second time, and once again no move was

270

made to couple them up. I had been travelling in the carriage, feeling . . . what was the word? A sort of continuous *oscillation*.

Our camp was at a ring of palms. They ought to have enclosed a beautiful lagoon. In fact, only our campfire burned in the middle of them, with cooking things and water bottles nearby — also canvas chairs and King's crate of champagne which, since it had practically boiled and was undrinkable, he had made generally available. We had chosen a spot near a feature of interest, namely some sand-coloured rocks, and the Royal Engineers had been walking about on them as if they'd never seen rocks before. They all had on keffiyahs, rather fancying themselves in them, and Wallace King and his assistant had been filming and photographing them. King had kept shouting to the man on the topmost rock: "Scan the horizon!" but the fellow couldn't do it for laughing. King had explained, "This footage is to be preceded by a placard reading, 'A forward patrol reconnoitres'," at which one of the Engineers had shouted back, "Why not change the bally placard? 'A forward patrol larks about on some rocks.'" That hadn't gone down well.

As for Shepherd: he and a couple of spare Engineers had walked a quarter mile along the line in order to inspect a second branch going off at a wide angle. The branch had been in a bad state; had apparently petered out in the desert, but three further Turkish wagons had been berthed upon it, and these held wooden crates that had contained, strange to say, an aeroplane, or parts thereof. It was not thought possible to run *The*

271

Elephant along the branch in order to collect this booty. I had viewed the wagons myself, through binoculars borrowed by the campfire.

After his return from that jaunt, Shepherd had got hold of a rifle and shot a gazelle, parts of which were now roasting on the stones in the fire. The fat would spurt from the meat — it was very fatty — with red sparks. Otherwise the flames were invisible in the white light.

Watching Shepherd slay the beautiful animal, I was reminded that he must still be a suspect in the case of the murdered Captain Boyd. His explanation of the Turkish "treasure" might have held water (I was inclined to think so), but that didn't mean he hadn't become aware that Boyd thought him a traitor.

Now, at the end of his exertions, Shepherd was taking a shower bath on the other side of *The Elephant*, which had been kept in steam as before. A Royal Engineer and one of the privates stood on top of the tender. They'd removed the cap off the water-filler hole, and were lowering into it at regular intervals a bucket on a rope. This they would then upend on to the man below. It was a service open to all comers.

Major Findlay, looking one degree redder than he had that morning, sat opposite me, on the other side of the fire, looking at a back number of *The Times*. I read, "New British Thrust East of the Vimy Ridge". Turning the page, he caught my eye. There was nothing for it: he would have to speak to me.

"You feeling better?"

"A little."

"I was sorry to hear about your man — Jarvis, wasn't it?"

I nodded, gave a mumbled "Sir."

"He was demoralised by the heat, no doubt . . . Or was it the attack? I suppose he'd never been under fire before."

I felt the need to defend Jarvis. "He *had* been, sir. At Kut-al-Amara."

Shepherd was approaching, fresh from his shower bath, hair combed back. He might have been stepping into the cocktail lounge of the Midland Grand Hotel, except that he wore his gun.

"Were you there, sir?" I asked Findlay.

"Where?"

"Kut."

He shook his head. "Came up straight from Basrah. I've never eaten antelope before," he went on, looking at the spluttering meat. "I'm looking forward to it. Well, I think I am."

Shepherd took hold of one of the folding seats. He'd caught the drift of our earlier conversation, and he wouldn't let Findlay change the course of it, for he asked, "Did you happen to see Jarvis after the meeting broke up?"

"Did I see *Jarvis*?" said Findlay. "I was attempting to protect the lady. Not that she takes kindly to any sort of chivalrous display," he added, with great regret.

I spent the next little while revolving this answer, as no doubt did Shepherd. Findlay *must* have seen Jarvis, since Jarvis had taken the photograph from the club room and then we'd found it in Findlay's pocket.

Shepherd offered a cigarette to Findlay, who took it, and began to smoke it rather crossly, it seemed to me. I had not seen him smoke before; I myself could not face a cigarette.

I looked up and saw a van speeding across the horizon. To my somewhat dazed mind it seemed to be towing behind it — sideways on — a gigantic cone. But it was only the sand that the wheels threw up. Captain Ferry was in that motor, I knew, together with a driver we'd picked up at Samarrah. It was one of the two radio vans. The other was also flying about in the vicinity. Sometimes the two would converge, and there would be a conference; then they'd roar off in opposite directions and attempt a wireless communication.

Findlay was now pacing near the rocks, while Shepherd was turning over the antelope steaks. It would soon be supper time, and all the party seemed to know it. At any rate, the Royal Engineers were converging on the fire, and I now saw that the two radio cars were racing towards us, dragging half the desert with them. They gave us a wide berth, so as to spare us the dust cloud, and came to a stop near *The Elephant*, where the four men climbed out. As the dust around them subsided, it was Captain Bob Ferry that I had my eye on. He went behind the engine, whereas the other three stayed by the vans. Since a stalemate seemed to have set in between Shepherd and Findlay, and since I didn't feel like eating, I walked somewhat unsteadily towards *The Elephant*. I knew that telegraphy was somehow important in the case of Captain Boyd, and I meant to draw Ferry out about who had sent what to whom.

One fellow remained standing on the water tank of the tender, and as I walked around the rear of it, I saw Ferry standing naked. He looked if anything neater without clothes than he did with, and when the bucket of fairly cold and fairly clean water was pitched down on him, he looked neater still, for all the black hairs on his long brown body were immediately aligned by it. He'd got hold of a cake of soap, and he was lathering his bald brown head. I registered the gold signet ring on his left little finger, and I saw, nestling amid his chest hairs, another item of jewellery: a small gold crucifix on a thin gold chain.

The Royal Engineer called down to Ferry: "Ready for your second?"

Ferry glanced upwards, and in doing so, he saw me: "I . . . am," he said.

The water came down, and all the hairs were straight again. Ferry had closed his eyes to take the deluge. He opened them again to see me still staring at him. He must think me a queer, but I didn't care. What had Captain Boyd's Arab servant, the amiable but half-witted Farhan, said? That the British soldier who'd visited Boyd on the day before his last day had had "religion in his heart" — the Christian religion. Farhan had also disclosed that Boyd had made frequent visits to "the home of the British" — surely the British Residency. Surely, also, he had gone there to send telegrams.

Ferry stepped forward to where his uniform was neatly folded on top of his kit bag together with Colt revolver, belt and holster.

I had seen the carbon copy, albeit too faint to read, of one of Boyd's messages, or one of his attempted messages. A line had been put through it. Was it that Ferry had refused to send it? Was it that the message constituted what Ferry had called "tittle-tattle"? Or did he have some deeper reason for disapproving? Ferry was religious. He had the crucifix, and was therefore most likely Catholic. If you were Church of England, you didn't go in for jewellery. Not if you were a man, anyhow. He had been first to arrive at both the club meetings I'd attended, and the Church of the Saviour's Mother was just around the corner from the clubhouse. Catholics — keen ones — would go to a service held on a Saturday evening as well as the Sunday ones. They went on a Saturday evening because it was *nearly* Sunday.

Ferry put on his shorts first, and no wonder, the way I was looking at him. He said, "Are you . . .?"

He buckled up his gun next, and I could see the logic of that, too, given that I still stared.

"Am I what?" I said.

Ferry put on his shirt. As he sat down ready to put on his socks, puttees and boots, he leant forwards and I could easily see the crucifix between the buttons of his shirt. It would be in plain sight every time he leant over. It was a wonder I hadn't noticed it before. The point was that he wouldn't have had to strip off for Ahmad to notice it.

276

"The peculiar . . . code you employ," he said, and the rest came with horrific fluency: "Are you working for Manners at the War Office?"

He was lacing the first of his boots. It seemed to me he'd set himself the task of doing it in not more than half a dozen precise movements. It made me feel sick to watch him, for I knew I was not up to that sort of effort.

Ferry said, "Are you . . ."

Sock, boot, puttee. Ferry had completed his left leg; he now turned his attention to the right one. He was horribly in control of himself. He began by making an inspection of his long left foot, pulling apart the toes. Beyond the smoke box of *The Elephant*, the sun was going down, but not without protest, not without having started a great many other fires in the sky around it. I wanted to say to Ferry, "You had a run-in with Boyd. What happened?" But I was too hot to speak, so Ferry did instead:

"Are you . . . on a secret job?"

It was the cool cheek of the question that I found distressing. Ferry was not turning out how I expected. But this was my fault, for I had seen the steeliness in him.

Fifty yards off, Wallace King and Wilson were filming the sunset. King was a little way in advance of Wilson, perhaps taking a closer look at the sunset. "It's not up to much!" I could hear him calling. "We've got plenty of sunsets anyway! What we need is a good sunrise!"

It made no difference of course, the going down of the sun, and I thought of the one day of my childhood when I'd been overwhelmed by the heat. Baytown, the place of my birth, stood on the Yorkshire coast, not too far from Jarvis's Scarborough. It wasn't easy to be overwhelmed by heat on the Yorkshire coast. Knocked over by the east wind, yes. I was six years old or so; the sun was raying down on the beach, and I was screaming. My father held my hand. Being only a man — a widower — he did not quite understand young children, and I believe my distress had been increased by the woman who had come up and shouted at him, ordering him to take me indoors. He had immediately removed me into the lifeboat house, which was always dark, and smelt of paint, for they were always painting the lifeboat. There was a bench you could sit on to watch them do it. I had been placed on the bench and given a penny lick . . .

Ferry was asking another question: "Are you quite . . ."

An expression came to me all the way from Yorkshire, and I believed that I said out loud, "I feel like I don't know what."

And then I keeled over, and I continued to watch the sunset from sideways on.

They — I didn't know exactly who — put me back on the sofa in the carriage. I was given bottled water, more quinine; I dropped asleep.

I awoke to see Findlay descending from the carriage. I had been somehow aware of him not sleeping, fretting with *The Times* — thrashing at it. He would now, I supposed, be making for the camp around the fire in the palms. As he opened the door, I made out the red glow rising above the single-fly tents. Shepherd was over there. It was no cooler in the open but uncomfortable in a different way, preferable to some. I took it for granted that the military arrangements had been made to guard us — that a couple of men were on sentry go, that someone was keeping the steam up in *The Elephant*. I could not see Ferry in the carriage, but an hour later, when I next awoke, he was there, and he was there perhaps six more times as I came out of fitful dozes, always with his pipe in his mouth and his eyes upon me. Evidently, he lived without sleep. Maybe that was the way of it with the brainier sorts of fellows. He was an Oxford man. He taught there, as did Harriet Bailey's husband. He was Professor Bailey. Perhaps Prof. Bailey and Ferry were more than colleagues. Perhaps they were fast friends, in which case Ferry would have another reason — on top of his own strict morality — to warn Boyd off The Lady. I thought of the message I'd seen in the telegraphic office at the Residency: "Religion has a great influence over the Arab." Well, it had a great influence over some white men, too.

I had many dreams — dozens of them, but the principal one concerned a nest of mosquitoes in the corner of the carriage. In the dream, one of the engineers explained that mosquitoes did not as a general rule go in for nest-building, but this particular lot had decided to club together. Later, in what may or may not have been a dream, I saw through the carriage window facing opposite to the camp a lavender-coloured sky containing three stars and a crescent moon. The cigarette packet of Shepherd was assembling itself, but no man in a fez and no woman in a red dress came wandering into view to complete it. I looked away, looked back again, and this time it seemed reasonably certain that I was awake. Beyond the window, an exchange had now occurred. The crescent moon remained, but there were a million stars instead of four, and in place of the imaginary vision of the walking couple there was a single walking man in khaki, and, as if to prove that he had somehow evolved from a cigarette packet he himself was smoking. He was about a quarter of a mile off. I ought not to have been able to make him out at that distance, and the reason I could was because of the dawn.

I rose from the couch, stepped down from the carriage. Even after I'd walked twenty-five yards, I still wasn't sure I was on the ground, but I was making towards the smoking figure. This dawn, I realised, came with complications, namely a constant swirling of hot sand. I had to keep my hand over my eyes, and I would periodically tip it, in order to see — so the world came in flashes. The smoking figure did better than me, for even though he too staggered somewhat, he had a cloth about his neck that he now put over his head: a keffiyah. It was Lieutenant Colonel Shepherd that I was following: a thin and small, bow-legged figure. He had the ready-for-anything look of a jockey. He wore his gun of course, and his haversack, but that evidently contained little if anything.

He was making towards a long, low object that seemed to lie near the source of the swirling. This was the branching railway line, and Shepherd was approaching the three wagons sitting upon it, as I had somehow known he would be without quite being able to say why — and it was this knowledge that had made me rise from the couch. I turned about with my hand over my eye. I lifted my hand. Another man approached — another staggerer. He wore a sun helmet, and walked leaning forwards with his hand upon it. Findlay.

The wind whined as it swirled the sand. It *sounded* like a cold wind just as the waters of the Tigris *looked* cold but it, and they, were not. Lieutenant Colonel Shepherd had now arrived at the wagons. He gave a half glance back, and I dived for the protection of a gravel ridge — the kind of thing that I might once, before coming to the desert, have named as a dune. I did not believe I had been seen. I looked over my shoulder, and Findlay had also gone to ground, doubtless for the same reason. I peered forward again. Shepherd had gone between the bogies, beneath the rearmost wagon. In there was darkness; I couldn't see what he was about. Presently, he re-emerged and stood upright. He began walking towards where I lay. He looked no different. But wait a minute. His haversack was *not* the same. It had hung more or less limp before. It now contained some new article.

Shepherd now stood ten feet away from me. I had my gun pointed at him. I could not help noticing that the train behind him seemed to have tilted to about thirty degrees. It held on to the track very well, considering.

I said, "Throw down your gun, sir." He took the Colt from its holster — pitched it away. "What are you thinking of, Jim?" he said, as if really curious.

"You know, sir," I said.

He said, "Shall I show you what's in the bag?"

Whether I blacked out or not I can't say, but a minute later he had jewellery in his hands: a tangle of gold, emeralds, rubies. I heard a footfall.

"Here comes a murderer, Jim," said Shepherd.

I whisked around, Findlay was removing his revolver. He was now aiming it at me, but I let fly with a bullet and his piece went spinning out of his hand — not quite what I'd intended (I did not quite *know* what I had intended), but it had come out all right. Beyond Findlay, I saw a particular illumination: a gap in the whirling, and it held numerous Arabs on horses. They then disappeared. I motioned Findlay towards Shepherd. The major and the lieutenant colonel were now opposite to me.

"I will face you down!" I called over the storm to both of them. I was judge and jury, albeit with malaria.

Shepherd said, "May I put these down?", meaning the jewels. I eyed him. "Of course, I will be delivering them to the Corps HQ," he said.

"Nonsense," said Findlay.

"I'm sorry I couldn't tell you everything, Jim," Shepherd said, setting down the jewels. "I've been let in on an extraordinary adventure, and I wanted to follow it through in my own way."

"The Turkish officer," I said. "The bimbashi. He *did* offer you treasure."

"Not at the station," said Shepherd. "He said there would be gems to be found. They would be attached to the underside of the rearmost wagons of the abandoned trains in this territory."

The wind rose and he had to shout louder, but there was now a lesser quantity of sand in the skies. Or rather the colour of the storm had changed: it was becoming golden.

"A system of exchange would be set up," said Shepherd. "Jewels for military information. At the last train, a week ago, I found some rubies. In return, I left a document about the disposition of our forces and future plans. Naturally, it was one long lie from beginning to end. I saw the chance to make a great score. Well, to throw the Turks off. I about doubled the size of our force in the city for one thing . . . It was all lies, as I say."

"And so is this," said Findlay. "You will be on a charge yourself, by the way, Stringer, if you don't put that damned gun down."

It seemed to me that, *in extremis* and removed from the presence of Miss Bailey, Findlay was reverting to type: an upperclass man, irritated at the situation in which he found himself.

"I gave the first haul into the safe keeping of Brigadier General Barnes," said Shepherd.

"Hogwash," said Findlay.

"Of course," said Shepherd, "they weren't real. They were paste, and I'm pretty sure these are too." He indicated the jewels at his feet.

I turned towards Findlay, and my gun wavered that way too.

I said, "You took the photograph."

"There was a connection," he began, "I have no idea of the details of it — an *association* — between Mrs Bailey and Captain Boyd. It was Mrs Bailey's business alone. I felt that she was entitled to her privacy. I need hardly mention that Mrs Bailey did *not* kill Captain Boyd."

"No," said Shepherd with a half smile, "she did not. But you did."

The sun was rising fast on us, and I could hear a new sound: a distant singing.

"Oh, do come off it," said Findlay.

"Why are you here?" I asked Findlay.

"To keep cases on *him*."

"Why?" I said again.

"Look," he said. "He killed Boyd. Boyd had seen him take a Turkish bribe. He's just taken another one."

Shepherd said, "You adore Mrs Harriet Bailey. You are in love with her. Unfortunately for you so was Boyd, and probably she with him. He had met her in Basrah, as you knew quite well. When he came up to Baghdad, he telegraphed to her repeatedly — Jarvis told me. He had a run-in with Ferry of the telegraph office about sending wires of a personal nature. Boyd wouldn't leave her alone. You arranged to meet him at the station. I don't know what happened, but it ended by you killing him. You knew he had this idea about me — that he considered me a traitor. He misinterpreted what he saw at the station on the night the town fell. I suppose I can't blame him for that. As a result, you thought I'd be blamed for his murder."

"All nonsense," said Findlay. "I only learnt of his theory about you — well, it's more than a theory isn't it? I only learnt that late on Saturday night when Jarvis told me."

"You took the photograph off Jarvis," Shepherd said. "You knew that it might ultimately help make a case against you. I don't know what you told the fellow when you forced him to give it over — what sort of pressure you put him under. He was overstrained in any case."

Findlay was about to reply, but in that instant, it seemed to me that I had at long last cottoned on.

"No," I said to Shepherd, "Jarvis *gave* him the photograph."

"Of course he damn well gave me it," said Findlay.

"I don't know *exactly* why," I said to Shepherd. "But he felt guilty about something to do with Boyd. I believe he had helped you, and that's why he shot himself."

The desert revolved once again, bringing the Arabs into clear view — all these natives coming up with the sun. Unfortunately, Shepherd now had a second gun in his hand. He was like a magician. Where the hell did they keep coming from? It was another Colt, but this one a much handsomer piece. It must have been Captain Boyd's of course, and it had been in

Shepherd's haversack. So it was the Webley against the Colt: one pull on the trigger of the Webley and I would do for him, whereas he would have to cock the hammer of the Colt.

With a half smile, this he now smoothly did, so that we became evenly matched.

"My dear Jim," he said, blushing.

The shot came. I reeled away and in the instant of falling I saw that one rider from the crowd of Arabs was approaching fast, evidently bringing important news from the rising sun. But whatever news was too late for me, for I was spinning, spinning away into blackness and the end of Mesopotamia.

Part Three

York Again

CHAPTER
EIGHTEEN

In the railway police office at York station, I opened my eyes. The thin fire in the grate was much the same as when I'd last looked at it. Therefore I hadn't been out for more than a few minutes. As for the letter before me, that was exactly the same. To the man recovering from malaria, the mystery is not so much his own drowsiness as how anyone at all can keep awake for an entire day — not to mention the question of why they would *want* to. I read over the letter again.

It must have been sent to the War Office by the diplomatic bag, which is to say via the man Lennon — at a price no doubt, but evidently one affordable to Jarvis. (I supposed that Lennon's rates were variable according to the customer's rank.) It had then been forwarded to me at the police office by the ordinary mail, courtesy of Lennon's brother and partner in crime if crime it was. The envelope was date-stamped May 30th, which was the day he and I had had our conversation about Kut. We'd gone soon afterwards to see Boyd's Arab servant, Farhan, and it must have been after that encounter that Jarvis had written and posted.

Dear Capt. Stringer,

You told me you worked before the war in the police office at York station so that is where I am writing to you.

I am writing to you to point out that Lt. Col. Shepherd killed Captain Boyd at about six o'clock on the evening of Wednesday May 23rd 1917. I was there so I know. Capt. Boyd had asked me kindly if I would drive him to the station, not saying why he wanted to go there. Lt. Col. Shepherd, who I knew a little from the HQ, was already there walking up and down the platform. I did not think I was supposed to see him but he didn't seem to mind very much about it. They went together into the station buffet as was, and I walked some distance away but still heard a little of their talk. Shepherd challenged Capt. Boyd. He said Capt. Boyd had been giving him dirty looks when they had passed by each other at the Hotel. Capt. Boyd said well don't pretend you don't know why. Capt. Boyd then called Shepherd a Turkish spy paid for in gold. He had seen and heard an arrangement made with a Turkish officer at the station where he and Shepherd had been on the day of our entry into the city. They started an argument, and then Capt. Boyd fell silent. As to how Shepherd did it, I believe it was by stabbing, for there was no gun shot. I had glimpsed a quantity of knives on the floor of the place on first arriving. Shepherd came hurrying out, saying would I mind very much giving him a lift back to town, for he is very polite as you know as well as a killer. I said what about Captain Boyd, and he said he would be remaining behind at the station. I said why — not taking much trouble by now to be respectful, and he smiled, saying Oh he's rather brooding you know. I still stared at him, and he went red saying I think he means to walk over to the range shortly. He admitted they'd had a bit of a row, and I was amazed at how he didn't try to cover up. But then this is a man who likes to put his whole life in hazard from time to time. Not to mention the lives of others.

When the body was turned up, Shepherd got me involved in trying to investigate the crime even though he'd done it, and so began a lot of play-acting. Shepherd said he had a suspicion of the culprit (as if it wasn't himself) and wanted to pursue the matter secretly it being sensitive. It was painful to me to go along with this because you know what Capt. Boyd meant to me because I have told you. Shepherd would have me believe Capt. Boyd was a man likely to get into hot water over the ladies, but he himself I believe to be a QUEER.

I am hoping you will be in a safe place when you get this news. I pray God Capt. Stringer that you will be able to read this in your home town of York which I consider on a par with my home town of Scarborough. (This is meant complimentary.)

But I will NOT.

Capt. Stringer they say nothing lasts for ever but I don't think so. I have been out here for two years straight no leave. I find it to be far too hot. My back which I have never showed you is covered with black fly bites and I can not sleep at all without taking more than is good for me in strong drink. On top of this, I let down my friend by not going to his aid, and by not speaking out until now. So I will in time do what I know must be done, and the writing of this letter will clear the way for me.

What exactly are we doing here? Building a nation it is said and who for? Not us. We already have one. But for the Arabs I ask you. Well it won't happen overnight.

So we sit here waiting for the Turk to come back. Let him build the nation I say.

Why am I writing to you of all people?

It is because you asked about my experiences near the town of Kut-al-Amara which nobody has ever done.

In closing Capt. Stringer please find enclosed two tokens of my estimation. You will know which one Shepherd gave me after he came back from your run north saying here's a trinket for you but I knew it was in order to keep silence about the events at the station.

Yours ever, Stanley Jarvis (Private)

The letter had come two days before in a package together with *The City of the Khalifs* (somewhat battered) and a sizeable brooch or pendant tightly wrapped about with newspaper, and consisting of three large green stones, each about the diameter of a shilling, surrounded by a larger quantity of smaller red ones, each about the diameter of a farthing. A glittering tassel hung down from it. I had immediately telephoned Manners at the War Office, and read over the letter. With his say-so, I had taken the brooch or pendant (rewrapped in its paper) into the best York jeweller, Pearson and Sons, in St Helen's Square. Rather to my disappointment — because I'd been hoping to cause an immediate stir by handing over the thing — old Mr Pearson had said he was too busy to look at the brooch just then. I was to call back later in the week.

I knew the letter practically off by heart now. It was not quite clear on whether Shepherd had invited Boyd to the station or the other way around, or whose choice the station might have been. Shepherd might have chosen it, meaning to show Boyd the remaining Berlin-Baghdad railway medallions, and to fob him off with that tale. Then again Boyd might have chosen it, since he regarded it as a safe meeting place, as proved by the fact that he'd been planning to meet me there.

Boyd, it was becoming clear to me, must have influenced the allocation of Jarvis to me as batman. It would have been a way of opening up a channel of communication between us without our having to meet directly after that proposed first rendezvous.

Repocketing the letter, my thoughts turned to Jarvis himself. He had gone through the charade of playing detective when he knew the culprit all along. That might have brought him near to doing the deed promised in his letter — and he would have felt *obliged* to do it once having written and despatched the letter. The last straw had been the business over the photograph; the attempt to incriminate an innocent man. In the aftermath of the attack on the Railway Club — when giving over the photograph — Jarvis had told Findlay what Shepherd had done, and it was evidently to keep tabs on Shepherd — to catch him in the act of going under the Turkish trains to leave the data and collect the treasure — that Findlay had gone on the trip to Samarrah.

Beyond the window an express had pulled in.

I had the police office to myself, and I was cold, hence the fire I had lit, even though it was July. Baghdad had got into my blood, in more than one sense. Yet I had been away for no more than twelve weeks, and ten of those had been spent travelling, and five days in the packed army hospital behind the cavalry barracks. I had never smoked the narghile, never been to the bazaar. On the other hand I had also never been shot. Much to my shame it had been a faint that had keeled me over when Shepherd had pointed the Colt single-action at me. I blamed my malarial condition.

The stationary express was somehow making the sound of a rainstorm.

I began to think of my five days in Baghdad military hospital. Existing on a diet of quinine and bad dreams, I had slept in a sort of dark cave, for my cot had been surrounded by a thicket of mosquito nets — three of them. It had been a case, as I had confusedly told the gentlemen of the Royal Army Medical Corps (apparently many times), of "bolting the stable door after the horse had locked". Yet I had kept parting the curtains, in hopes of letting in a draught. How I had longed for coolness, yet now I was contemplating walking out to the driver of that northbound express and asking him for a few lumps of good anthracite to get a blaze started in the police-office grate which held only screwed-up six-month-old pages from the *Yorkshire Evening Press*.

Towards the end of my stay in the hospital, Ahmad had visited me with ginger biscuits, two sticks of chocolate, and a quantity of raisins. I'd told him I was feeling better. He'd said, "I prayed for you so what do you expect?" I'd said, "Thank you," and he'd said, "Now you pray for me. Goodbye."

It broke in on me that this express train fuming away must be the one the Chief had said he was going to meet. He was expecting a special visitor and this was somehow related to "a real treat" that was in store for me. Knowing the Chief, that might mean any number of things not normally counted as treats. For instance, a trip to the Police Court to see some bad lad sent down for a few years' hard.

I stood up and put on my suit-coat, still thinking of the Baghdad hospital. Lieutenant Colonel Shepherd was still in there. He'd taken an Arab bullet, but according to Manners he would recover fully from his wounds. He would then be taken from the hospital and be shot again, this time by the British Army as a murderer and traitor. Naturally, there would be a court martial first. The treasure he'd taken was being held as evidence. (He'd disclosed its whereabouts to the investigators. He'd simply stowed it in a trunk in his quarters, but not the one whose lid I had myself lifted. I thought it typical of Shepherd to have been so reckless in his choice of hiding place.)

No treasure had been lodged with Brigadier General Barnes.

The documents that Shepherd had admitted to leaving under the first train — the one carrying the motor launches — had been looked for and not found, having fallen into Turkish hands. The second lot of documents — the ones left by Shepherd under the train carrying the crated aeroplane — had been discovered, and all I knew of these was that they had been scrawled in French, and that they would be part of the body of evidence against Shepherd.

The express was still fuming away outside. They must be changing the engine. I heard a footfall, and the door opened. It was the Chief.

"Hey!" he said, "follow me."

I might be a British Army captain and an intelligence agent of sorts, but this was still how he commanded me. I followed the Chief, who was lighting a cigar as he walked, towards the First Class end of the train, and there, stepping down from the farthest carriage, was Manners of the War Office.

"Is this the special guest?" I called ahead to the Chief.

"Try to sound a bit more enthusiastic," he said, half turning around.

I had only recently been speaking to Manners on the phone, and I'd sent him two full reports of the events of my Baghdad investigation. The novelty was beginning to wear off the man. I had not forgiven him for furnishing me with such a bloody daft cipher, and it had seemed that on my return I had given him a sight more data than he had given me. For instance, I couldn't get out of him whether Captain Ferry of the Residency telegraph office was suspected of any corruption. But I did not believe so. Ferry guessed I had been sent to Baghdad on a secret job, hence his asking whether I was sending to Manners. But I believed he had not told anyone else — and indeed that my secret role had *remained* secret, except in so far as I had deliberately given it away to Lennon of the Residency post room, a man I had trusted at the time and still trusted in recollection.

Captain Bob Ferry was not corrupt. He was if anything too moral. He had visited Boyd and given him a rating for his repeated attempts to send to Miss Bailey when she was down in Basrah. Word of this had no doubt leaked out (the British force in Baghdad being a sort of round-the-clock rumour factory), and had reached the ears of Shepherd, who had then tried to paint Boyd as a man who'd come to grief because of his connection with Miss Bailey.

I *supposed* that was how it had worked, anyhow.

Manners had also failed to fill me in on what had happened after I'd keeled over in the desert. I believed

I had come to very soon after, but memory loss was known to be a symptom of malaria, and it appeared that it had been so in my case.

On top of these grievances, Manners's tone of amusement also went against him. And he certainly seemed to find York station *highly* amusing, as he stood waiting for us with the train finally drawing away behind him. Whisking off his bowler, thus shamelessly revealing the entirety of his long, shining head, he said, "Lunch, gentlemen?"

Well, it had apparently all been pre-arranged with the Chief, and we wheeled about and headed for platform seven, on which stood a side entrance to the Station Hotel.

"I believe the new offensive has begun brilliantly," said Manners as we entered the hotel.

"Has it bollocks," said the Chief. (In London, the Chief had been rather quelled by Manners, but here he was on his own turf.)

"You think it's propaganda, Saul?"

"If you read it in the paper," said the Chief, "then it's propaganda. Or is it something you know in an official capacity?"

"Unfortunately not," Manners said cheerfully. His amusement at the world was out in the open now, whereas in London it had been kept somewhat it check.

The York Station Hotel was a red-padded, silent world, but the war had made a few intrusions. A sign on the reception desk, which we were now passing in front of, read, "Guests are reminded to close their room curtains at or before 8.30p.m." Manners had stopped at the desk, where he was now buying postcards of York. "I always do this when I come to a new town," he said. "It saves me walking around the place." He seemed to be in holiday mood.

A waitress came up, and even before we'd been seated the Chief had ordered beer.

"Don't you select the food first, Saul?" said Manners. "I mean, you order the drink that goes with the food."

"I find that beer goes with any food, Peter," said the Chief.

This business of "Saul" and "Peter" — I didn't care for it.

(I did not myself drink any beer. On my return from Baghdad, I'd told the wife all my adventures, adding that since being put on a course of quinine, which was very bitter, I had quite lost my taste for bitter beer, to which she had said simply, "Good. Because you drank far too much of it before.")

The waitress gave out the menus.

"Any war restrictions, dear?" enquired the Chief, in a resigned sort of way.

"No potatoes except Wednesday and Friday, and no meat on Wednesday," she said, speaking like an automaton.

"But today", said Manners, with happy realisation dawning, "is Thursday. We could have meat *and* potatoes. Cottage pie!"

And that's what we did order, just because we could. The waitress said, "Shall I send over the sommelier?"

"The bloody what?" said the Chief.

"Yes do," said Manners.

It was a jolly enough lunch, and over the second bottle of good claret, a few "Jim's began to be floated amongst the Sauls and Peters. Manners asked whether I had heard from the Medical Board (I had not), and there was some speculation about my future. The Chief said he wanted me back in the police office; that I had more than "done my bit". We then talked over the case. It appeared from what Manners said that Shepherd had always been a loose cannon, prone to getting into scrapes whether at school, university or in the army. As a young man, he had travelled in Turkey, and formed an affection for the place. "And an affection," Manners added, "for its gold and silver." The court martial, he said, would be held in conditions of the utmost secrecy. It would be held "in camera".

Manners paid for the meal, and I said, "I'm obliged to you. I was promised a royal time, and that certainly fitted the bill."

"Your treat is still to come, lad," said the Chief, and he looked at his watch and grinned at Manners.

"Really?" I said.

We crossed Ouse Bridge under a blue sky and a light rain. The Chief was in the lead, and he was telling Manners how, the night before, he'd attended a party at the Railway Institute, a leave-taking for the timekeeper of the carriage works who'd finally got round to joining the army — the West Yorkshire Regiment. There were speeches, and the fellow had been given a present. Manners asked what it was. "A clock of course," said the Chief, and that tickled Manners no end. Well, he had at least a pint of claret inside him.

We walked along Lendal, coming to St Helen's Square, where we passed Pearson and Sons, Gold and Silversmiths. I looked in the window as we went by. It was a small shop, pretty like a jewellery box, only with bars on the window. (And a guard sat in it all night.) I wondered whether they'd got around to looking at the package I'd given in.

We walked along Coney Street, along Pavement, and we came to the start of Fossgate. The Blue Bell was to our right. Its smoke room was the Chief's home-from-home, and I thought a drink-up in there might be the *real* treat. But not after all that claret, surely? That would be going it a bit even for the Chief. But instead, we crossed the road . . . and there stood the wife, looking at her watch.

She'd been doing her marketing, and carried her basket. She stood right in front of the Electric Theatre.

"Chief Inspector Weatherill told me a cinema show was to be held in your honour," she said. "He let on about it when I bumped into him last week, but I was to say nothing to you. He didn't *really* want me to come."

"Now that's not quite right, Mrs Stringer," said the Chief.

". . . But I forced the details out of him, and here I am," said the wife.

A cinema show in my honour . . .

With its highly decorated front, the Electric Theatre might have looked quite at home in Baghdad. It was the very place the wife and I and the children had seen *Ali Baba and the Forty Thieves*, and I thought I might be in for another showing. I looked at the placards in front of the cinema. Under the familiar words "To-Night To-Night" was advertised "The Gentleman Rider" and "In the Hands of the London Crooks".

"We're *all* in the hands of the London crooks," said the wife, and Manners came up to me, speaking confidentially. "I've been told your good lady wife works for the Co-Operative movement, but I had no idea she was actually a communist."

He grinned and wheeled away to greet two fellows who'd just stepped out of the door by the pay box. The first was a fat chap called P. T. Buckley, and he was the owner of the Electric Theatre, and was forever being featured in the *Yorkshire Evening Press* as "the man who brought cinema to York". Of late though, he'd been up in arms about the Council having given the go-ahead for a new cinema: the Picture House in Coney Street. The second fellow was Wilson, assistant to Wallace King. He wore a bright blue blazer and a straw boater, and I realised how wrong he'd looked in that baggy, badge-less uniform in Baghdad.

I shook his hand, and he said, "You look a good deal brighter than when I last saw you."

Behind him, I glimpsed a third placard: "Closed this afternoon for showing of a special item."

"Where's Wallace King?" I asked Wilson.

"Oh, Mr King's never available at short notice . . . But I am," he added, offering me a cigarette; I took the cigarette; everyone smoked outside the Electric, since

302

you couldn't smoke inside. "He's in meetings all this month with some of the production companies is Mr King," said Wilson.

"*The Battle of Trafalgar?*" I said, dazed.

Wilson shook his head. "He's going all out with a new treatment he's worked up: *The Great Fire of London.*"

"And what's this special item?" I said, indicating the third placard.

"You'll see," said Wilson. "You're the star."

The wife was talking to Buckley.

"So you've been to the Picture House?" he was saying, looking worried.

"It's really gorgeous," said the wife, "tip-up seats, two programmes a week continuous daily, all the latest American pictures, ice-cream parlour, balcony, gallery, fancy plasterwork — a lovely scheme of decoration, it is — and an orchestra!" And then she remembered herself, so she indicated the Electric and said, "But this is my favourite."

Inside, the Electric was fairly plain. It was painted brown. As we crossed the entrance hall, the Chief was looking all around.

"Ever been here before?" Buckley was anxiously enquiring.

The Chief shook his head, saying, "You don't have an alcoholic licence, do you?"

And there in a nutshell was the reason.

We entered the auditorium and I heard the Chief asking Buckley, "Where's the lantern operated from?"

He then shot me a look that told me he was taking the rise out of Buckley.

The projection box was at the rear. It was dark. I sat next to the wife on the front row. We *all* sat on the front row. The wife said, "Your Chief wanted me to sign the Official Secrets Act before I came here."

"And did you?"

"I told him not to be so daft. But I think Buckley may've had to sign it. And the fellow in there," she added, gesturing towards the projection box.

Buckley was turning about, signalling that way. The room then became darker still, and the whirring started. On the picture screen appeared the words "WALLACE KING BRINGS THE WORLD TO YOU", and then there was the desert of Mesopotamia, and something was happening beyond the furthest extent of it.

"The sunrise," Wilson was whispering to the Chief. "That's why we were there, you see: to film the sunrise." After a few minutes he leant over to Buckley, saying, "Not a flicker! Not a flicker!" at which Buckley nodded rather graciously. "It's a good job we don't have sound," Wilson continued after a further half minute or so of the sun rising, "because just now you'd be hearing Mr King saying, 'Pan right, you idiot, pan right!'"

And the camera now began its travel, bringing the abandoned train into view.

"Nice work," Buckley whispered to Wilson.

"Not bad," said Wilson. "Well, I've been in the camera trade since I was a boy."

The camera came to rest on three figures, all blurred. The focus was adjusted and I saw myself with gun pointing at Shepherd. I was wavering, staggering somewhat. A man came into view — Findlay. He drew his gun; I turned as he was aiming it, and fired my own revolver — in complete silence of course — whereupon Findlay's piece went spinning from his hand.

"Good shot, lad," said the Chief, from three seats along.

On the screen, I now had my gun aimed at both Findlay and Shepherd, and we were all speaking. The wife, next to me, was looking on, fascinated. Then Shepherd had his gun pointed at me, and she turned and stared at me in horror. Beyond Shepherd's right shoulder, I could make out the muster of mounted Arabs. They were out of focus, but not completely so, and I saw a small figure in the middle of them gesturing to another of the tribe (if that be the word), who aimed a rifle. The small figure signalled to the marksman, and Shepherd fell down at that moment.

"Is this real?" gasped Buckley.

"Better than *The Gentleman Rider*, eh?" said Wilson.

"But he's not dead is he?" said the wife, who'd had the whole story from me several times over.

"He will be soon," I said, and the Chief leant towards the wife, kindly explaining, "The bullet went clean through his upper arm, shattered two ribs and — fortunately for him — lodged in the lung. If you're going to be shot," he added, "be shot in the lung. It's very seldom fatal."

I had fallen at the same time as Shepherd.

Wilson said, "At this moment I was saying to Mr King, 'Hadn't we better go and help?' and he was saying, 'If you leave off cranking, I'll bloody shoot *you!*'"

On the screen, I was attempting to stagger to my feet, which I had not remembered doing. In the course of that action, I faced the camera.

"Oh, Jim," said the wife, "you look like nothing on earth."

But I wasn't looking at me. I was watching the approaching rider — the one that had broken away from the Arabs; the one who had indicated to the marksman.

"So *that's* Harriet Bailey," said the Chief. "She's quite a looker."

"Hold on a minute." I was saying, "Hold on a minute."

On the screen, I'd fallen down again. I was on the desert floor alongside Shepherd — looked like I was lying in bed with him. Major Findlay had approached Harriet Bailey, who had remained mounted, and who wore a keffiyah. The focus was again adjusted, and I could clearly see Findlay in profile, speaking to Harriet Bailey. He then gave a thin smile. But Miss Bailey did not return it. She pulled at the keffiyah, so that it fell away from her face, and she glowered down at Findlay. She then spoke to him, and his smile disappeared. Other men came running into the picture — Royal Engineers — and the screen went black.

Silence in the auditorium.

The lights came up, and I turned to Manners, who said, "She protected you, do you see? She ordered her Arab pal to shoot when Shepherd pulled the gun on you."

"What was she *doing* with those Arabs?"

"Oh you know, buttering them up, arguing the British case. I can't quite recall what lot they were, but her dealings with them were a matter of absolute confidentiality. I believe it was pure coincidence that she was in the same region of the desert as your party, and in order to come to your aid she had to break cover so to speak. As you could tell, she wasn't very happy about it. You see, it was above all important that the Arabs should believe her to be quite independent of the British secret service, whereas in fact of course . . ."

"She was the other agent."

"Correct."

"She was the one you wouldn't let me speak to."

"Right again. I'm sorry about it all. We ought never to have mentioned any other agent in the first place."

"So before my arrival," I said, "Captain Boyd was in contact with Harriet Bailey only because they were both intelligence agents?"

Manners nodded. "Unfortunately, Boyd was rather too overt — kept trying to telegraph to her, and when she came up from Basrah, he insisted on meeting her a couple of times."

"So word got out that they were lovers?"

"I suppose so. And that gave Shepherd his cue to develop the clever tale about Major Findlay — who clearly *was* enamoured of Miss Bailey — having done for Captain Boyd."

My thoughts raced. Had Miss Bailey known I was investigating Shepherd? She'd given me a good look over on our first meeting. That might have been because I resembled Boyd, or because he had told her I would be arriving in order to work with Shepherd and keep tabs on him. She had asked me, with some concern, the whereabouts of my revolver.

The wife stood up. She faced Buckley. "I want to see it again," she said.

Manners was looking at his watch. He said, "Be my guest, Mrs Stringer. I'm sure you'd all like to see it again before it goes under lock and key. But I have a train to catch."

He shook all our hands, and I believe he had already quit the Electric Theatre by the time the lights dimmed once more, the whirring began again, and "WALLACE KING BRINGS THE WORLD TO YOU" reappeared before us.

This time we watched the reel in silence, and there was no sound in the auditorium but the flickering of the projection machine — until, that is, Harriet Bailey removed her keffiyah and glared down at Major Findlay, at which point her words were suddenly and very clearly audible: "No. I believe *you* did it."

It was the wife who had spoken. I turned to her. "What did you say?"

"It's what *she* said."

"You told me in your letter," I said, stunned. "You can see speech."

"Not as well as Margaret Lawson, I can't."

"I knew!" I said, "I *knew!*" I turned to the Chief. "Did you see Findlay when he drew his gun? There was a delay. He *cocked the trigger*. It was a single-action. *He* had Boyd's gun, not Shepherd. What time is Manners's train?"

"Half three," said the Chief. "London express."

It was twenty past.

With a clamour of raised voices and questions behind me I was out of the auditorium, out of the Electric Theatre and into Fossgate. I began to run, as fast as my crocked right leg would allow. Shepherd had told me he meant to get hold of a Colt single-action. He would doubtless have put in for one at the armoury. A man wasn't supposed to have two pieces but Shepherd was a lieutenant colonel and very persuasive with it. What he had told Jarvis about his meeting with Boyd at the railway station had all been true. Boyd *had* gone back to the range afterwards. He spent half his time at the range, after all. Findlay might easily have found him there, or intercepted him on the way. They had returned to the station to talk privately, just as Boyd had talked privately with Shepherd. Findlay would have challenged Boyd over his connection with Miss Bailey and Boyd would not have been able to tell the truth because the truth — that they were in Intelligence work — was a secret. And so they would have started a fight.

I skittered into Parliament Street.

Miss Bailey, too, would have wanted to guard the secret of the reason for the connection with Boyd.

309

Perhaps she would rather Findlay thought it a romance than know the truth. Findlay must have thought that, as well as protecting himself, he was saving the lady's reputation by going back into the club room for the photograph. Perhaps that had been in his mind when he'd killed Boyd — that he was saving the lady from herself. Well, she was a married woman.

I doubted that she'd known what he'd done — not at first. Her declaration in the desert had seemed like a moment of revelation, prompted by Findlay saying something like "We have run to ground the killer of Captain Boyd."

Jarvis had had no need to commit suicide. He had not stood by while Shepherd had killed Boyd because Shepherd had *not* killed Boyd. But Jarvis had . . . what was the word? He had misconstrued, and what he had misconstrued he had passed on to Findlay. No doubt Findlay did believe Shepherd was a traitor on the strength of what Jarvis had told him, but he couldn't have believed Shepherd was the killer of Boyd, because *he* was the killer of Boyd.

Pushing through the crowds in the square, I repeated to myself out loud, "Everything Shepherd said was true." Everything he had said was true, *as far as it went*. But he had covered up as well. He *had* heard of the rumour of his treachery as proved by his decision to confront Boyd, yet he'd let on that he was hearing it from me for the first time. And no doubt he *had* taken Baghdad railway medals from the bimbashi at the station . . . But he had left out the rest: the arrangement he had made to give over information in return for

310

treasure. He had only come round to discussing this in our desert stand-off, where he'd said he wanted to string the Turks along, to play a private game with them in return for supposed treasure that he insisted was really nothing more than . . .

I was alongside the window of Pearson's. I had five minutes before Manners's express departed for London. It was a four-minute run to the station. I pushed at the shop door. Old man Pearson stood behind the counter. When he saw me, he froze.

"I'm Stringer," I said, panting. "I brought in the brooch or whatever it was."

"I know you did," he said, eyeing me steadily.

"Well?" I said. "Have you looked at it?"

"I have. Do you want to sit down?"

"No. Look, is it real?"

"How do you mean 'real'?"

"Is it valuable?"

"You might say that," he said. "Where did you lay hands on it?"

"I'll tell you later. Look, I'm in a hurry."

"Yes," he said, "I can see that. Shall I start with the stones or the tassel?"

"The stones."

"Pastes," he said. "You can tell by the tiny air bubbles in the . . ."

I made a dart for the door, but checked myself. "And the tassel?"

"Fake pearls. A combination of glass and fish scales believe it or not, a very curious and antique formula."

I believed that I heard old Pearson say, as the door clanged behind me, "I'll give you two pounds for it if you like!"

I raced pell-mell over Ouse Bridge and along Station Rise. At half past three exactly, I clattered through the ticket gate on to platform four, and the express was drawing away. I began chasing it. A platform guard stood in my way, and I just floored him. When the train cleared the platform, I did too, running over the black rubble of the Holgate sidings. The express was approaching Holgate Junction. In a moment, the curvature of the line would take it from my sight. I gave it up, sat down on the rubble half dead, but as the train began to bend, a head appeared from the window. The head was bald. It disappeared back into the carriage.

A moment later, the train began to brake.

CHAPTER
NINETEEN

The express from York whirled my First Class carriage fast through the night. It was heading . . . Well, it makes no odds. Let's say I was on War Business. I might mention that it was towards the end of that summer of 1917 — a season of blaring and indeed murderous sun in Mesopotamia and rather weak sun and frequent showers in Blighty. The rain was lashing at the windows as we flew along; the fields seemed grey-blue rather than green, and the gas was up.

I caught up my *Railway Magazine*, opening it at the page marked "At the Club Room" and "Forthcoming Talks".

"On Thursday October 9th," I read, "Mr John Maycroft will give his talk, *Humour on the Rails*, together with lantern slides. This was unavoidably postponed in January. Mr Maycroft is the author of *Humours of a Country Station, Our Booking Office, Down or Up* & c. & c., and is widely considered our principal railway comedian. Tea and coffee will be served."

This was not the page I had wanted to see. I had in any case already read of the promised coming of Maycroft, so I turned to the article I'd been halfway through: "Some Developments at Crewe". My place was marked with a picture postcard I'd received a week before. It was of the booklet type, with attached leaf for longer messages. It had come from Manners and was doubtless one of the ones he'd bought in the York Station Hotel. It featured a grid of photographs showing parts of the Bar Walls and parts of the Minster. Underneath the pictures was written "Did you know that York is a jewel of the North?"

"Well . . . did you?" began the message from the ever more flippant Manners:

> . . . I believe you did. A tedious report will be despatched to you shortly, but I thought you should know that Major Findlay is dead. He was given pretty fair warning that he would be taken in charge for the murder of Boyd, and that Miss (or should I say Mrs) Bailey would give evidence against him. He did the right thing. Your York surmises proved quite correct, and we did not have to press the lady too hard. She had already resolved to speak out about her suspicions of Findlay, not that any of it really amounted to evidence, but in the end it didn't need to. He had not spoken to her since they'd returned together to the clubhouse to look for the photograph. Findlay had then gone off on his own after Jarvis, who'd given him his wrong account of what had happened between Boyd and Shepherd. Findlay was thus encouraged in thinking he'd got away with what he'd done, and it seems he urged Jarvis

314

to come out publicly against Shepherd. It was all too much for Jarvis. Anyhow later on, in the desert, Findlay announced the wounded Shepherd as the killer of Boyd, and all of Harriet Bailey's doubts came together, resulting in her outburst.

You are to be congratulated on provoking the crisis that brought this end about. The Chief had told me you would do something of the sort — that while you were not quite Sherlock Holmes, you were nothing if not dogged. I believe I am also indebted to your dear lady wife and a certain Miss Lawson, a typewriter by profession.

As for Lieutenant Colonel Shepherd, he is pretty well patched up and out of Baghdad. He took it all like a sportsman, I must say, but of course he should have let on about the jewels even if they were fake. The fellow is what is called a lone wolf; he is also incorrigible. Of his present whereabouts I have absolutely no idea, and would rather like to keep it like that.

Good luck to you, Captain Stringer,
Peter Manners.

I pocketed the card, and the train and I and the world raced on into the night.

Historical Note

My description of the British occupation of Baghdad in the summer of 1917, including the events leading up to that occupation, the disposition of British and Turkish forces, and the development of railways around Baghdad, is, I hope, roughly accurate. By the end of the war, the British had established full control over what would become the state of Iraq, at a cost of 92,000 British and Indian lives and an unknown number of Turkish and Arab lives. Iraq was established as a British mandate, but a nationalist revolt of 1920 showed the impossibility of direct colonial rule. The British therefore installed a monarchy under the Hashemite King Faisal. However, the regime was unpopular with Shia Muslims (Faisal was a Sunni), also with Kurds and nationalists. In 1958 it was overthrown in favour of a military dictatorship.

Also available in ISIS Large Print:

Sidney Chambers and the Shadow of Death

James Runcie

Sidney Chambers, the Vicar of Grantchester, is a 32-year-old bachelor. Tall, with eyes the colour of hazelnuts, he is both an unconventional clergyman and a reluctant detective. Working in association with his friend, Inspector Geordie Keating, Sidney is able to go where the Police cannot, eliciting surprise revelations and confessions from his parishioners; whether it involves the apparent suicide of a local solicitor, a scandalous jewellery theft at a New Year's Eve dinner party, or the unexplained death of a jazz promoter's daughter. Alongside his inquiries, Sidney also manages to find time to enjoy cricket, warm beer, hot jazz, and the company of an attractive, lively young woman called Amanda.

ISBN 978-0-7531-9044-9 (hb)
ISBN 978-0-7531-9045-6 (pb)

Killed at the Whim of a Hat

Colin Cotterill

When Jimm Juree is forced to quit the city for a fishing village off the Gulf of Siam, she's convinced her career as a crime reporter is over. After all, what crimes could possibly take place in such an out-of-the-way location? No sooner does she think this than two skeletons are found during the excavation of a well. They are sitting side by side in a rotting camper van, and one of them, curiously, is wearing a hat. Shortly afterwards, a monk is murdered in the nearby town of Lang Suan.

On top of bizarre connections between this killing and several others around the globe, where do the newly uncovered skeletons fit in? Suddenly Jimm's new life becomes more exciting — and, before long, a great deal more dangerous.

ISBN 978-0-7531-8972-6 (hb)
ISBN 978-0-7531-8973-3 (pb)

The Somme Stations

Andrew Martin

A notice is pinned up in the railway police office on Platform Four at York Station. Detective Sergeant Jim Stringer recognises immediately that he must do his patriotic duty, and join what would become known as the Railway Pals and to set sail for France.

July 1916, the first day of the Somme, and Jim lies trapped in a too-shallow shell hole as bullets fly overhead. Friendships and enmities have already been born among the supposed pals. Even before they departed for France, a member of Jim's unit had been found murdered. Jim and his comrades must operate by night the vitally important trains carrying munitions to the Front. Close co-operation and trust are vital. Yet proof piles up of an enemy within, and as a military policeman pursues the original killing, the finger of accusation begins to point towards Jim himself . . .

ISBN 978-0-7531-8896-5 (hb)
ISBN 978-0-7531-8897-2 (pb)

Murder at Deviation Junction

Andrew Martin

December, 1909. A train hits a snowdrift in the frozen Cleveland Hills. In the process of clearing the line a body is discovered, and so begins a dangerous case for struggling railway detective Jim Stringer.

His new investigation takes him to the mighty blast furnaces of Ironopolis; to Fleet Street in the company of a cynical reporter from The Railway Rover; and to a nightmarish spot in the Highlands. Jim's faltering career in the railway police hangs on whether he can solve the murder — but before long, the pursuer becomes the pursued, and Jim finds himself fighting not just for his job, but for his very life . . .

ISBN 978-0-7531-8130-0 (hb)
ISBN 978-0-7531-8131-7 (pb)

The Lost Luggage Porter

Andrew Martin

Winter, 1906. After his adventures as an amateur sleuth, Jim Stringer is now an official railway detective, working from York Station for the mighty North Eastern Railway Company. As the rain falls incessantly on the city's ancient, neglected streets, the local paper carries a highly unusual story: two brothers have been shot to death.

Meanwhile, on the station platforms, Jim Stringer meets the Lost Luggage Porter, humblest among the employees of the North Eastern Railway Company. He tells Jim a tale which leads him to the roughest part of town, hot on the trail of pickpockets, "station loungers" and other small fry of the York underworld.

But then in a tiny, one-room pub with a badly smoking fire he enters the orbit of a dangerous villain who is playing for much higher stakes.

ISBN 978-0-7531-7904-8 (hb)
ISBN 978-0-7531-7905-5 (pb)